Praise for *The Iron Witch*

"Dark and beautiful, sensual
and dangerous, utterly enthralling."
—Richelle Mead, *New York Times*
bestselling author

"Teen girls will love the descriptions of Donna's
feelings about her new love interest, and the details
about clothing, friendship, and her attempts to fit in.
Fantasy lovers will enjoy reading about a different
world trying to hide in ours. This book should
prove to be the beginning of a popular series."
—*School Library Journal*

"Mahoney's debut sizzles with romance and
alchemical swashbuckling...A captivating read."
—Tiffany Trent, author of *In the Serpent's Coils*

"Dark around the edges, but shiny at heart, this
is a worthy addition to the YA paranormal shelf."
—Michael M. Jones

"This story has it all for fans of (sub)urban
[fantasy]: vicious adversaries, devoted friendship
and first romance."
—*Kirkus Reviews*

The Stone Demon

KAREN MAHONEY

The Stone Demon

AN IRON WITCH NOVEL

Flux™

Woodbury, Minnesota

First Edition
Second Printing, 2013

Book design by Bob Gaul
Cover design by Lisa Novak
Cover image of: Curtain © iStockphoto.com/Steve Debenport
          Mask © iStockphoto.com/Dominik Pabis
          Woman © iStockphoto.com/teamtime

Flux, an imprint of Llewellyn Worldwide Ltd.

Library of Congress Cataloging-in-Publication Data
Mahoney, Karen.
   The Stone Demon: An Iron Witch Novel/Karen Mahoney—1st ed.
      p. cm.
   Summary: "In order to produce the Philosopher's Stone, as the demon hordes demand, alchemist apprentice Donna Underwood pits her unpredictable powers against a vengeful demon king, two maleficent faery queens, and an immortal magus with his own shadowy agenda"—Provided by publisher.
   ISBN 978-0-7387-3340-1
   [1. Magic—Fiction. 2. Alchemists—Fiction. 3. Demonology—Fiction. 4. Fairies—Fiction. 5. Kings, queens, rulers, etc.—Fiction. 6. Fantasy.]
   I. Title.
   PZ7.M27713Sto 2013
   [Fic]—dc23

                              2012035619

Flux
Llewellyn Worldwide Ltd.
2143 Wooddale Drive
Woodbury, MN 55125-2989
www.fluxnow.com

Printed in the United States of America

For Mum, who was there at the very beginning
and couldn't wait to see how the story ends.

They say that the truth sets you free.

Whoever "they" are, they have no idea how far off base that is. Free? I don't think so.

Now that I know the truth—some of it—my life is more restricted than ever. I want out. Out of the Order of the Dragon. Out of the Order of the Crow. Out of this crazy world of alchemists hidden in the shadows. I feel as though I'm living in a MMORPG, only my character is running low on food, weapons, and life force all at the same time. She's crashing and burning, and I'm not sure I can save her. Save ME.

Seems like the more I thrash around trying to find some kind of escape from the alchemists, the tighter the threads bind me. I'm stuck in the middle of a web of lies, just waiting for Simon Gaunt, the Magus, to scuttle over and deliver a poisonous bite. He's the spider at the center of all this crap, but unlike Anansi he is way more than a trickster and teller of tales. He's dangerous.

I thought I'd stopped believing in "good" and "evil" a long time ago—it's so reductive and small. But Simon's immortality has come at a terrible price. Not so much a price exacted on himself, as far as I can figure it, but on way too many other people. Possibly even on Quentin.

And then there's Demian.

He may be a demon—the king of the demons—but at least he's true to his nature. There are no secrets. He simply is what he is. A force of nature. A vengeful god that I'm responsible for unleashing on the world. Aliette is cunning, but I can't really blame her for setting me up—I can only blame myself for being stupid enough to trust her. The Wood Queen and I have tangled too many times, now, and somehow she doesn't scare me. At least, not as much as she used to. But she did trick me into releasing the demons on our world.

Demons... it's a whole new ball game, one I'm not sure that any of us are ready for. I wish I knew the rules, but every time it feels like I'm finding my footing, somebody pulls the rug out from under me and I have to learn how to stand all over again.

All this, and my dreams are getting more vivid with each night that I spend in London. The pain in my arms from the iron tattoos that used to bind my power grows worse. Some mornings I wake up screaming, and I remember that the Demon King is gathering his army and the whole world is in danger... and I just want to run away and hide. Miranda speaks of the reaper storm of demons as though it's something that we all face together, even though I know I have to take responsibility for opening the door to Hell. I set things in motion— doesn't that mean that I should be the one to fix it?

The only problem is, I'm not even sure I know where to begin...

From: Donna Underwood
To: Navin Sharma
Subject: Use The Force

Nav,

I was being serious in that last email. Stop trying to cheer me up with *Star Wars* quotes.

I wish you would come visit. Didn't you say your dad was into the idea of you spending some time in London? I'd love to see you. I know it's a lot to ask, but I don't have any friends here and I just don't feel like I fit in—I know it's only been three weeks, but still. And anyway, I thought you'd want an excuse to skip school! :-)

Everybody in the Order of the Crow is so English. (Yeah, I know, I'm stating the obvious.) I feel like I'm living in a real-life version of Mary Poppins. Only without the singing and dancing. You know, the cool stuff.

Miranda's nice, don't get me wrong, but she's very *efficient*. Since her promotion she's pretty senior in the ranks—not quite on the same level as Quentin, but she's quickly approaching that. I thought I'd have gotten to know her better by now, but she's only really focused on the task of training me to be an alchemist. Honestly? So far, that mostly involves spending way too much time reading dusty old books. Being stuck in this house is starting to drive me crazy, too, though the upside is that it's pretty cozy for somewhere so big. Winter in London is colder than I thought it would be, and I miss the open fires at the Frost Estate. Never thought I'd hear myself say that...

Robert's around more, now that he's recovered from that demon shadow attack in the Ironwood, but he's not you. And he's way too serious about training me!

Anyway, I won't mention the fact that there's been news of demon activity up in Scotland. That's not something I should be bothering you with, and if anybody hacks into my emails they'll probably have me put away somewhere nice and "safe"...

Could you, possibly, if it's not too much trouble (!!) check on Xan for me? I guess he might be at Maker's workshop if he's not at home. I just want to know he's okay, that's all. I haven't heard from him in ages.

I miss you.

Love,
Donna

From: Navin Sharma
To: Donna Underwood
Subject: Trust Your Feelings

Donna,

Stop sending me such miserable emails, would you? You're depressing the crap out of me.

It's bad enough that you're not here, but then the only communication I get from you is filled with doom, gloom, and typos. (Wo)man up! What happened to the Donna Underwood who can open inter-dimensional doorways and rescue her mom's soul from the Wood Queen? Okay, so you probably started the apocalypse while doing that, but we're focusing on the positive here. And anyway, who says demons always have to be the bad guys?

Oh, and about what you asked me: no, I haven't seen or heard anything from the Wingless Wonder. (That's Xan, just in case you were confused.) Sorry, but I don't expect to. I think the guy was always threatened by my good looks, charm, and manly physique, if you really want the truth. He's hardly likely to want to hang out with me while you're not here, you know? I'm surprised he hasn't visited you yet. Doesn't his mom live somewhere in England?

Anyway, I'm stuck with school and homework and—ugh—exams. Some of us are destined to save the world, while others have to write essays on Macbeth's primal wound. Personally, I think you might actually have the best deal. This shit is messed up, yo.

Don, I'm worried about you. You haven't sounded like your normal self (and I use the word "normal" with caution) in ages. The last couple weeks, I mean. Don't make me get on a plane just so I can kick your ass.

I'm not sure the English laydeez are ready for me.

I'll Skype you soon.

Your buddy,
Nav

One

The British Museum was on fire.

Donna gazed in horror at the television screen, which showed the entire museum complex ablaze. Hungry flames licked the night sky, staining it the color of dried blood. Firefighters were beaten back by a wall of heat, smoke billowed in choking black clouds, and sirens split the air like screams of terror.

She shifted on the couch in Miranda's den. It was the homiest room in her mentor's grand old Victorian house, which was serving as a temporary headquarters for the

Order of the Crow. Grabbing the TV remote, Donna turned up the sound.

The newscaster's voice shook as she attempted to report from the scene. Or, at least, from as near to the site of the devastation as the news crews were permitted to get. Donna had never seen so many police in one place; blockades were set up on multiple streets, and it was reported that neighboring buildings had been evacuated, with talk of the evacuation zone being moved out to a two-mile radius.

There was chaos on the streets. Panic on the faces of the few people who stopped to be interviewed.

Miranda Backhouse touched Donna's shoulder, making her jump. The alchemist—Donna's new mentor—smiled gently. "Sorry, I thought you heard me."

She sat down on the couch beside her apprentice. The older woman's eyes reflected the burning buildings. Shadows played across her strained face, both from the television and from the candles that flickered throughout the room.

Donna shivered. "This is messed up. They're talking about a terrorist attack."

"Yes," Miranda said, her tone bleak. "A new 9/11."

"You don't sound convinced."

The alchemist shrugged. "Does that fire look like anything man-made to you?"

Donna remembered the Twin Towers. She'd watched the coverage as a child, from her bed in Ironbridge while recovering from one of the many magical operations that had rebuilt her ruined hands and arms.

"I don't know," she replied. "I think people can do some pretty terrible things."

Miranda fixed Donna with her clear blue gaze. "Of course they can. But can they also create flames that fly in the shape of dragons?"

"What?" Donna leaned forward, gazing harder at the ribbons of fire that coiled in the smoke-filled air. She narrowed her eyes, trying to see what Miranda saw.

That curl of smoke, like a tail. Tongues of flame, like giant wings. A column of fire that formed a neck, supporting a burning head with black eyes and nostrils that billowed some sort of noxious gas...

How had she missed it? Donna looked sharply at her mentor, raising her eyebrows, waiting for an explanation.

Miranda didn't disappoint. "Before, you could only see what everyone else saw. That's part of the illusion."

Hope gripped Donna's chest. "Illusion? You mean, this isn't real? There aren't really people who are hurt...or dead?"

"No, no, you misunderstand me. This is completely real. The only illusion is in hiding the true nature of the fire."

Donna squeezed her iron-clad hands into fists, clenching the soft fabric of the gloves she always wore to cover them. "It's the demons, isn't it?" She tried not to think of how beautiful the Demon King's voice had sounded the last time he'd spoken her name. She remembered the cruel turn of his mouth, and realized that in using dragon-shaped flames in his attack, Demian was mocking the alchemists. All the Orders, not just the Order of the Dragon, held the mythical creature sacred. For the alchemists, the dragon was a symbol of transformation.

"Yes, it seems that Demian has made his first move." Miranda's reply was so matter-of-fact, it chilled Donna to the bone. "He's calling us out. Look—the image is changing."

Now the flashing flames split off into multiple figures. This time they became smaller, winged creatures, their fiery beaks open as they swooped and soared in a strangely chaotic formation—a murder of crows.

"But why the museum? What the hell does Demian gain by attacking the British Museum, of all places?"

Miranda smiled grimly. "The alchemists have had many artifacts on display there over the years, especially in the Enlightenment Gallery."

Donna turned back to the TV screen, watching as a wall crumbled and hit the ground in a cloud of dust and flying debris. There was no sound, just shaky camera images filled with a historic landmark's destruction on a scale that London probably hadn't seen since the Second World War. The silence made it even creepier.

She swallowed. "I don't think the Enlightenment Gallery exists any more."

"No," Miranda agreed. "I don't think it does."

Banished to her room "for her own safety," Donna tried not to dwell on how this was all her fault. But how could she *not* think about the way that the Wood Queen had tricked her into opening the doorway to Hell? She wanted to call her mom, but knew her mother would be part of the emergency meeting that was taking place upstairs.

The conference between the four alchemical Orders—of the Crow, Dragon, Rose, and Lion—was supposedly to figure out what the Demon King's next move would be. They were communicating via *Skype*, of all things. Donna would have laughed at that, if she didn't feel sick every time she thought about the people who'd died in the museum fire. While the news reports said there'd been minimal fatalities because the attack took place after closing, that hadn't meant the building had been entirely empty; a handful of office workers, night security, and cleaners were still inside. Six human lives had ended. And of course even more people were injured, although those figures hadn't yet been officially confirmed. Maybe a dozen. Maybe more.

Donna hated that she wasn't involved in the alchemists' discussion. Shouldn't she be part of things? Sure, she knew it wasn't All About Donna Underwood, but what was she even doing in London if they weren't going to talk to her when Demian—whom *she* had released—attacked? It was crazy, although she should hardly be surprised given the super-secretive way the alchemists always acted. She'd just hoped things would be different in London. Even Robert was at the meeting.

Thinking of Robert Lee made Donna remember how lucky they'd both been to escape from the Ironwood last month. They *did* make it out in one piece, but Robert had been barely hanging on to life when the alchemists admitted him to their super-secret, super-private wing of Ironbridge Hospital, back home in Massachusetts. *Her* home, that is. Robert was about as American as tea and scones.

It had taken him more than a week to be considered well enough to travel, but now that he was back in London, his recovery had been faster than ever. Once Donna knew he was out of the woods (so to speak), her relief had been overwhelming. Robert had helped *her* when they'd faced down the demon shadows, after all.

Lying on her bed, Donna wanted to cry, but she found herself unable to squeeze out a single drop of emotion. She was so frustrated it made her jaw ache, and she realized that she'd been grinding her teeth.

This was pathetic. She had to do something.

Deciding to take some sort of action calmed her down, at least enough for her to sit up and swing her feet off the bed. She sat down at her computer and jiggled the mouse, waiting for the screensaver to clear.

If she was responsible for letting all the horrors of mankind out of Pandora's Box, well then … maybe she could find a way to put them back where they belonged—deep beneath the earth, in their Underworld home. Maybe there was a magical method of locking Demian up again. The alchemists had said it was impossible, now that he was free to roam once more, and that it had taken too much power when they'd done it two hundred years ago. But they didn't know everything. And they didn't have Donna's ability to open doors to other realms, or teleport to anywhere in the world.

Of course, she needed to be able to *control* her new-found powers to be able to use them effectively. And she was learning how, thanks to guidance from Maker back home and intense "training" sessions with Robert. As a new alchemical initiate, Donna had hoped to be casting spells by now or at the very least mixing a few potions, but she'd spent much of her time in London either reading dusty old books with Miranda or locked in martial arts combat with Robert—which involved sweating a lot and falling over at the end of lessons because she was so exhausted. Robert seemed to be on a Mr. Miyagi–style mission to prove that plain old self-defense techniques were somehow going to help her with the wacked-out "Iron Witch" abilities that everybody seemed so afraid of.

Well then, maybe she could learn more about the demons. There were books on demonology in Miranda's library, although she'd had been forbidden access to the darkest texts.

Donna smiled to herself, remembering the way Miranda had kept her out of the conference earlier. *Fine.* Let them keep her out of the loop. It seemed they still didn't trust her, which wasn't really surprising, considering what she'd done. And of course she'd grown up in the Order of the Dragon, which had been compromised, in the other Orders' eyes, by Simon Gaunt's machinations.

So, perhaps if she could get some insight into the nature of demons, she might be able to figure out a way to stop Demian and his hordes. She needed to look for weaknesses ... or maybe even something that she could use to negotiate with the demons. It wasn't like she didn't have experience making deals with otherworldly creatures, after all.

And if she couldn't put Demian back in his box, maybe she could figure out a way to kill him.

Donna wanted to be surprised by how easily she was even contemplating such extreme possibilities. She should at least be shocked at herself for *wanting* to end another being's life. But no matter how hard she tried, she couldn't manage to feel guilty. Not when it came to protecting the people she loved. And the Demon King wouldn't blink when it came to destroying human cities filled with millions of people. Among those people were Rachel Underwood, Navin Sharma, and Alexander Grayson—three lives she would do almost anything to protect.

She focused again on the computer screen in front of her. Another news update was the first thing she saw when she refreshed the BBC page. The fire was finally under control, but it was far too late to save the main buildings of the British Museum. Nobody could understand how the fire had spread so quickly and so totally. There were wild speculations about this in various comment threads and on Twitter, including talk of an "apocalypse," but mostly people seemed pretty sure it was a terrorist attack. Which, Donna thought, it *is*. Only carried out by a vengeful Demon King rather than religious fundamentalists or political extremists.

According to the reports, there had definitely been some kind of explosion, but nobody could agree on what exactly could have caused it. There would be all the usual investigations, of course, but while various experts were wheeled out to outline their ideas, not a single one of their theories matched. The explosion—if that's what it had been—was being classified as "mysterious" and "highly unusual."

Yeah, Donna thought. A *highly unusual* demon attack.

She flipped over to Google, typing in "enlightenment gallery british museum."

After scrolling past all the news reports about the blast, she came across several sites with information about the gallery Miranda had mentioned. The Enlightenment Gallery was where some of Dr. John Dee's mystical equipment was displayed. Dr. Dee was the creepy sixteenth-century astrologer, mathematician, and Master Magus who had played a pivotal role—unknown to most academics and historians—in the founding of the current alchemical Orders. One of the collection's centerpieces was Dee's famous obsidian scrying mirror. The British Museum also held alchemical grimoires and other manuscripts, all of which would undoubtedly be nothing more than ash by now.

Sighing, Donna decided she'd had enough of staring at a computer screen. It wasn't like she was learning anything *useful*. She headed down two flights of stairs to the library, hoping that the alchemists' conference would last a good while longer. It was unusual for her to have some time to herself, and now she was glad of it.

There had to be *some* sort of weapon that could be used against Demian and his kind—she just needed to find out what it was.

Two

S tepping quietly into Miranda's impressive library, Donna surveyed the eclectic décor. In the evenings, the room was dimly lit by iron chandeliers that hung from the high ceilings. Paintings adorned the walls—canvases of all sizes, framed prints of esoteric symbols—and gilt mirrors shone with reflected candlelight. The library was one of the grandest spaces, and yet also one of the most intimate, in the impressive old house.

Although Donna had been in London for almost a month, she still hadn't been shown anything that related to the creation of the Philosopher's Stone—even though this was, supposedly, the main reason she'd been sent to London in the first place. The alchemists needed the Stone before they could set to work re-creating the elixir of life, which Donna had (unfortunately yet necessarily) lost. But beyond the dry alchemical reading she'd been assigned, her so-called apprenticeship seemed to consist mostly of polishing ancient equipment and listening to Miranda's stories of "English Alchemy Across the Centuries." Donna was beginning to think that Robert's lessons on how to control her powers were actually more interesting, even if they didn't seem to have anything to do with alchemy.

True, it hadn't been all boring, but she wanted to know when she was actually going to learn the *real* secrets. Robert had quickly disabused her of that notion when he'd told her, "Alchemy is all about the individual's journey to transformation. We each find a different path to the truth."

"But *how* am I supposed to find that?" After having spent two hours cleaning out a closet of esoteric test tubes, Donna was tired of dust and even more tired of being told what to do.

Robert had grinned. "Use your initiative, Initiate Underwood."

So here she was, using her initiative. Miranda had given her the keys to the library and told her to shelve books whenever she had spare time. Fine. She would shelve books. She would take great care to examine even the ones that she wasn't supposed to touch.

There was a locked cabinet of antiquarian books against the north wall. Donna knew it wasn't just secured with an ordinary key; there were magical wards placed on it so that Miranda would know if anyone had disturbed the Order's most precious volumes. Donna remembered thinking that that was pretty strange, when Robert gave her a tour of the house on her first full day here. Quentin Frost, the Archmaster back home in Ironbridge, had never forbidden her from touching any of the books in the Blue Room, his own personal library. He'd loved to see her enjoy reading when she was a kid; it was something they shared.

Seeing books under lock and key—and protected by magic—gave Donna an uncomfortable feeling. It was as if they were dangerous in some way... as though, if allowed to go free, they could cause unknowable damage and destruction. Which was a weird thing to think, but nothing was outside the realm of possibility in her experience. Seventeen years on this earth had shown her plenty of danger already, and a whole lot of *weird* to go with it.

Before she could change her mind, Donna tugged off the black velvet glove that covered the ironwork on her right hand. She turned the small bronze key in the cabinet lock and rested her fingers against the mechanism. She had no idea what she was actually doing, but if she could open doorways between dimensions, surely she could open a freaking cabinet.

She examined her knuckles, willing something to happen. *Anything.* The iron tattoos that held her together—and which had bound her power for so long, as she'd recently discovered—were at peace for the moment, still and silent against her pale skin. Sometimes the silver swirls and markings would move, winding around her wrists and hands, up her arms to her elbows. Apart from how strange it was to see, the movement hurt her in a bone-deep sort of ache. Maker once told her it was because some of the iron was lacing together her actual *bones*. His alchemical magic had been the only thing that had saved her, after the Wood Monster's jaws had almost destroyed her arms and hands.

Thinking about it still made her shudder, even after all these years.

As she hesitated, the key in the lock, Donna saw her tattoos begin to move. She held her breath—the strange sensation made it feel as though the bones themselves were moving, shifting position and reshaping themselves into something new. It was something that she had no real control over. Watching the tattoos twist and writhe, sort of like soundwaves around the small amount of pale flesh still visible, made her feel nauseated.

She watched in fascination as the shimmering iron across her fingers curled around her hands and seemed to flick toward the lock. Then there was a sharp *click* and a sudden release of pressure inside her chest, like a balloon had just burst. The cabinet door jumped open.

Donna's ears popped and the tattoos stopped moving.

She'd done it! She'd actually managed to break Miranda's protective wards. Donna was pretty sure she'd also alerted her mentor to what she was up to. *Well, it's not like Miranda doesn't have more important things to think about right now*, she thought as she carefully opened the door wider to examine the contents of the shelves.

She lifted down one of the heavy volumes. It was bound in cracked leather and the pages were yellow and musty. Flipping through, she was surprised to see that it was hand-lettered in a barely legible script. The ink was a rusty brown, and some of the pages were filled with columns of numbers and unfamiliar equations.

Turning another page, her attention was immediately drawn to a sinister line drawing of some kind of small creature. It was twisted and knobbly, a bit like a wood elf but even more alien. She'd never seen anything like it before, and she traced the word underneath the illustration with her finger.

"*Homunculi,*" she read aloud. She'd heard that term before, but this was the first time she'd seen an illustration. "*Artificial life forms, based on human physiology, created with the aid of the Philosopher's Stone.*"

Donna shivered. Whoever the artist was, he or she hadn't seemed to believe that *homunculi* were all *that* closely based on human physiology. The creature was weird and lumpy, and about as far from a person as it was possible to get while still having a head, a torso, two arms, and two legs. Yet Donna wasn't surprised that the Philosopher's Stone was needed to make these beings, just as the stone was necessary in the creation of the elixir of life. She hoped she'd learn more about the Philosopher's Stone soon.

The book was arranged alphabetically, and she turned to the B section to look for "British Museum." There was no entry for it, so she tried "Dee." She found two pages of cramped, spidery text devoted to Dr. John Dee. Scanning the information, she came to a section that made her pause:

Dee's Mirror:
A polished piece of volcanic glass (obsidian), used
by Dr. John Dee to contact spirits and gain knowl-
edge of Other Worlds.

That sounded familiar ... she bit her lip and thought for a moment. Oh, right. John Dee's scrying mirror was one of the alchemical artifacts stored in the British Museum. Did that mean it was gone now, thanks to the fire? She flipped through some more pages before putting the volume aside. It was full of alchemical terms and definitions, and perhaps it would be useful later in her studies, but for now she wanted demon intel.

There was a smaller book, at the end of the top shelf, that drew her attention. It had one of those stupid locks holding it shut, like on her very first diary, which you knew was never going to keep anybody out. Not if they really wanted to read it.

This lock had long since worn away and was hanging by a few cotton threads and a thin strip of leather. She fiddled with the rotting metal until she could open the book without tearing the binding.

A handwritten title page declared, *Encyclopaedia Demonica*. She raised her eyebrows. Interesting title.

She looked for "Shadows," but there was no entry with that heading. Then she tried "Skriker," just out of curiosity. Of course, that wasn't in the book either. The Skriker was a fey creature, not a demon. But a couple pages further on, she found an entry that caught her eye:

"*Strix*,'" she read. "*About the size of an adolescent human, these demonic birds are hunters, just like their counterparts in the animal kingdom. Often seen in folklore as a bad omen, particularly known to foretell death. In Roman mythology they were believed to nest in desolate area, abandoned buildings, and ruins such as castles. In the demon world, they are known to feed on human flesh.*'"

Donna shivered and sat down on the floor, pulling the book into her lap and making herself comfortable.

Time slipped away as she read, flipping through various sections with foreboding subheadings and growing increasingly absorbed. No wonder Miranda kept these books locked away. There was some creepy stuff in them. Creepy and fascinating, in a car-crash kind of way. But useful? She wasn't so sure about that.

Until she came to something marked "Demon Locales." That sounded like it had some possibilities. Donna rubbed her aching back and shifted position, her eyes scanning pages more quickly. She half-expected Miranda to come bursting in at any moment, eyes filled with reproach for what she would see as her apprentice's blatant disregard for authority.

"*The Otherworld holds an unknown and potentially infinite number of different realms,*" she read. "*Commonly referred to as the Underworld in many world mythologies, the Land of the Dead is said to be the domain of the Demon King.*"

This is it! Donna thought, only just managing to hold back her cry of excitement. It had to be what she was looking for. Well, she didn't really know what exactly she *was* looking for—but perhaps she would find something useful here. Something that she could file away and use against Demian when the time came. The alchemists needed weapons, and one of the best weapons was knowledge. Quentin had taught her that. She hastily returned to the page, scanning parts that looked particularly interesting:

The Grove of Thorns:
Recognizable by its protective wall of black roses,
the Grove of Thorns is believed to be the one part of
the Underworld that even demons may not enter.
Alchemical scholars cannot agree on what is hidden
at its heart, but some ancient texts display crude
drawings of a pear tree. The fruit of this tree is
believed to be silver in color, and the tree itself has
many names, the most commonly found being—

Crack!
Something sharp tapped at one of the high windows, almost making Donna's heart burst through her chest. She dropped the book with a clatter as her mind flashed to a not-particularly-comforting image of demon-owls carrying babies in their beaks. Springing to her feet, she half-expected a reaper storm of demon shadows to smash through the glass and fly into the room.

All she could see, however, was a single crow. Or a raven? It stared in at her with coal-black eyes that glittered with disturbing intelligence.

Tap-tap-tap!

Donna jumped again, annoyed with herself for being so nervous about a stupid bird. She pushed aside disturbing thoughts of Edgar Allan Poe and climbed onto the carved wooden bench beneath the window. Her nose was just about level with the bottom of the glass, and she got a close-up view of the creature's scaly talons as it gripped the ledge outside. *What was a crow doing out at night?*

Attached to the bird's ankle was a rolled-up piece of paper or parchment, like a scroll. But the paper was black instead of ivory, or cream, or whatever color those things were supposed to be. Donna wondered if she'd fallen asleep over Miranda's dusty old books. Was this one of those disturbingly vivid dreams she sometimes found herself having? Maybe the crow was a messenger from her subconscious. Or maybe she was just hallucinating.

The "hallucination" squawked loudly and almost seemed to glare at her through the lightly frosted glass.

"You're not dreaming, Underwood," Donna told herself. "You're just going crazy."

And now I'm talking to myself.

She rolled her eyes. Definitely crazy. Not that she'd admit it to Nav when she told him about this.

Telling herself to get a grip, she opened the window and tentatively removed the paper on the crow's leg from its bindings. Her hand accidently brushed warm feathers. The moment the scroll was in her hand, the bird blinked once and then flew back up into the indigo sky.

Donna watched its inky wings blot out a section of stars for a moment, and then it was gone.

She unrolled the ebony parchment, but froze when footsteps sounded outside the library. *Great.* Either the meeting was already over, or Miranda was about to kick her ass for breaking into her secret book stash.

The scroll contained a simple but elegant invitation, and Donna quickly read it before her mentor entered the room. She could practically *feel* her face drain of color as she wordlessly handed the paper to Miranda. At least now, she was less likely to get into trouble for touching those forbidden texts.

It seemed that the crow-messenger had brought something far more important for the alchemists to worry about.

INVITATION

To: Donna Underwood, member of the Order
of the Dragon, care of the Order of the Crow
(London, United Kingdom—Human Realm)

His Highness Demian, King of the Demon Realm
invites you to a
Masquerade Ball
at
Pandemonium Crypt
(Beneath St Martin-in-the-Fields Church)

Time: Midnight. Tomorrow.
Dress: Formal. Masks must be worn.

Three

"I'm not going," Donna said, standing tall in the center of the library and glaring at Miranda as though it were *her* fault.

The heavy black paper in her mentor's hand looked like a shadow that didn't belong, almost appearing to mock her as the silver lettering shimmered in the candlelight.

Miranda placed the invitation on the nearby long wooden table. She blinked at Donna's outburst, but that was her only outward reaction. "This isn't the only communication that was delivered tonight. Other alchemists have already received their own invitations."

Donna raised her eyebrows. Waiting.

Miranda closed the book that Donna had dropped and slid it back into its rightful place on the shelf.

"Nobody said you have to attend," Miranda said in her typically mild tone.

"Good."

"You might want to *consider* it, though."

Donna snorted, for once not caring about being unladylike in front of Miranda. "Why am I not surprised?"

Her mentor shook her head, as though disappointed. "I'm just thinking about what's best for everybody."

"What about what's best for *me*?"

"I believe," Miranda said dryly, "that I was including you when I said 'everybody.'"

Donna dug the toe of her sneaker into the floor, wishing she could gouge a big-enough hole to escape through. "How could attending this thing possibly be good for me?"

"Because the Demon King seems to have taken rather a shine to you, and if he wants you to attend his masquerade, there must be a reason. We want to know what that reason is."

Donna picked up the invitation again. "But this... why would Demian's party have anything to do with me? And why is he even holding a masquerade ball? It seems kind of trivial for someone who supposedly has revenge on his mind."

"The intelligence we've gathered indicates that the demons are maneuvering for something specific—why do you think they haven't attacked the alchemists directly yet?"

Donna stared at Miranda for a beat. "Um…what do you call burning down the British Museum? I'd call that a direct attack."

"On humanity, yes. Not on the alchemists themselves."

"But there are alchemical artifacts in the museum. Maybe they were going after those."

Miranda waved her hand, irritation passing briefly across her face. "Either way, we have reason to believe there's a lot more going on here. We just don't know exactly what that might be. Not yet, anyway."

"The demons are probably still gathering their forces," Donna said. "That's got to take a while, after being trapped for two centuries."

Miranda frowned. "The demons are powerful—*Demian* is powerful—you really think he wouldn't have everything settled by now? No. Whatever it is they want, there's more to it than war. More even than simple revenge."

Simple? Donna didn't think there was anything "simple" about revenge, but she chose not to argue the point.

She forced out a breath. "Right. And you want me to find out what he's really up to?"

"If you can, yes."

"I'll just dance with him at some stupid ball, ask him all about his demonic plans, and he'll tell me…just like that. That's what you think?" Donna shook her head. "Somehow I don't think it's going to work."

Miranda shrugged. "It's worth a try. You may have more influence with him than you want to believe."

"Why? Because he's taken a *shine* to me?"

"Perhaps," her mentor replied.

"You're telling me that the Order of the Crow is willingly sending me to hang out with a demon king? You're quite happy to use me as bait?" Not that Donna was surprised, she just wanted to make sure she knew exactly where she stood.

Miranda tucked a strand of blonde hair behind her ear. A vaguely guilty expression crossed her face. "There will be other alchemists present, keeping watch over you. We're treating it as a diplomatic event—possibly even an opportunity to divert a war. At the very least, we can gather important information."

Robert chose that moment to enter the library, catching the tail end of their conversation. "Miranda's right," he said. "All of the alchemists received a similar messenger."

He looked more well-groomed tonight than usual, although for Robert that wasn't saying much considering his general Goth appearance. He was tall and willowy, his half-Chinese heritage evident in his dark eyes and glossy black hair, which tonight was tied back into a partial ponytail—all the better to show off his cobalt-blue highlights. He actually looked like he might have been out for the evening before getting called to the meeting upstairs, and Donna remembered that it had been his night off. Maybe Robert had had a date with a cute guy—he totally deserved some fun, given how close to death he'd come just weeks ago.

Donna immediately latched onto a hope she hadn't dared to believe might come true this soon. "Quentin and my mom—will they be at this ball?"

"Well, the Order of the Dragon has been invited to send representatives," Robert replied. "As have the other Orders."

"How are they going to get here in time for tomorrow night?" Donna had visions of them using her wildly untested abilities to somehow transport people, and her stomach tightened.

Miranda smiled grimly. "Demian says that arrangements for that will be made. I don't doubt that our colleagues will be there."

Donna scowled at the invitation. "Part of me doesn't want to go, but the other part... well, *she* wants to kick Demian's ass."

Robert flashed her a quick grin. "He'd probably enjoy that."

"What are you talking about?" Donna snapped, annoyed at the flush of warmth in her cheeks.

He ignored her, then turned to Miranda. "Don't you think you should get some rest? It's already gone midnight and there will be a lot of work to do tomorrow."

Miranda checked her watch. "There's no time for me to sleep yet. I have to start getting things organized. Not the least of which is finding a ball gown for you, Donna."

Donna blanched. "A ball gown?"

"Yes. Never fear, it's all under control." Miranda turned on her heel.

Donna watched the petite woman stride from the room before turning on the tall alchemist standing in front of her. A slow smile was spreading across Robert's face. Despite how irritating he could be, Donna couldn't help liking him.

"So, what did you mean?" she asked, knowing she'd probably regret asking. "About Demian enjoying it if I kicked his ass?"

Robert rolled his eyes. "Isn't it obvious? He fancies you."

Fancies? "Who even says that?"

"Doesn't change the fact."

"It's not a fact. It's your theory. A very bad one."

"Well, it's a theory that Miranda clearly shares. I didn't hear you arguing with *her* about it when she said something about how the Demon King has taken a shine to you."

Donna crossed her arms. "That's because she's currently my boss. Sort of. And Miranda's choice of words was far less annoying."

"I realize how *annoying* it must be that I'm right all the time, but I told you as much when you first opened the Gate to Hell," Robert replied. "The look in Demian's eyes when he spoke to you was pretty weird. Creepy, even. Like you were a commodity rather than a person."

Donna knew something about that look, but not from Robert's description of the demon. She remembered what her mother had written in her journal—about Simon Gaunt's expression when he noticed the young Donna's growing power. She shivered.

"We're not just talking about some guy here, Robert. He's a demon. The Demon *King*. Do you honestly think that's what this is about?" Donna picked up the invitation and tossed it at him.

He ducked as the heavy paper fluttered to the ground like a dead, black thing. "Ah, so serious." Seeing that she really was mad at him, Robert sobered. "Sorry, Donna. I was just kidding. Trying to take the edge off all this bloody tension."

Her shoulders were still tight with anger. Or perhaps with fear. "Well, then, you're doing a shitty job of it."

He ran his tongue over the silver lip ring that caught the candlelight, a nervous habit. "Right. I got that. Once again, my apologies."

Donna forced herself to relax. "Demian only cares about power. If he *fancies* anything, that's what this is all about."

"He wants something from you," Robert said. "That's certainly true."

"Yeah," she snapped. "Maybe he does, but it sure as hell isn't a date."

❧

Donna stomped out of the library and ran upstairs to her bedroom. She wanted privacy for the phone call she was about to make.

When her mother picked up on the second ring, Donna's face broke into a grin of pure relief.

"Hey, Mom."

"Donna." The smile was evident in her mother's voice, although Donna could also detect a note of strain. "It's good to hear from you."

The strange bird with its invitation from Demian was the first thing on Donna's mind, but she tried to wait. At least for a moment. "I miss you."

"You didn't call just to catch up." Rachel Underwood's tone was suddenly all business. "This is about that so-called ball the Demon King has dreamed up. Any excuse to get us all in one place, I'm sure."

"So, everybody got invitations?"

"Yes. The Order of the Rose in Prague—they aren't too happy about it, let me tell you! It takes something special to dig them out of that mausoleum they call a home. Even an alchemist from the Order of the Lion was found by Demian's messengers. We don't know how he managed it, but I would imagine that a demon has his ways."

The Order of the Lion was the most clandestine branch of alchemy; the members were more like spies or super-secret agents. Half the time, nobody was even sure where their latest base of operations was—whether or not they were on covert missions or just sitting around somewhere sipping martinis (shaken, not stirred). Locating one of their members out in the middle of nowhere and deep under-cover—to personally deliver an invitation to something as ordinary as a party—was pretty impressive. Demian clearly hadn't had any trouble finding them, which was just another demonstration of his effortless power.

"At least we'll find out what he wants—he may be about to offer terms," Rachel added.

Donna immediately felt shards of ice smash any pleasure she felt at speaking with her mom. "Terms? Maybe he's just feeling destructive. The British Museum is pretty much gone."

"It's terrible, of course, but this is exactly the kind of behavior we expect from a creature like that. Why do you think the alchemists worked so hard to lock him away for two centuries?"

Which made Donna feel guilty all over again for letting such a potentially powerful being loose on the world. She guessed it was a feeling that wasn't going to disappear any time soon.

"So, Mom, how are you feeling?" If the change of subject was unsubtle, her mother didn't call her on it.

"Better. Much better."

"Are you sure?" Donna couldn't help her constant anxiety about her mom's illness and recovery. She wished she could have stayed with her in Ironbridge, just to keep an eye on her, but here she was stuck in England serving out her "sentence" for all the mistakes she'd made. It didn't help any that her mom had a tendency to brush her sickness aside as though it had been a minor thing, rather than a ten-year trip around the bend to Crazy. Half the time, Donna wondered whether her mother's recovery was yet another of the Wood Queen's tricks, but so far things seemed to be moving in the right direction.

"You worry too much," Rachel said. "I'm feeling almost back to my old self. I've been spending a lot of time with Quentin."

"That's great," Donna replied. "I bet he's happy to see you back."

Her mother laughed. "He's the only one."

Donna couldn't help her own snort of laughter. Aunt Paige and Simon Gaunt had been shocked to witness Rachel's magical recovery. They'd tried to look and sound pleased, but neither of them did a very good job of it. Even Aunt Paige, who was experienced at putting a positive spin on things in her day job working for Ironbridge's mayor, had looked shell-shocked.

Her mother sighed, filling the silence between them. "I'm just sorry you're having to deal with any of this. You've already had a decade of secrets and lies to come to terms with. Now this."

Donna's fingers tightened on the phone. "I'm not even sure I *have* come to terms with it."

"So you don't want to try?"

"Not really, no." She lowered her voice. "I want to leave, Mom. You know that, right?"

"I do," her mother replied steadily. "I'm not surprised, and I certainly don't blame you."

"I'm just trying to figure out the best way to ... "

"Make your escape?" There was the hint of a smile in Rachel's voice.

"Something like that." Donna blew out a breath, relieved to be having this conversation, while at the same time regretting that it was happening while her mother was so far away. "I'm sorry. Are you mad?"

"Why should I be? I love you, no matter what. I never wanted this life for you."

It was far too late for that, Donna thought. This was the life she had, and the only thing left was to make the best of it. At least until she turned eighteen this summer. *Not long,* she thought. *Not too long to wait.*

She wondered if she would even *reach* her birthday before the world ended at the hands of a reaper storm of demons. She'd probably die a virgin, knowing her luck; she smiled faintly as she remembered how close she'd come to sleeping with Xan, that night she'd teleported to his house.

Not like she could think about romance when there was a demon king knocking at the door. Pushing images of Alexander Grayson from her mind, Donna pressed the phone against her ear and focused on her mother's gentle voice again as she recounted what had happened at the alchemists' meeting. Anything to ground her, to take away the feeling of despair that suddenly hit her in the gut and made her dizzy.

Not many people her age had to worry about stuff like a demonic apocalypse, but it didn't make Donna feel in any way special. She was tired. She felt old and worn out and cynical. She wanted the chance to be a kid again, before it was too late. She dreamed of traveling the world and going to college and doing normal teenage things. Perhaps those things would always remain just out of reach—more like a cruel mirage than a dream—but if she didn't hold on to hope, what else was there?

Donna paced up and down the street, just outside the little row of Victorian houses in the heart of Pimlico. The lights of the city still burned, even at this time of night, and the sky was full of stars. Miranda hadn't wanted her to go out alone, but Donna needed air before she could even think of going to bed. She'd promised to stay within sight of the house, but even this tiny slice of liberation lifted her spirits. She'd declined Robert's offer to join her for an "early hours" walk around the neighborhood—she was still pissed at him for talking about Demian the way that he had. Sure, he meant well, but that didn't mean he knew what he was talking about.

Power was the only currency that someone like the Demon King cared about. As Miranda had already indicated, it wasn't about something as ... *banal* as destruction; there was more to it than that. It wasn't even about revenge. Donna had felt it that night in the Ironwood, when Demian had first stepped free of his prison—and then once again, that day on the bridge when he'd given her the first of many black roses.

She shivered, remembering once again his gaze and the way he'd spoken to her. As that thought crossed her mind, she saw a pale shape coalesce out of nothing but cool night air.

He stood waiting for her, three doors down from Miranda's house.

She instantly recognized the tall, slender figure, who was motionless except for his silver hair, which was blowing slightly in the sudden wind. It felt like something out of a movie, and Donna had no doubt that this was the effect Demian was going for.

Donna knew that Robert was watching out for her from one of the top-floor windows, but she wondered how much he would really be able to see. Demons were masters of illusion—more so than the fey with their glamour, and perhaps even possessed a more powerful kind of magic than the alchemists. At least, once they were at full strength again.

Demian was beautiful, as before. But it was a dangerous beauty. The sort of beauty that you could cut yourself on if you weren't careful. He stood with his shoulders back, in the black suit that matched his glittering eyes. His skin was very pale, his features all sharp planes beneath the shadows cast by the silver hair sweeping back from his face.

The Demon King smiled as she watched him. Somehow, his smile was more terrifying than any other expression he might have chosen to wear on his wicked face.

"What are you doing here?" Donna managed to say.

"Am I not free to visit my subjects when it pleases me?"

Subjects? Donna clenched her jaw and gave him the most scary look she could. "You are beyond arrogant."

His eyes flashed. "And you are *beyond* discourteous."

Her stomach dropped to somewhere down near her knees, but she stood her ground. "We got your invitation, if that's what you're here to check up on."

He shrugged one shoulder, a gesture she was already familiar with from their previous meetings. "Indeed. I have received a reply from your Archmaster and the Order of the Dragon, as well as from the alchemists here."

"Oh. Right." Donna wondered how the alchemists managed to RSVP when there hadn't been a return address included with the invite. "I'm going back inside," she added. "So you might as well leave."

"Won't you stay and talk for a few moments?"

"It's cold."

The air around her instantly heated. For some reason, that made her shiver even more. Demian was powerful— exactly how powerful was anybody's guess. Two hundred years of incarceration didn't seem to have slowed him down too much.

"Better?" he asked, raising his eyebrows in challenge.

Donna glared at him. "Please, just leave me alone."

She felt for the elusive shard of first matter—alchemical *prima materia*—that lived within her, just in case. Catching the very edge of the unpredictable power she had yet to fully understand, she prepared to tug on it, to use it if the Demon King attacked. Her own personal brand of magic was her only defense against him. Donna wasn't sure what she could really do with it, but at the very least she might be able to escape. The enhanced physical strength of her arms would be pretty much useless against a demon.

"I'll leave you alone," Demian said, "when I get what I want."

Donna crossed her arms. "Which is?"

His lips widened in a sensual smile. "You, Donna Underwood. I will have you for my own. You ... interest me."

Her legs went weak, but she managed to remain upright. What was he talking about? "I'm not a belonging," she ground out. "I am not your pet. You can't talk about human beings like that."

"Nevertheless," he said, "I'll make you mine and you will thank me for it."

Donna dug her nails into her palms. "What do you mean, 'have' me? In what way?"

"In *every* way." His eyes glinted.

Crap. She had to stop baiting him. Up until now, he'd seemed civil enough, but that could change at any moment. He was a demon, after all. What was to stop him from just taking her into the Underworld by force, Persephone-style?

Demian bowed. "I look forward to seeing you at the masquerade."

"I'm not going," Donna said. The treacherous words were out before she could drag them back and lock them away.

"You *will* attend."

"I'm busy tomorrow night."

He showed her the edge of his teeth. "Change your plans, or I'll be forced to change them for you. This ball is more than a social event. It is not a trifle. Negotiations will take place there."

"At a masquerade ball? Really? Is that how demons do business these days?"

He moved so quickly, she didn't even realize it until he was almost on top of her. She felt the heat radiating from his body. "Demons always mix business with pleasure. Haven't your little books told you that?"

Donna tried to hide the shudder that ran through her at just having him so close. It was a strange and sickening mixture of disgust and desire. She knew the pleasure wasn't real; Maker and Quentin had told her it came from Demian's natural pheromones and that all she could do was fight against it. So she tried to focus on a thread of fear instead, her pure terror that she was nothing more than prey.

His head tilted to one side as he examined her. "You are ... afraid."

She didn't have the energy to laugh. "You think?"

"You freed me. You gave my people—what remains of them—hope. Why would I hurt you?"

Donna clenched her hands. "Maybe because I didn't mean to set you free. I know that's not what you want to hear, but it's the truth. Aliette tricked me. I never meant to open the door to your realm."

"Accident or not, the door opened, and you were the one responsible. Therefore, I owe you a great debt."

Her throat felt impossibly dry. "You owe me nothing. I intend to put you back where you belong." *If I can*, she added to herself.

His lips curved into a wicked smile. "You will fail."

"But at least I'll have tried."

Demian grabbed her hands and pulled her toward him so that they were standing face to face. "I won't allow you to send us back. Not after two centuries. Not after I have tasted freedom again."

"Then kill me," she said, amazed that her voice remained steady.

"No," he said, his own voice like stone.

Donna looked Demian right in the eye and summoned defiance—she was her father's daughter, after all, heir to Patrick Underwood, a legend in his time. "So, what is it about me that keeps you from just ... snuffing me out?" she asked.

"Do not presume to question me."

All his charm had disappeared—Demian was as change-able as the night sky above London. It was terrifying, but she wouldn't let him intimidate her. Donna hated bullies, even Otherworldly bullies who were simply being who they were. Demian only knew how to throw his weight around because he was born a king. And although she couldn't beat him in any kind of direct confrontation, Donna still had a few sur-prises up her sleeve. Or, more precisely, hidden beneath her gloves.

She let her whole body go limp, hoping to sucker him into a mistake. As she relaxed, the only thing keeping her upright was Demian's hold on her.

He reacted to her "fall" instantly, releasing her hands and wrapping his arms around her body in a lightning-fast movement that took her breath away. Donna placed her now free hands against his chest and pushed, with all of the iron-clad strength in her arms. She gritted her teeth and put everything she had into it, gasping with the effort of trying to move what seemed to be an immoveable object.

Releasing her, Demian rocked backward, stumbled on the edge of the sidewalk, and adjusted his balance all in one fluid move. His expression was almost comically shocked.

Donna pulled herself upright. "Don't touch me again, *Majesty*."

"I do as I like," he said, clearly shaken. "I could destroy your whole pathetic race. Every human being would serve me. I could rule this world!"

All his courtly manners were gone. Fury remained, sharp-edged like a blade.

"You *could* rule," Donna replied, feeling the color drain from her face. "But you would be a lonely king. A heartless, pathetic dictator."

"You will not speak to me this way," he snarled.

"Why not? What have I got to lose? If you're going to kill everyone on this planet, there's not a lot I can do about it. You've already made that pretty clear." She took a step forward, pressing on despite the numb terror that hovered on the edge of her awareness. "And I'm not sure you'll do it, anyway."

"And what makes you think you know me so well, young alchemist?"

"I don't know you. Not even a little." She took a deep breath. "But if you really were going to destroy everything in a fit of demonic rage—just to get your *revenge*—I think you would already have done it."

Demian smiled, but it was a terrible expression. "You have no idea what I'm capable of. Your tiny mind would break under the weight of all I have done. If I told you … "

He let his voice trail off suggestively, but Donna was getting the picture. Demian might be quick to lose his temper, but he was still a manipulative control freak. She recognized all the signs, after spending a lifetime around creeps like Simon Gaunt.

"Yeah," she heard herself say in a bored voice she almost didn't recognize as her own. "I'm so impressed by you. Wow, you're amazing."

His lip curled. "Hide behind your human sarcasm if it pleases you. I will see you at the ball, and after we have danced and celebrated my freedom, then we will speak of the future. What remains of it, at least. There is much to be discussed after all these years."

"You don't need me for negotiations."

"On the contrary," he replied, his voice becoming implacable. "You are the one person we cannot do without."

"*If* I attend."

"As I have already made clear, you *will* attend the masquerade or I will make you regret it."

Donna touched the center of her chest, as she'd frequently done these past months as she connected to the power inside her. "Are you threatening me?"

His expression darkened. "I don't need to make threats."

"Because you're so used to people doing your bidding, your Majesty?"

"They usually do," he said.

"Well, then, you can expect me to buck that trend," she said.

Demian's mouth twitched—with annoyance or amusement, Donna couldn't decide.

"We'll see," was all he said. "I am certainly used to having to convince people that my way is the *best* way to do things."

Donna resisted the temptation to punch the Demon King in his perfect face. He was such a psycho. "You mean, the way you convinced the Order of the Crow to take your 'invitation' so seriously? By *murdering* innocent people in London?"

"There are always casualties in war." His eyes were completely unreadable black spaces. "It is regrettable, but necessary."

Before she could reply with an appropriate level of contempt, Demian turned and walked away from her. His movements were smooth and sure. Nothing troubled him now—least of all her.

Donna's heart was pounding so hard it blocked out the distant sounds of the city.

As the king of the demons reached the garden gate of the next house, he stopped and looked over his shoulder at her. It was one of the most incongruous scenes she had ever seen—and it wasn't like she hadn't seen a lot of strangeness in her life.

"Until next time, Donna Underwood," he said.

She shivered as he said her name, hating him for his power. Or maybe she didn't hate him for that—it was easy to resent power, but she really wasn't the sort of person who "hated." No, the thing she disliked in Demian was the way he used his power. The abuse of it.

He disappeared, leaving behind a single black rose on the sidewalk. Of course.

"Show-off," she muttered, turning on her heel and leaving the flower exactly where it was.

❧

There were several missed calls and a text message from Xan waiting for her when she got back to her room. Cursing herself for being so careless as to leave her phone behind, she scrolled through to the new message. It read:

> I heard about what happened. If you get this in
> the next hour ping me back and I'll call you.

Worrying that she might have missed her chance to speak to him, Donna fumbled to text back a quick reply and then sat waiting anxiously, her cell phone in her lap. She knew Xan had been hiding something from her these past few weeks—something important—but as usual, she knew not to push him. He would probably talk when he was ready. At least, she hoped he would. He'd been brought up with as many secrets as she had, having to bury his half-fey heritage and practically live a lie. She knew it was a hard habit to break … that natural desire to keep things safely hidden and hold your emotions inside, to fear what might happen if you reached out and trusted someone else.

Maybe hearing from him tonight was a good sign. At the very least, she'd be able to talk to him about everything that had happened in London tonight.

She tried not to think about Demian while she waited, but of course that was impossible. It seemed almost like a dream—a nightmare—that only minutes ago she'd been talking to the king of the demons outside in the street. A regular London street, where passersby had no clue what was going on right under their noses.

The phone rang and she snatched it up, her heart pounding.

"Hey, Donna," Xan said.

"Xan," she replied, holding the phone more tightly and savoring the sound of his voice. "How are you?"

Four

Alexander Grayson sat in his beaten up old car on the edge of the freeway, where he'd pulled over so he could call Donna. He had trouble hearing her to begin with, what with all the traffic zooming past and the low-flying airplane that chose that precise moment to pass overhead.

"What did you say?" He wished the window on the passenger side could actually be closed fully.

"I said," she repeated, "how are you?"

"Fine. I'm fine. It's you I was worried about. I miss you."

"What was that?"

"Wait a sec," he said, climbing into the back of the car, in hopes of cutting out the traffic noise by moving farther away from the busted window.

"*Where* are you?" Donna asked.

"Just running an errand for my dad." The lie tripped easily off his tongue, and he tried to tell himself it was for the best. That he just didn't want to worry the girl he'd so quickly fallen for.

It was true what he'd just said—he did miss her. All the time. Every day. But he found it hard to say that kind of thing—especially right now, when he was sneaking around behind her back, doing stuff she wouldn't exactly approve of. Xan liked to think of himself as the kind of guy who took action first and worried about the consequences later. He wasn't much for planning. Or at least, he wasn't into *sharing* his plans, because that just gave people the opportunity to talk him out of whatever he was going to do next.

Donna's voice was faint on the other end of the phone, making her sound far away. Which, he supposed, she was. "Xan? Are you still there?"

Her voice yanked him out of his thoughts. "Yeah, sorry. Hearing your voice again ... it's been too long."

"And whose fault is that, Mr. Grayson?" Donna's tone was playful, but he could detect the edge beneath the surface.

Sighing, Xan tucked his cell phone into a more comfortable position and leaned back. "I know, I know. I really am sorry."

"It's fine," she replied. "I'm happy to hear from you. Things have been crazy here."

"I heard about the British Museum on the news. That's why I called—I needed to make sure you were okay."

"We're all fine," Donna said. Her voice lowered and he could hear the emotion in it. "I can't say the same for the people who died in the explosion."

"And it was definitely him? Demian?"

"What do *you* think?"

He shrugged, even though she couldn't see the gesture. "I just wanted to make sure. You know, just in case there was a chance it was ... something else."

"He wanted to get our attention." She laughed bitterly. "And then he invited us all to a stupid *ball*."

"I heard a little about that, too," he admitted, wondering if he was already saying too much. "I saw Maker earlier and he let something slip."

"Maker does like to talk."

"Yeah, I was surprised he told me anything at all, but I guess it was hard to hide that something major had happened. I mean, that Demian had actually made his first move."

If she was surprised he'd spent time with Maker, Donna hid it well. "What did he tell you?"

"About the masquerade, and that there's going to be a big meeting there of alchemists, demons, and wood elves."

There was silence on the other end of the line for a moment, but she quickly recovered herself. "Sounds like he told you more than 'a little.' It actually sounds like you know more than *me*."

Shit. He knew he'd said too much. "Which part didn't you know?"

"I thought it was just the alchemists meeting with Demian," she said. "How did he know about the wood elves?"

"I don't know. He just said it was like peace negotiations, and that all the major factions would be involved. They're trying to avoid a war, but I'm not sure how much hope everyone is really holding out for that."

"Did he specify *which* elves would be there?"

Xan rubbed his eyes. He was getting a headache. "No… he definitely didn't mention the Wood Queen to me— not by name—but I guess I assumed that's who he meant when he said 'wood elves.'"

"Oh." Donna went quiet after that.

"You're not mad because Maker told me something you didn't know, are you?"

"Well, it's not exactly your fault." There was a smile in her voice, which filled him with relief.

"Donna," he said, a sudden rush of anxiety hitting him full in the chest. "You're not going to it, right? The ball, I mean."

"I don't want to, but it's not looking like I have much of a choice."

"You have the choice to walk away. From all of it."

Donna sighed. "I'm sort of stuck here, Xan. This was the result of the tribunal—you know that. I'm serving under Miranda now."

He hit the back of the passenger seat with his free hand. "That doesn't mean you have to do what they tell you *all* the time. Take back some control!"

"I'm only seventeen. I'm a member of a secret order of alchemists. I have cold iron running through my arms and a piece of the first matter inside me. My life is so far away from being under my control that, most days, I feel like screaming." Donna's voice was rising in pitch. "Don't start lecturing me, okay? Please. I ... I don't think I can take it."

He pressed his lips together for a moment, pushing down on his rising temper. "Sorry."

There was silence between them for a moment.

Donna said, "Let's not talk about that anymore. How are things with you? Seriously, I've hardly heard from you, and when I do ... I don't know, Xan. I know there's something you're not telling me."

"Everything's fine," he replied. It was an automatic response. A response he'd learned in childhood.

"I wish you'd tell me about how things are going with Maker."

"There's not much to tell."

"Xan ... "

He shoved his hair back from his face and looked out the window at the busy freeway. "The only reason I don't say much is because I know how you feel about it. About what I want Maker to do for me."

"You mean, helping you to get your wings back? If he can."

"Exactly. *If* he can. That's the point. There aren't any guarantees at all."

She paused. Then, "It's not that I don't want you to get his help. You know that, right?"

"I know."

"I just don't want the Order to use you," she continued. "The way they wanted to use me."

"I get it," he said. And he did. He understood that her concern was totally for him—that she was afraid that if he took Maker's help, it would only come with a huge price. Debts to be paid. All of that. "You don't trust Maker."

"I don't trust anyone," Donna said. "God, I sound totally paranoid."

"It's not like I can blame you."

"I guess."

He cleared his throat, curious. "Why don't you trust Maker? He seems the most okay out of all of them to me."

"*He's* the one who bound my powers." Donna sounded annoyed that he'd even asked. But before he could say something, apologize or whatever, she was speaking again. "Maybe he was telling the truth when he told me how dangerous my powers would have been while I was so young. I was only seven when my abilities began to manifest—that's what it said in Mom's journal. But that doesn't mean I can trust him again. Not just like that."

"I know."

"And they're still all trying to hide the truth about me. About what I might be able to do with this power inside me."

"They're afraid," he said. "That's all."

"It hurts, Xan," she admitted quietly, and he had to struggle to hear. "Sometimes, it felt like Maker was the only one in the Order of the Dragon who was truly on my side."

"What about Quentin?"

"I don't know." She sighed, and he could almost swear he felt it vibrate through the cell phone pressed against his ear. "Sometimes. Maybe. I *love* Quentin, sort of like a grandfather, there's no doubt about that. But he's with Simon."

"The guy clearly has excellent taste," Xan said, totally deadpan.

She laughed. "Right."

Xan thought about Simon Gaunt and felt his whole body tense with dislike. The guy was a fucking snake. A man who summoned and trapped *demons*, then blamed Donna for the current threat posed by her mistake in opening the door to Hell. How many of the alchemists knew that the Magus had the essence of a minor demon trapped inside a bronze statue in his laboratory?

He leaned forward and checked the time on the dashboard. "Hey, I have to go."

"It's okay. This is probably costing you a fortune."

"Rich dad, remember? He still helps me out."

"I didn't think you guys talked much."

He thought about that for a moment. His adoptive father was a distant man—which was putting it kindly. Sometimes he wondered why his human parents had even adopted him, what with his mother being back in England since the divorce. They really *didn't* talk much. None of them did.

"We don't," he said. "But he must feel guilty on some level, because he's pretty generous with his money."

Money was the answer to most of Charles Grayson's problems. Xan just wished that his father didn't see him as simply another problem to be solved in his busy life. Not that it should matter now, anyway—now that Xan was old enough to do what he wanted. If he even knew what that was.

Filling the aching hole inside him would be a pretty good start. All he wanted was the chance to recover what he'd lost: the life he never had the chance to know. It was all gone, now, and the only thing he had left were the scars on his back.

He said goodbye to Donna, knowing she was still unhappy with him for how secretive he was being. Xan couldn't blame her for that.

He just hoped that she'd forgive him.

That night, Donna had another of the unsettling lucid dreams that were becoming a regular feature in her life. Ever since her powers had been unbound last fall, her dreams were becoming something she was witnessing rather than experiencing. And yet, at the same time, she knew it was herself in the dreams. She was a participant even as she watched herself, a shadow Donna, gliding through her mind like a ghost…

She walks through hallways and more hallways. There is no end, just straight lines going on and on into the dark. No windows. No doors.

No way out.

She finally reaches a corner. She feels excited that something has finally changed in her surroundings—she knows that what she is about to see must be very important, something that might help her to solve the riddle of demons in this world.

Demian whispers to her, a shadowy presence with impossible stony wings half-unfurled against his shoulders. They move and shimmer with a life of their own.

"Look," he says. "All the ghosts are dancing in the ballroom."

And she looks at where he's pointing and sees that he's right—there are indeed ghosts gliding across the polished obsidian floor. Strange shadows flicker around the edges of the room. Her father is there among the dancers, but he doesn't see her, even when she calls out to him. Donna draws closer, trying to move around the revelers, but each time she takes a step somebody gets in her way. The sound of music and laughter fills her ears. She tries to get her father's attention by screaming, waving her arms, anything to pull his gaze around. But he dances on by with a serene expression on his face. The woman in his arms is not her mother.

The woman in his arms is not even human.

Patrick Underwood hasn't changed at all—he looks just the same as he did when she last saw him ten years ago. He wraps his arms more tightly around the monster he dances with, resting his head on her bony shoulder.

The woman stares directly at Donna and smiles with a mouth full of blood-stained teeth. Her eyes are strange . . . inhuman. The pupils are shaped like hourglasses, and sand is slipping through them like tears.

"We all die," the woman says. "That's the secret of life."

"Wait," Donna whispers, because her voice isn't working right after all that screaming. "What do you mean?"

But the monstrous woman just dances away, spinning Patrick around and around until Donna feels dizzy from watching.

She tries to wake herself up, because she knows that she is dreaming.

"We all die. That's the secret of life." The words seem to echo inside her head for a very long time and the sands keep falling, but even then she can't wake up.

She wonders if she ever will.

Five

Donna sat up in bed, feeling her heart race and listening to the clatter of an early morning trash collection in the street. "Dustbin men," as they called them over here. She tried to focus on the sound of ordinary life outside, tried to let it seep into her consciousness and bring her back from the bright terror of the nightmare. Words of death lingered on the edge of her memory. A warning.

She rubbed her cold arms and looked across the bedroom that still didn't feel like hers, letting her gaze fall on the elegant, full-length black satin evening gown that now hung on the outside of her huge oak wardrobe. Miranda certainly worked fast. And although Donna might have liked to shop for the dress herself, having never before had the opportunity to pick out a ball gown, it was hardly a priority.

Quietly crossing the room, she slipped into the dress. It had an off-the-shoulder cut and fell in graduated folds to her ankles, the satin material shining like polished onyx. It made her feel very grown up, even though she wished there was more color in the outfit. *Well, I can fix that with my favorite pairs of gloves*, she thought with a slight smile. She didn't see any evidence that they'd bought her a mask. Of course, Miranda had said not to worry—it was all "under control." That wasn't very reassuring, but hopefully they wouldn't get her anything *too* crazy.

Somebody knocked at her door.

"Donna, are you up?" Miranda called. "Your training session with Robert is still on for today. And then I'll need your help in the library. *Somebody* appears to have damaged the antiquarian cabinet, and I have to reset the wards..."

Donna grimaced. *Oh, that.* "I'll be there in ten minutes, Miranda," she called. At least helping her mentor would keep her mind off whatever was coming her way tonight. And she could also make amends for breaking into the private collection of alchemical texts. Miranda obviously knew it was her, but she was being amazingly cool about the whole incident. She certainly handled breaking-and-entering better than Simon Gaunt did.

Gazing at her elegant silhouette in the mirror, Donna tried not to think too much about what Demian had meant when he'd said she would be an important part of "negoti-ations." She was way past tired of being used as a pawn in games she didn't understand—didn't *want* to understand. The ball loomed ahead of her like a storm threatening the sky.

The only positive part about the upcoming event was that she might actually get to see her mother. Donna didn't know how Demian intended to bring everybody together in such a short space of time, but he could probably just snap his fingers.

And there was definitely something specific that the Demon King wanted, something far greater than he was let-ting on. Demian was full of trickery, of course, but Donna suspected he was after something that only the alchemists could give him. And from what he'd said during their encounter last night, she felt pretty sure that she was some-how part of it.

This slice of knowledge filled her with sickly dread. She did her best to push it out of her mind, but that was an impossible task. At least she'd find out the answer soon—which wasn't exactly a comforting thought, either.

But right now she was late for yet another training ses-sion with Robert Lee, and she didn't want to give him an excuse to be any tougher on her than usual. Donna changed into some comfortable clothes, hastily tied her hair back, and ran downstairs to meet him.

Donna hit the mat hard, biting her tongue in the process. Tears of pain burned her eyes, but she blinked them away fast.

"Holy crap," she said, tasting blood in her mouth. "You're like a ninja."

Robert put his hands on his hips and gave her a look that clearly meant she was a moron. "Ninjas are Japanese," he said. "I'm half Chinese. There's a difference, you know."

"I know. I was just kidding."

"L O L," he deadpanned.

"Sorry," Donna said, feeling bad for making such a dumb joke. "Help me up and we'll try again."

"Sure." Robert grabbed her hand and pulled her to her feet, but he didn't stop there. He sort of twisted his body to the side—still pulling—and then flipped her over his hip so she went crashing down again. She wound up on her hands and knees, gasping for breath.

"Oops," he said. "I put a little bit too much into that one. You okay, Donna?" He held out a hand to haul her up, concern warring with amusement on his face.

"Aren't you supposed to call me Initiate Underwood?" Donna asked, pleased that her voice sounded steady despite how winded she felt. She supposed she deserved that particular move, so she didn't complain that he'd totally tricked her. She took Robert's hand and allowed him to drag her back on her feet. This time, he gave her time to recover.

Learning to fight was tougher than it looked on TV, but after encountering the demon shadows in the Ironwood, she'd promised herself—and Robert—that she'd put in the work. She needed to discover how to bring her unique abilities into the process.

Of course, she hadn't expected Robert to be so hard on her, today of all days. Usually he gave her time to react as she reached for her newly awakened powers, but today he'd decided they'd try something a bit different. "Just in case it comes in handy during the coming apocalypse," he said, almost cheerfully. "You're doing really well with the magical stuff. Let's see what you're made of when the fight comes at you fast. Will you still be able to access the first matter and bend steel bars with your bare hands?"

Donna almost smiled, despite her aching shoulders and sore backside. Robert was kicking her ass way too easily right now, considering he'd only gotten out of the hospital a couple of weeks ago, not to mention how naturally strong she was. The guy was determined, she'd give him that. And determination was something she could relate to—kind of like the single-minded focus she'd used to save her mother's soul. Even if she *had* ended up falling right into Aliette's trap.

It was so obvious with the gift of hindsight, Donna thought. She wasn't surprised that the alchemists weren't letting her off the hook so easily, and for once she could hardly blame them. Even Simon Gaunt.

Robert stood in a "ready" posture. "Again?"

At least he was making it a question. Donna wondered what would happen if she said, "Actually, could we just forget this for the day and maybe go get a coffee?"

"Again," she replied.

Robert moved toward her, his willowy frame giving him a huge advantage in height and reach, and leaving her enhanced strength all but useless. Just because she could "bend steel bars," as Robert put it, didn't mean she was good at fighting. Even after three weeks she had absolutely no idea what she was doing.

Stepping back, Donna tried to "hold her center" as he'd taught her, maintaining her balance while being ready to dodge or parry his attack.

She almost tripped over her own feet, and Robert struck at her right shoulder with his right hand, across her body. It wasn't a hard blow—he was aiming to demonstrate ways that she could deflect an attack, whether a punch or a grab of some kind—but still, instinctively, she tried to backpedal instead of using the defensive block he'd been trying to drill into her without much success. Just stepping away from the strike was a big mistake.

Robert flicked out a long leg and swept it behind the one foot she currently had anchored to the floor—

—and down she went.

"Shit!" Donna pounded the bright red mat with her fist, forgetting to control her strength. Despite how padded the training mats were, she managed to leave behind a clear imprint of her fist. The mat would probably never recover, but at least the floor beneath was intact. *Small mercies*, she thought.

Robert raised his eyebrows. "Considering that the floor didn't do anything to you, that seems a little extreme."

Donna pulled a face. "Better the floor than you."

"Why *didn't* you do that to me? Or at least," he added, "*try* to do that to me. It would have made a far better defense than just falling over."

"Ha, ha." Donna pulled off her glove and examined her knuckle.

"Donna, are you sure you're okay?" Robert actually did sound worried this time.

"I'm fine," she replied briskly, pulling the glove back on and hiding the flash of silver tattoos.

"Phew. I thought I was going to have to make some kind of rubbish joke about how the gloves were coming off for the next round."

Donna laughed. "When the gloves come off, Adept Lee, you'll know about it."

Robert nodded approvingly as he sat beside her, crossing his long legs. "I like this new Donna Underwood."

"'New'? What's so *new* about me?" She searched his face to see if he was teasing her, but he looked completely serious.

"Ever since you came here—to the Order of the Crow, I mean—you've seemed different. More self-assured than in Ironbridge. It's good to see."

Donna half smiled, feeling uncomfortable under his scrutiny. "I don't *feel* more self-assured."

He laughed. "Trust me. I can see it in your eyes. In the way you carry yourself."

"You'd think I'd be *less* confident, given my release of the demon hordes."

"Why is it so hard for you to believe in yourself?" Robert touched her shoulder, taking her by surprise. "You were brave, and you did your best under the worst possible circumstances. Seriously, you're way too hard on yourself."

She let out a long breath and met his dark eyes. "Thanks."

"For what?"

"For being the only person—apart from my mom—who hasn't rubbed my nose in what I did."

"What would be the point in that? What's done is done. It's how we react to the new status quo that counts."

"Next thing you know, you'll be telling me to trust my feelings ... "

Robert smiled a confused sort of smile. "Okay, *now* what film are you referencing?"

She grinned. "Please don't tell me you don't recognize it."

"I was never allowed to watch movies as a kid. I've got a lot of catching up to do, now that my dad's gone back to China."

"Dude. We're *totally* watching *Star Wars* together."

"Okay. Only if you'll watch my favorite Bruce Lee film afterwards."

"I thought you said I was bowing to stereotypes, making that Bruce Lee reference last week?" She mock-glared at him.

Robert's lips quirked. "I didn't say I wasn't a fan now, did I?"

"Oh, you're *good* ... "

"I know," he replied, nodding emphatically.

Donna laughed, wondering that she could still do something so ... frivolous. Laughter seemed a long time ago (in a galaxy far, far away—or at least as far away as Ironbridge, with Nav). Having fun seemed wrong, somehow, what with everything that was threatening on the horizon.

"You must miss them," Robert said, breaking into her thoughts. Almost reading her mind, it seemed.

"Who?" she asked, just to make sure.

"Navin and Xan." He rolled his eyes. "Who did you think I was talking about? Simon and your aunt?

"Yeah, right." She shrugged. "I've been staying in contact with Nav pretty much all the time."

"And Xan?"

She shrugged, uncomfortable as to how to address *that* particular situation. "Off and on, you know? What about you—do you have anyone special? You were pretty dressed up last night. For you."

He smiled, but the expression didn't reach his eyes. "I did at one time. Or at least, I thought I did. It was years ago, back when I was at school."

"How old?"

"Sixteen," he replied. His eyes had gone somewhere else.

"It wasn't that long ago. You make it sound like you're ancient."

"Five years feels like a lifetime."

"You wanna share?" Donna smiled encouragingly at him, trying to shake him out of the suddenly serious mood that had taken hold. She was genuinely interested—she really was—but she was also glad of the chance to take a breather.

Robert shrugged. "Things didn't end well."

"So tell me how they began."

"With a kiss," he replied, a faint smile appearing and disappearing, blink-and-you'll-miss-it fast.

Donna grinned. "Was he hot?"

This time he really did smile. "Yes. He was..." He shook his head. "Yeah. He was *hot*."

"Was that supposed to be an imitation of me?" she asked, mock-offended.

"I thought it was rather good," Robert replied.

"Oh, was it?" Donna laughed. "*Rather good*."

And then they were both laughing together, and somehow the laughter didn't feel so wrong to Donna anymore. There had to be light to balance the darkness in life—otherwise, what was the point? She'd read that somewhere. Or maybe she was just thinking about *Star Wars* again.

"Seriously," she said, taking a breath. "What happened?"

Robert looked away. "He told the other guys that it was me who'd tried to kiss *him*. The worst part of it was that I would never have told them anything. Even if he wanted to stay closeted for the rest of his stupid life, that's his business. Not mine. But *he* kissed *me*, I kissed him back, and he was happy about it. There was a moment where I saw it in his eyes."

"What did they say? Your other friends." Donna had a horrible feeling she already knew.

"They called me 'queer' and 'fairy' and made my life a living hell for the better part of a year. They weren't my friends, not anymore. I kept thinking, something else will happen to take their attention off me. Somebody else will screw up and become the focus of all their crap." He shook his head. "I actually *hoped* that would happen. What kind of person does that make me? I hoped that one of my classmates would do something wrong in their eyes and start taking the heat so I'd get a break."

Donna shook her head. "Nobody who's been bullied would blame you for that."

He didn't reply, and she didn't push him on it.

"So," she said, poking him playfully in the arm.

He leaned back and stretched his legs out in front of them on the mat.

"So ... what?" he asked.

"Considering that your not-so-friendly friend lied to everyone about what happened, why didn't you just tell them the truth?"

"You think they would have believed me? I doubt they'd even have listened."

"But you didn't even try," Donna repeated. "It wasn't fair, what they did."

Robert shook his head, his wide shoulders filled with tension. "You don't understand. I was different from them, right? Too different."

"You think I don't get being *different*?"

He didn't look at her. "I know you understand that. That's why I like you."

"Then, what? Tell me. Please?"

"I don't even know how to say it. I'm not as good at getting things off my chest as you are." He smiled sadly. "Maybe it's my British half."

Donna touched his hand and was intensely glad when he didn't move it away.

"I get it," she said.

He raised his eyebrows, his gaze meeting hers and filling with scepticism.

Donna's voice was quiet. "You didn't explain what really happened because you cared about him. Despite what he'd done."

Robert's cheeks flushed, and Donna knew she'd hit home. "Maybe I did still care. I'm an idiot, though. Look how well it worked out for me."

"I think maybe it worked out better than you realize."

"What does that mean?"

Donna held his hand. "Where's this guy now? What's he doing with his life?"

"Honestly? I don't have the first bloody clue."

"And what are you doing with *yours*?"

He gave her a crooked smile. "Saving the world?"

She bumped his shoulder with hers. "I rest my case."

They sat in comfortable silence for another minute before Robert's voice broke into her thoughts once more. "Hey, listen," he said. "Maybe we should call it a day—I don't mind letting you off early for once, considering everything that's going on. Do you want to get cleaned up before breakfast?"

"Are you kidding?" she replied, jumping up and striking the "ready" pose. "I'm only just getting started."

Six

St. Martin-in-the-Fields stood directly across the busy street that ran past Trafalgar Square. At night, the building seemed even more impressive than usual, but it wasn't the church itself that Donna needed to enter. Somehow it didn't seem right to be attending a demon's party so close to a place devoted to worship. Not because Donna was particularly religious—which she wasn't, having been brought up as an alchemist—but just … *because*. Wasn't this sacred ground or something?

She pulled her wrap more tightly around her shoulders as the chauffeur-driven limo, sent by Demian, left her on the sidewalk. As she looked for the entrance to the crypt, the clock, high above her on the church spire, began to strike midnight. Donna felt a bit like a fairy-tale princess. She could even hear Big Ben tolling the hour, just down the road in Westminster.

The ride over had been surreal—the demon driver had kept changing his appearance in a disconcerting display of power. Donna was only able to see the side of his face from where she'd been sitting in the back of the spacious vehicle, but he'd cycled through at least six different personas in the space of the short ride. As his face flickered in the eerie light of the dashboard, it was like watching one of those old-fashioned movie reels.

When the limousine had first arrived at Miranda's house, with a message from Demian that Donna was his "date" for the night and would therefore be traveling to the ball with his personal chauffeur, nobody had asked the obvious question. Well, nobody except Donna. "What does the king of the demons need with a freaking chauffeur?"

Robert had laughed while Miranda was busy looking for a way out of this particular demand. "Demian is trying to separate us," she'd said. "I won't have you going to that place alone. You're under my protection."

The driver—who'd looked human to begin with—had spoken up. "Actually, Donna Underwood is under His Majesty's protection. She is guaranteed safe passage."

Miranda had tried further delaying tactics, but the tall man was having none of it. He spoke as though controlled from far away, outside of him—as though he was nothing more than a puppet. If that was the case, it was pretty obvious to Donna who was pulling the strings. She wondered if the words he spoke were even his own; it was probably Demian's voice filtered through another's mouth. The chauffeur certainly sounded pompous enough.

"Well, I suppose we'll just see you there," Miranda had finally said, grimly.

"I'll be fine," Donna had replied, wondering if it was true.

Now, following her mentor's directions, she walked around to the pedestrianized area alongside the main church building, her black satin heels clicking against the pavement. She was usually way more comfortable in sneakers and didn't feel like herself at all, dressed up like this. The only colors in her ensemble were her long emerald gloves and the red feathers on the mask Robert had given her at the last moment. Not that she was wearing it quite yet. She clutched the exquisitely carved decoration in her hands, wondering whether or not this was the moment she was supposed to put it on.

The golden mask had a sinister sort of beauty. It was a traditional Venetian Carnival mask, which she'd seen in paintings and movies. Hers was apparently called a "Columbina" and would cover only half of her face, which she was glad of—masks that covered the whole face creeped her out and, for some reason, made her think of death. With the bright crimson feathers waving from the top, she expected to look as if she had a plume of fire billowing above her head.

The London streets were still busy, despite the late hour, and many groups of people looked like they were only just getting started on their evening. Black taxis hurtled through the streets, narrowly avoiding the cluster of cycle-rickshaws lining the Square, waiting for Londoners and tourists alike to grow tired of walking. Homeless men and women had already settled themselves beneath their cardboard-and-news-paper blankets on the steps of the church.

The entrance to the crypt—or as Demian had referred to it, "Pandemonium Crypt"—was down a spiral staircase enclosed within a separate glass structure that, to Donna, looked exactly like Willy Wonka's glass elevator. Even though the public café that was situated beneath the church should have closed several hours ago, she wasn't surprised when the doors to the glass enclosure opened for her.

The St Martin-in-the-Fields crypt wasn't called "Pande-monium Crypt" at all, of course. It was most likely some kind of sick demon joke. Donna couldn't say she found it particularly funny.

But it seemed Demian had selected the location for his masquerade with care. The eighteenth-century crypt was more than just a tourist hot spot—it was a historical site of some significance for the alchemists. Miranda had told her that at one time, at least three important alchemists were interred there. When Donna asked where those remains were now, Miranda had simply shrugged, saying that she didn't know. And then she'd quickly changed the subject.

Yeah, right. It seemed that Miranda wasn't going to tell her anything about anything.

The staircase wound down and around, the steps narrow and the journey seemingly never-ending. Donna remembered her dream from the night before, with its eternal corridors. She shuddered and walked more quickly. The descent really was taking a long time, which confirmed her suspicions that she wasn't just heading to the popular café.

She wondered how Demian could mould reality like this, making it be whatever he wanted to be. And, if he could do something like this—shift everything just a little to one side, so that a previously "fixed" spiral staircase now led to his own personal ballroom—then what *couldn't* he do? Why did he even need to negotiate with the alchemists?

And what did he truly want with her?

Her stomach fluttered with nervous energy. So many things to think about. Not just where Demian was concerned, but regarding this whole setup in general. Miranda's warnings still rang in her ears: *"Keep your mask on once you're inside the crypt, try not to talk to anyone until we're called into the private meeting room, and whatever you do, don't eat or drink anything, not until we're all there together."*

Not that Donna felt like eating anything right now. If she was honest, she'd have to admit to feeling pretty sick.

Just as she was wondering whether or not she'd been deceived—yet again—by a maleficent being, and if it really was possible to enter Hell while you were technically still alive, she reached the bottom of the stairs. She took a deep breath to steady herself.

Two silent women, wearing plain black robes and ornate golden masks, stepped forward to greet her. They turned and escorted her through a candlelit tunnel. The ground was made of smooth stone, and Donna, not used to wearing heels, almost slipped over on the polished surface.

"Please," one of her faceless guides said. "Put on your mask."

Donna stared at her but kept walking, still trying to catch her breath. "Where are we?"

"Pandemonium," the same woman replied, as though that explained everything.

"Put on your mask please, Miss Underwood," the second woman said. She spoke in exactly the same voice as the first. They were like creepy living dolls.

Swallowing more arguments, Donna slipped on her mask and shivered as the cold metal touched her face. Her vision was immediately constricted by the carved eyeholes. She felt both claustrophobic and strangely safe, as though she could hide from anything that might attempt to hurt her down here. The mask was secured to her face with a black satin ribbon that tied at the back of her head, which she tried to disguise by pulling pieces of her freshly curled, chestnut-colored hair over it.

The distant sound of music reached her as they finally stopped at a pair of huge double doors.

"Welcome to Pandemonium Crypt," both women intoned. "Enjoy the masquerade and let yourself be seduced..." They bowed in unison, gesturing that Donna should enter.

The great black doors swung open and she walked through, alone.

As she stepped into the room, Donna immediately forgot how much her shoes pinched her toes. She decided this must have been how Alice felt when she first set eyes on Wonderland.

The air was thick with a cloying sweetness that almost made her choke. The ceiling swept far above her head, much of its wide expanse lost in shadows cast by flickering candles and the chandeliers that seemed to float suspended in the air. The ballroom seemed endless, in all directions, as if she could get lost if she wasn't careful.

There were floor-to-ceiling ivory pillars lining each wall. The floor was decorated with a mosaic in every shade of red that Donna could think of—and a few she'd never seen before. It looked as though someone had spilled blood across the entire space and then frozen it in place. The parts of the ceiling that *were* visible were midnight blue, and studded with tiny stars.

It was stunning and macabre, and just a little over-whelming.

The room was full of revelers of the sort she'd never even imagined. Donna had seen strange—she'd seen magical. But this…this was something else. Alien, twisted, and yet beauti-ful in spite of its strangeness. Perhaps even *because* of it. It was like walking into a storybook, where monsters really did exist and, if you looked hard enough, you might find a beanstalk.

As that thought crossed her mind, Donna felt her gaze drawn to what looked like tree roots climbing the walls and spreading across the dome ceiling. She hoped there weren't any giants around.

Some of the people who filled the ballroom were dancing, whirling and spinning on the crowded floor. Others stood at the edges of the room, their masked faces close together as they shared secrets and laughed behind their hands. It was impossible to recognize anybody, but that was the point of a masquerade. Mystery. Magic.

The masks took the shapes of wolves and goblins, bears and eagles, stags and foxes and dragons. But many of the masks depicted beings that Donna had never seen before, and she wasn't sure these creatures actually existed—perhaps only in her nightmares. Some of them were so bizarre, she hoped she'd never come across them whether waking *or* sleeping.

She walked cautiously in the direction of a small raised dais against one wall, waving away the servers, all dressed in black, as she remembered Miranda's warning about not eating or drinking anything. The smell of sweet pastries and sticky-red wine was intoxicating, and she wished she could taste something, but the thought of being enchanted by demon curses was enough to squash that visceral urge. Donna knew that this kind of hunger wasn't real; it was a hunger for oblivion rather than sustenance.

On the dais, Demian sat on a throne that was carved from silver bones and threaded with black roses. His white suit made him look monochromatic, highlighted only by his onyx eyes and the single black rose in the lapel of his jacket. He was attended by beings who might have been demons or faeries, or even humans glamoured to within an inch of their lives. It was difficult to tell, what with everyone wearing such ornately carved masks.

The Demon King was the only person in the room not wearing one. His face seemed made of marble anyway, Donna thought as she surreptitiously examined him, so it wasn't like he needed to. It looked like someone had taken the sharpest knife in the world and carved his features, taking great care to get all the angles just right.

His eyes came to rest on her and she saw the corner of his mouth flicker. He looked away and said something to a tall man standing beside him. The man nodded behind his silver goat-mask and slid from the dais with inhuman speed, disappearing through a doorway that appeared out of nowhere.

"May I have this dance?" a low voice said in her ear.

Donna turned, and found herself looking into familiar green eyes. Everything around her seemed to stop, caught in a spell that could almost have frozen time. She knew she was being way over-the-top corny, but, in that disorienting moment—while her brain tried to catch up with what her eyes were seeing—the disconnect between dream and reality felt exactly like that. There was no way that the person asking her to dance could possibly be there.

And yet… here he was.

"Xan," she whispered, suddenly feeling light-headed. But not in the silly, giddy-girly way that she used to feel around him—she was just so surprised he was there, and so happy to see him, that the emotions all sort of crashed together like a wave that left her breathless.

She'd never imagined he would travel all the way here. For her.

"Donna," he said, his eyes burning viridian bright in the atmospheric lighting. "You look beautiful."

Then Xan stepped back, holding her gloved hands in his, examining her as if she was something precious. With the way he was looking at her, Donna actually *did* feel beautiful—for the first time in her life. She didn't think about the iron tattoos that covered her arms, or about all the things that made her feel different and like she didn't belong; she just soaked up his attention like a plant starved of sunlight. One happy moment amid all the craziness was allowed—right?

"Seriously," he said, grinning at her. "You look amazing."

His appreciative expression told Donna that he truly meant every word, and despite how much his quiet sincerity made her squirm, she was pleased he'd said it. Warmth spread through her body, chasing away some of the night's tension and fear.

She smiled, trying to own the belief that she might actually look halfway cute. In Xan's eyes, at the very least.

"You look pretty amazing, yourself," she said.

And that, too, was true. Xan was wearing a simple, charcoal-gray suit that fitted him to perfection. His hair was slicked back from his face, showing off his beautiful cheekbones and flashing eyes even more than usual. The forest-green shirt added to the effect, and, honestly, Donna couldn't imagine that he didn't know how stunning he looked. But then, she thought, maybe he really didn't. Xan had faults, sure, but vanity wasn't one of them.

When she glanced down at his feet, she couldn't help smiling. He was wearing his regular black boots beneath the sharply tailored pants, which should have spoiled the effect but actually made him look even hotter.

Xan raised an eyebrow. "What are you smiling at?"

"Oh, nothing." She bit her lip in an effort to stop grinning. A lot of the past month had been spent wondering how things stood between them, and yet all it took was for Alexander Grayson to get on a plane and turn up at a party looking dashing to sweep all that from her mind.

Well, maybe not entirely, but it was a start.

"Why didn't you tell me you were coming?" she finally asked.

He smiled. "Honestly, I didn't know if I could make it in time. Not with how packed the flights were."

"But you found a way," she said, gazing at him wonderingly. How had he managed to gain entry? Surely Demian would have a problem with gate-crashers.

"There's always a way," he said, and then crooked his arm, indicating that she should take it. "Shall we, *mademoiselle?*"

"Why thank you, kind sir." Donna hooked her arm through his and let him help her down an awkwardly placed marble step. She was glad of the support, considering the stupid heels she was wearing.

"Where did all these people come from?" Xan whispered, bending so that his mouth was by her ear. His breath tickled the sensitive flesh there, making her shiver.

"I have no idea. I haven't seen anyone from the Order of the Crow at all. Miranda should be here by now."

"Maybe we're just early."

"Yeah," she said. "Because I was so keen to hang out with a bunch of demons."

His lips twitched. "Well, I was keen to hang out with you, Miss Underwood. I waited outside for half an hour."

"Xan! It's freezing." She shook her head. "Why were you waiting out there?"

He gave her what he probably thought was a very mysterious look. "Well, I'd better not say. You'd tell me off for destroying my lungs."

Donna rolled her eyes but said nothing. She'd already smelled the tobacco on him. It wasn't her job to tell him what to do, no matter how much she might worry. She wasn't his mother.

"I still can't believe you came all this way..."

"Really? I thought you knew how I felt about you." Xan's eyes were filled with warmth.

More people entered the hall, and the noise levels rose. Grand orchestral music filtered through hidden speakers, and a band appeared to be completing their equipment checks up on a huge stage in the center of the room. Donna was sure she'd just seen the Prime Minister of England remove his ivory Punch mask and wipe sweat from his brow. She did a double take, and there was his stylish wife beside him, hidden behind a demonic-looking Judy.

It was surreal. How had Demian gotten all these humans to come? Was he using his magic to influence them? His natural charisma, the result of Otherworldly pheromones, was powerful enough to turn her to mush each time he even looked at her, so who knew what he could achieve by talking to humans in positions of power in the world? The possibilities were horrifying.

Perhaps she should start hoping that Demian really *was* only interested in revenge on the alchemists. Whatever else he might have planned for the world, she couldn't begin to imagine.

Xan said something that she didn't catch. She tucked strands of hair behind her ear and adjusted her mask, leaning toward him, trying to hear over the music. But before he could repeat what he'd said, the crowds parted and a lone figure appeared on the main stage. And "appeared" was the right word. Demian was obviously intent on making a dramatic entrance; he materialized out of the already magic-stained air.

Donna squeezed her hands into fists, prepared for anything.

Xan glanced at her, concern creasing his brow. "What's the matter?"

"You didn't see that?"

He grinned. "Oh, *him*. Sorry, I was too busy looking over there."

She followed the direction of his gaze and shook her head. Three immaculately groomed women had taken to the floor, each wearing a low-cut, backless gown. They looked gorgeous—almost unreal visions of female perfection. Each wore a jeweled bird mask, which made them look predatory and ever-so-slightly scary.

She elbowed him. "Be serious. We don't know what Demian's up to."

"Seems like the dude's just having a party, to me."

"You don't believe that for a minute. Stop trying to put me at ease."

He shrugged. "It was worth a try. I know how much you've been missing Navin. I guess I should try to take on his role for you, right?"

Donna continued watching Demian through narrowed eyes. "Maybe you should leave the humor to him. And honestly, I'm glad he's not here. I don't want Nav anywhere near Demian."

Xan squeezed her shoulder gently. "But it's okay for me to be in the same room as a demon king?"

"You know what I mean."

"If you mean that you think I can handle myself, I'll take that as a compliment. We all know that Sharma would probably run screaming."

Donna glared at him, finally taking her eyes off the stage. "That's not true! Nav is one of the bravest people I know."

"Hey, relax. I'm just messing with you. I know you've got a soft spot for him. For some reason … "

He was grinning again, so Donna chose to ignore his teasing. When she looked back at the stage, Demian had already gone. She couldn't see him anymore, but the band looked ready to play their first number.

Xan nudged her. "So, shall we dance?"

Donna was suddenly self-conscious. She didn't know the first thing about ballroom dancing. "Sure."

It had been weeks since she'd last been in Xan's arms, and her heart automatically began to speed up in anticipation. Maybe he was acting a little strange, but he could still make her melt with that smile.

His left hand circled her waist and he took her right hand in his. He pulled her gently against him and they began to move to the music, entering the flow of dancers swishing around the floor. A minute had barely passed before the music changed to something slow and seductive. Xan's hand was warm against the small of her back as he pulled her more firmly against him.

The lights flickered and dimmed. Donna frowned and tried to look over her shoulder, but Xan spun her and she had to concentrate on her footwork to keep up. She might not know what she was doing but *he* seemed surprisingly adept, leading her around the floor as though he'd had lessons.

As they swayed with the music, Donna began to feel hot—unnaturally hot. Her tattoos were quiet beneath her long gloves, otherwise she might have thought something weird was going on with them. Her powers had seemed to settle down over the last couple weeks, which was a huge relief, but even so ... she was always prepared for that to change.

"Xan, I think I need to stop for a moment," she said, beginning to step back.

"Let's keep going!" he replied, spinning her again, faster and faster.

Too fast.

Impossibly fast.

Donna looked into his eyes and watched as they flickered from green to black and then back again.

"Xan? Where's your mask gone?" And then she realized something she should have noticed immediately—he hadn't been wearing one. No mask. She narrowed her eyes. "Answer me."

He shook his head, as though trying to clear it, but there was no hiding the fact that his golden skin was much paler than normal. His eyes flashed ebony again. Donna tried to pull herself free, but his arms held her with unfamiliar cruelty. She couldn't get away, even with her own strength, and it was pissing her off.

And then Alexander Grayson's face began to fade.

His flesh rippled and glowed. In fact, his entire body was momentarily surrounded by an aura of crimson light, making him look as though someone had doused him in blood. It now seemed he had been wearing a "mask" all along—Xan's features were sliding down his face, leaving behind the Demon King's harsh beauty.

"Ah," Demian said, "and we were having such a lovely time." He smiled, and his lips looked perfect and kissable.

Donna swallowed hard, dragging her gaze away from his mouth. "Let go of me. Now. I'll scream, and I'm sure you don't want to make a fuss in front of all your important guests."

"Important?" The king of the demons laughed. "They are nothing to me."

He kept his left arm around her waist, and with the other he swept an arc across the entire dance floor.

Everyone disappeared.

Seven

Donna stumbled, only staying upright thanks to Demian's grip. She was about to try freeing herself again when she realized what he'd done.

"You moved *us*, didn't you? Everyone else is still at the ball."

"Yes." He released her, taking her by surprise, and placed both palms gently on either side of her face. "You look like a queen tonight, Donna Underwood."

Donna shook her head and stepped back, ducking away from his surprisingly gentle hands. He smelled of cold stone. "Stop it," she said. "Take us back."

The demon folded his hands behind his back, and Donna watched a slow smile spread across his face. Demian appeared to enjoy her gaze on him, lifting his chin and basking in it as though it was his right. She had never denied that he was gorgeous—even *otherworldly* in his beauty—but that didn't mean she could be swept off her feet by him.

It's all illusion, Donna reminded herself, yet again. *None of it's real.* He probably had horns and a freaking tail when he was just hanging out in Hell. Thinking about that helped her to hold the pieces of herself together, tightly. Fiercely. She looked around, taking in their surroundings for the first time since Demian had transported them . . . here.

Wherever "here" was.

They were in what could only be described as a very high-class waiting room—like something that you'd find in the most expensive kind of lawyer's office. Minimalist décor, lots of white, geometrically designed furniture that definitely hadn't come from IKEA, potted plants, and glass tables polished to within an inch of their lives. If they *had* lives, of course.

Donna swallowed her fear. She tried to find the whisper of first matter deep inside her, but there was something about their surroundings that made her feel dizzy. Disoriented. She was also fighting the crushing disappointment that Demian had played her for a fool. Of course, Xan wasn't here at all. He never had been, and that realization was like a sharp knife to the gut.

That part made her more angry than afraid, so she grabbed hold of the feeling to anchor herself.

"Nice waiting room. Do we have an appointment with someone?" she asked, putting her hands on her hips to hide how much they were shaking.

The demon smiled indulgently. "This is Halfway. You're seeing whatever your human mind conjures up. It's different for everybody."

"*Halfway*? We're ... between realms?"

He shrugged, and Donna couldn't help noticing that even his clothes had changed. "Xan's" tailored gray suit had been replaced by a black velvet jacket and slim-fitting black pants. Demian's smart black shoes shone brightly enough to reflect the spotlights embedded in the ivory ceiling. But he'd been wearing white when she'd first seen him up on that dais in the ballroom.

His silver hair rested on his jacket collar, and his cheekbones were so defined she imagined she might cut herself if she dared to touch his face.

Which she had no intention of doing. Donna bit the inside of her cheek, trying to focus. The only reason she felt like this at all was because of his power. It was sick and twisted; something that he could use to manipulate humans to do things against their will. *Remember that*, she told herself fiercely.

"So this is like Limbo?"

"If that is what you prefer to call it. It is just a name, a label. As I said, we call it Halfway."

"Nice trick with the fake-Demian on stage, by the way. While I was dancing with fake-Xan, I mean."

"Thank you." He bowed, echoing the sarcasm he could surely hear in her voice. He unbuttoned his jacket and Donna held her breath, her eyes fixed on how his black shirt clung to his slender frame.

"Stop it," she said.

"I am not doing anything."

"I mean it. I'm not going to talk to you if you keep messing with my head."

Demian's eyes flashed coal-bright. "And I tell you again, this is simply who I am. I cannot change it."

He gestured to the crimson chair behind her. The chair that hadn't been there moments before. "Sit, Donna Underwood. Hear me out."

Donna set her shoulders, knowing that her stubbornness could be the death of her, but, in that moment, not caring. "And you really couldn't have done this at the ball? Or somewhere else? I thought we were supposed to be having a meeting. With *all* the alchemists. But, oh no, you had to prove how manly you are and whisk me away to an in-between world that I probably can't escape from."

Demian raised both eyebrows in a disturbingly human gesture. "Why would you want to leave? This is where the negotiations will take place."

"Well then, where's everyone else?" Donna's heart lifted at the thought of seeing her mother.

"Through there." He gestured at a solid-looking door that definitely hadn't been there a moment ago. "Or, they will be soon. I had to bring you here so that we could join them."

He was up to something, she just didn't know what it was. Yet. Or maybe he was simply playing games—he was a demon, after all. That's what they did.

"Fine," was all she said. "Let's go."

Donna gazed around the meeting chamber and hoped her jaw wasn't dragging on the floor. She couldn't help it; the paintings that covered three of the walls were so vivid—so *visceral*—that it hurt to look at them too long. The one that kept pulling her attention back, despite her best efforts to turn away, was of a young man, painted in an almost-photographic style to look as if he were inside a giant aquarium, staring into the chamber. He was pressed up against the glass of the tank, fully submerged so that his long black hair waved around his head like tentacles, and his eyes were wide with terror. Those panic-filled eyes seemed to move back and forth, watching her. She tried to convince herself that it was just one of those freaky illusions, that there wasn't really a man trapped in a painting, drowning for all eternity.

She sat down at a long table, and the Demon King took his place at the head of it. The guy in charge of the seating arrangements was the goat-faced man she'd seen speaking with Demian during the ball. His mask was one of the more realistic ones Donna had seen, and it seemed to move with his face as he talked. Watching him suspiciously, she wondered just how much of a "mask" it truly was.

Perhaps most surprising of all were the demon shadows, drifting back and forth around the peripheries of the room as though keeping watch over their master. They were completely silent, and Donna shivered every time she felt one of them move behind her. She suddenly hoped that Robert wouldn't come, after all—she didn't know what he'd do if faced with a group of these things again.

Then Demian's steward, the goat-faced man, began announcing each person in turn as they walked through a doorway that had simply materialized in the center of the only wall empty of demonic "art."

"Representing the human alchemists, Simon Gaunt, Magus from the Order of the Dragon, he whom we call Demon Slayer."

As he walked through the door, Simon removed his Venetian Plague Doctor's mask and smiled, showing the edge of his teeth. Donna shivered. How could she ever have found this man someone to be laughed at? Spending the past month with an ocean between them had been a luxury; but now she could see, more clearly than ever, how truly dangerous he was.

"Also here on behalf of the alchemists, Miranda Backhouse from the Order of the Crow, and her apprentice, Donna Underwood."

So it was just Miranda and Simon here at the meeting, apart from herself. What about the other invitations that had been sent? Where was her mother? She'd been hoping to see her so much, and the knowledge that Rachel wasn't there after all made Donna feel incredibly lonely. And what of Quentin? As Archmaster of the Order of the Dragon, he was spokesman for the Council—surely he needed to be here, to speak for all the alchemists. And then there was what Xan had told her. The *real* Xan. When they'd talked on the phone yesterday, he'd said that Maker believed the wood elves would be represented. Yet another thing that didn't make sense.

Demian's eyes rested on her, making her feel hot and cold all at once. She straightened her spine and refused to look in his direction. This was all getting to be far too much; she was overwhelmed by the importance of the event. She didn't know anything about diplomatic negotiations—if that's what this meeting was even about.

Well, Donna thought. *I need to get some answers, so I might as well start now.*

She glared at Simon. "Where's Quentin?" She knew it would do no good to ask about her mother, but he should at least answer for the Archmaster's absence. "Why isn't he here?"

The Magus sneered at her. "He is . . . unwell."

"I don't believe you," Donna said. "I think you made him stay at the Estate so that you could take over."

"Donna!" Miranda's eyes were wide. "You mustn't speak to the Magus that way."

Donna swung around to face her mentor. "Why not? You haven't had to live with him sticking his nose into your life for the past ten years. He's got some kind of plan, and I want to know what it is."

Demian narrowed his eyes as he watched them. "Donna Underwood speaks truly—Quentin Frost should be present. Perhaps he is afraid to face me. After all, it was his magic that contributed to the sealing of my realm two centuries ago."

Simon's hands were clenched on the table, his knuckles so white it looked almost as though the bones had burst through his skin. "He paid the price for it, demon. As you well know."

Donna was torn between standing up and demanding to know—there and then—what the hell they were talking about, and letting the argument take its course so she could learn more. She opted to keep her mouth shut.

The Demon King shrugged one shoulder. "He brought it on himself. No alchemist should have been able to wield such power. It is incredible that he even survived." Demian tilted his head, gazing intently at the Magus. "Though perhaps he has you to thank for that, hmm?"

Simon's lips tightened, but he said nothing. Donna could see a muscle flickering in his scrawny cheek.

"Perhaps," Demian continued, "your own ill-gained immortality is feeding both of you. Only I am given to understand that you are somewhat ... *mortal* once again. What a pity. I wonder how that affects your beloved Archmaster?"

Donna's eyes, by this stage in the verbal sparring, were almost bulging out of her head. She was suddenly glad to have been dragged into these so-called negotiations—especially if it meant she would find out more of Simon Gaunt's secrets. Was he "mortal" once again because of her? Because she'd destroyed the remains of the elixir of life? Should she feel guilty about that?

No way. She didn't feel guilty about doing anything to break Simon's power, but she did worry about the possible effects on Quentin.

Demian's steward continued the introductions, dragging her attention away from her fears for the elderly Archmaster. "From the Elflands, we welcome Aliette Winterthorn, Wood Queen and friend of the Otherworld."

Aliette entered the room, her unglamoured face splitting into a nasty grin as her narrow gaze met Donna's. She stood tall and straight, almost as though carved out of one of the tallest trees in the Ironwood. Her brown skin looked like the bark of an old tree, and her eyes were black slits of malice. She wore a cloak weaved of leaves and ivy, and she leaned on a tall staff made of sturdy-looking wood.

The Wood Queen was attended by two of her dark elves, hovering behind her as though they'd been left out of a particularly tricky round of musical chairs. The elves were much smaller than their queen, although they looked as much creatures of earth as she did with their tree-bark skin and mossy hair. One of them hissed at Donna when it caught her watching, and she quickly looked away.

"And from Faerie, it is our pleasure to welcome Queen Isolde's official representative, Taran, chief knight and advisor." The goat-faced steward sketched a mocking bow as the first of two tall men strode into the meeting room.

All heads turned toward them, and Donna caught her breath. She hadn't expected anyone from Faerie to be here.

High-born faery knights—which both of these men clearly were—brought all kinds of thoughts crashing down on her. When had the Queen of Faerie opened their door? *Why* had she done so? Was it because Demian had demanded it? Perhaps the fey thought their realm would be next on Demian's destructive agenda ... when the Demon King said "jump," everyone asked "how high?" for fear of being wiped out in a fit of demon rage.

But experience told Donna that it was unlikely to be something that simple. The fey had been free of Hell's reign for two centuries, not having to pay their tithe of human sacrifice to the demons while Demian was locked up. They could have just stayed safely in their own realm—the door to Faerie could only be opened from the inside, after all. Donna had found that out the hard way, when Aliette had manipulated her into opening the door to Hell instead.

Taran, the queen's advisor, had a long pale face, huge almond-shaped blue eyes, and black hair that reached the middle of his back. His hair was woven into an intricate braid threaded with green twine, and he was dressed in what looked like silver chainmail. But it wasn't anything like the armor that Donna was familiar with from history books—it might almost have been spun from spider's silk. It shone with its own inner light, glittering and sliding across the knight's body when he moved. There was a silver circlet resting on his brow, and he held himself with a stiff sort of arrogance.

His companion stood slightly behind him, but he was just as tall and dressed in similar armor. This faery's skin was more golden-hued and his eyes flashed green as he kept a careful watch on everyone in the room. His blond hair swung loosely at his shoulders. Both men wore swords sheathed in beautifully embellished scabbards.

Both men also had slightly pointed ears, and Donna tried hard not to stare.

Displeasure flashed across Demian's face. "Queen Isolde does not see fit to attend these negotiations herself, Taran?"

The dark-haired faery nodded, tilting his head just far enough to indicate respect. "Queen Isolde is also ... *unwell*, your Majesty."

Taran's companion shifted his stance, resting his right hand on the pommel of the silver sword that hung at his waist.

The steward stopped reading from the scroll. "Who is this other person with you, Knight of Faerie?"

"I bring Cathal, a favored knight from the Court of Air who volunteered for this duty."

The blond knight bowed, but his eyes were ever watchful. Donna noticed his gaze flicker in the Wood Queen's direction several times—and then in hers.

Volunteered? That was interesting. She filed the information away for later.

Aliette shook her head, spilling leaves onto the table. "Interesting that my cousin sends warriors to a peace negotiation."

Donna hated to agree with the Wood Queen on anything, but she couldn't really argue with her on that. It did seem strange that the monarch of Faerie would shun this gathering and send knights armed with grand swords in her place.

Taran raised an eyebrow. "Just as the outcast Court of Earth sees fit to send guards with their representative."

"My companions are unarmed," Aliette replied. "You are looking for trouble where none exists, Taran."

Everybody took their seats at the table and refreshments were brought by women dressed similarly to those whom Donna had met on her way into the crypt. She watched them, curious about what they looked like beneath their masks.

"My Lord, His Amaranthine Majesty Demian, King of Terror and of the Otherworld, returned from his exile of two centuries, bids you all welcome," the steward announced, gesturing to the head of the table. "Who would speak first?"

Miranda leaned forward. Her face was pale but composed. "I want to know what we're all here for. Why go through this charade when you could just kill us all with barely a thought?"

Demian's lips twisted into something resembling a smile. "You overestimate my power, alchemist."

"I don't think so," Miranda said. "You demonstrated your power when you destroyed the British Museum."

The Demon King waved his hand, dismissing the complete destruction of a British institution as though he'd kicked over a child's sandcastle. "That was nothing. I merely needed to get your attention."

Simon glared at the demon from behind his glasses. They magnified his eyes and made him look like a balding white bug. "You have our attention, demon."

Donna didn't want to be sitting at a table with Simon Gaunt. She didn't want to be on his "side." Truth be told, she didn't want to pick sides—not if it meant more innocent people were going to suffer. Or die.

She noticed Taran's companion, Cathal, watching her, and flushed when he didn't look away. He nodded, very slightly, as though acknowledging her in some way. She frowned at him. What did a faery knight want with her?

Demian stood up. Demon shadows stirred against the wall, their heads turning eerily in his direction.

"Let me make this simple," he said. "I want two things and I will get them. If I do *not* get them, I will grind the human world beneath my heel and turn every human that remains into a shadow, to serve me in my Court of Fire."

Simon was squeezing his hand so tightly around his goblet that Donna thought he would smash it, as if he were the one who had the iron tattoos and super-strength. "You cannot threaten us here," Simon declared. "This realm is neutral territory, and the only reason we agreed to come without a fight was because of your promises. You—"

"Do not presume to tell me what I can and cannot do, Magus," Demian spat. "You are fortunate, indeed, that we are Halfway. I would enjoy removing your head from your shoulders and keeping you alive, as you have done with my people."

Donna stifled a gasp, her mind flashing to Newton. Trapping demons in the human realm . . . was this something that other alchemists had done, too? She clenched her hands in her lap and stayed silent, thinking about the creepy head carved out of bronze that served as a half-alive security system in Simon Gaunt's laboratory. She'd first encountered Newton with Xan, when all the statue had done was scream to alert the Magus to their unauthorized entry into the lab. But then, during her trial, Donna and Navin had actually spoken with the statue, and discovered that a demon's essence was trapped inside—summoned and then snared by Simon, who used the demon to serve him and provide him with knowledge of the Otherworld.

Demian's steward slipped quietly away, and returned moments later.

"It seems we have a late arrival," he declared, sounding excited, bored, and put out all at the same time. Which was no mean feat, Donna thought.

Demian sighed. "Fine. Admit him."

"*Her*, My Lord."

The wall shimmered and the door appeared, allowing the newest member of the gathering to walk serenely into the room.

Rachel Underwood lowered the hood of her emerald cloak and shook out her unbound red hair. The strange lighting above her head made it look as though fire cascaded down her back.

"Mom!" Donna didn't give a damn about ceremony. Just let Miranda—or Simon—try to stop her.

She ran to her mother and the two women embraced. Rachel pressed a kiss to Donna's forehead and then another on her cheek, before they finally pulled apart and regarded one another. It had only been a month, but to Donna it seemed so much longer.

Her mother smiled, ignoring the irritated expression on Simon's face. "You look beautiful."

Donna shook her head. "No way, *you're* the one who looks beautiful. I see you got your dress back."

Rachel shrugged, still smiling. She'd unclasped her long cloak to reveal the forest-green dress that Donna had found in the chest in Aunt Paige's study.

"This is all very touching," the steward finally said, sounding anything but touched, "but can we proceed? You are late."

Rachel raised her eyebrows, full of a haughty grandeur that surprised Donna. "Please accept my apologies—I had some difficulties with my transportation." Donna couldn't miss the look in her mother's eyes when she glanced at Simon.

Simon, for his part, looked as though he were about to explode. His forehead had gone shiny and his cheeks were almost purple.

Miranda leaned toward him. "Is there a problem, Magus?" Her tone was deferential, but Donna was pretty sure she caught a hint of amusement.

The Magus seemed to have gotten himself back under control. "Rachel, what a pleasant surprise."

"Surely not a surprise, Simon," she replied, making no attempt to disguise her disdain. "I was scheduled to accompany you in Quentin's place, after all."

"I was unaware of that," Simon replied smoothly. "How fortunate that you were able to make alternative travel arrangements."

"Yes," Rachel said, glancing at Demian, who must surely have provided her "alternative travel." "Very fortunate."

Donna looked around the table, taking in the strange gathering and trying to keep calm. There was her mother, sitting with Simon and Miranda; Aliette and her wood elves watching her back; the two hot fey guys sent on behalf of the Queen of Faerie, casting furtive glances around them; and Demian sitting majestically at the head of the table, his demon shadows drifting close by like guttering candles in the nonexistent breeze. His steward stood calmly behind his chair.

It was Demian who broke the silence.

"I want the Philosopher's Stone," the Demon King announced. "Give it to me, and humanity will not suffer any further at my hands."

Eight

Everything clicked into place. Fear tightened Donna's chest, making it momentarily hard to breathe. A demon king in possession of the Philosopher's Stone? She couldn't bear to imagine that—not considering the power the Stone supposedly possessed. Apart from the obvious things—riches beyond imagining, immortality, its crucial role in creating the elixir of life—there was also the not-insignificant legend that whomever held the Philosopher's Stone could reshape reality. Manipulate matter...maybe even change history itself. Of course, these were stories that she had read in books, but that didn't mean there might not be some truth in them.

From the look on the Demon King's face, maybe a *lot* of truth.

Miranda had visibly paled, but her voice was steady. "I expected threats from you, especially after the destruction you caused in London."

Demian tilted his head to one side. "Human beings are quite capable of inflicting all kinds of creative forms of suffering on one another. They do not need the help of demons. However, we are perfectly ... *willing* to provide that help, should I not get what I desire."

Rachel and Miranda exchanged a look, but it was Simon who spoke for the alchemists. "That's what all this is about? The Stone has been missing for centuries, presumably destroyed long ago by our ancestors. And even if we *did* have it, we would never give it to you."

Demian narrowed his abyss-black eyes. "Then make another."

Simon nodded sardonically. "Oh yes, because it is so very easy to do ... "

Rachel leaned forward, resting her hands on the table. "We can't do what you're asking, Your Majesty. The alchemists no longer possess all of the ingredients needed to create the Stone."

Donna's head jerked up at this proclamation. She turned to Miranda and whispered, "I thought part of the reason for my being here was to help the Order of the Crow create a new Philosopher's Stone."

Miranda shook her head. "We'll discuss this later, Donna," she said in a low voice. "Now is not the time."

Demian steepled his white hands in front of him, clearly able to hear every word. "No," he said, "let Donna Underwood speak. I would like to hear what she has to say."

His steward turned his goat face in Donna's direction and gestured with one long-fingered hand. "Speak up, girl."

Rachel pursed her lips and looked away, and Miranda shrugged. Simon huffed.

Donna cleared her throat, suddenly nervous. She didn't want to make another mistake—she knew what those could cost the alchemists. What it could cost many other people. "It's nothing."

She looked away from all of the stares, wishing that the floor would swallow her up. She was confused. Wasn't her original "sentence," handed down at the tribunal in Iron-bridge, to go to London as Miranda's apprentice for one year—to help in the creation of a new Philosopher's Stone? There hadn't been much evidence of that so far, of course, but then again, she'd only been here a few weeks. She'd figured that her newly awakened power to open doors between realms was something the alchemists might draw upon, when working to replace the elixir she'd lost in her first skirmish with the Wood Queen.

Simon's face was set in rigid lines, his shoulders tense as he leaned back in his chair and glared at Demian. "We will never help you regain your strength, not when we were the ones to lock you away in the first place. You ask too much of us. You ask the impossible."

Demian raised his eyebrows. "I am not asking."

Simon muttered something, but he seemed surprisingly powerless. He glanced at Rachel who looked away, trying to hide her anger.

Demian swept his black gaze across the table. "This debate is pointless when the matter is so simple. You will deliver a new Philosopher's Stone to me, in the Ironwood, at a time of my choosing."

"Or what?" Simon asked, his voice filled with hate.

"Or I will raze both your cities to the ground." Demian smiled. "You may choose the first location to be destroyed: London or Ironbridge."

Donna tried to imagine a world without London, or without Ironbridge. What would happen? Would the world powers believe it was some sort of nuclear attack? What other option would there be? The governments of the U.K. and the U.S. surely weren't aware of the existence of other realms, of demons and faeries and elves, of alchemists who were supposed to be the keepers of a magical Stone that could bestow all kinds of power and riches on ordinary humans.

Miranda closed her eyes briefly. "What does that achieve, apart from mindless destruction and the death of innocents?"

"On the contrary," the demon replied, "it is very far from mindless. If I reduce both cities to rubble, we can be sure that you will take me seriously when I tell you that I *will* have the Stone. I am willing to destroy your world one city at a time until you agree to create a new one for me."

Donna's heart beat so fast she imagined her ribs actually hurt. "How can we do that, Majesty, if we're all dead?"

"I will of course transport the alchemists I need to this realm, first. I need to protect my assets." He leaned forward and pinned her with his gaze. "Perhaps I will even bring you to the Otherworld. You may find it more comfortable there with me."

Donna swallowed, wondering if it might be better to keep her mouth shut. Miranda answered for her.

"A human being cannot enter the Otherworld without dying," she said. "You'll need Donna alive to create a new Philosopher's Stone."

"Yes," Demian said. "Because she alone holds a shard of the *prima materia* in her soul."

The first matter. One of the building blocks of reality—and something that Donna was finally beginning to understand. It seemed that her ability to open doors between worlds was just one of the things she could do when drawing on the power of the first matter.

The Demon King smiled. "You will bring me the Stone before dawn on the festival of Imbolc."

Rachel's face had gone paler than Donna had ever seen it. "Imbolc is less than two days from now."

Simon banged his fist down on the table. "Two days? That's ridiculous. We can't possibly gather all the ingredients in time. Do you realize how long it took to make the previous one?"

"And you are well motivated to keep any such new Stone to yourself, are you not, Magus?" Taran, the dark knight, put in.

Simon glared at him. "You know nothing about me."

Taran shook his head. "You are mistaken. I see the Hand of Time upon your shoulder. You have lived beyond your nature and are now suffering the consequences."

Aliette, who had been surprisingly quiet, turned her inhuman gaze Simon's way. "Immortality has a price, does it not, Magus?"

Donna didn't understand everything that was being said, but she knew enough to fill in some gaps. Simon Gaunt had been drinking the elixir of life to prolong his normal human lifespan. She had no idea how old he actually was—he had the appearance of a middle-aged man—but who knew how long he'd looked that way. When Donna was bargaining with the Wood Queen for Navin's life, she'd had to resort to throwing away the final drops of the elixir, rather than hand it over to the dark elves.

And to make a new elixir, you needed the Philosopher's Stone.

Donna frowned at the Demon King. "Why would you want the Philosopher's Stone, anyway? You're already immortal."

Demian's steward hissed at her. "His Majesty does not answer to a child."

His Majesty raised a hand, stilling his attendant. "No, I will answer." He turned to Donna as if she were the only person in the room. "The wood elves are not the only race suffering the ravages of time and confinement. My people are weak as well. We are fewer in number than ever before, our ranks made up mostly of shadows. Pure-blood demons have sickened over the past two centuries of our captivity. I need the Stone to restore health to my people, and also to create new demons."

Donna swallowed. "You can do that? With the Philosopher's Stone? Create demons?

Rachel touched her arm. "The Stone can be used to make life. Alchemists of the past could make *homunculi*."

Donna remembered the book in Miranda's library. "But...what *are* the demon shadows? Are they sick demons?"

It was Taran who answered this question, taking Donna by surprise. "No. The shadows are all that remain of the humans we sacrificed in each tithe."

"The Tithe to Hell," Donna whispered, her mind racing.

Cathal nodded, taking up the story. "The tithe is how the demons swell their own ranks. Demons cannot procreate."

"Which is why they want the Stone," Donna said.

"But," continued Cathal, "what I want to know is this: why is Aliette Winterthorn here? What does the dying Court of Earth have to gain by being part of these negotiations?"

Aliette sat up straighter in her chair. "I was invited by the king of the demons. That is all you need to know, *cousin*."

The way she said the word "cousin" left Donna in no doubt that the Wood Queen wasn't speaking fondly to a family member.

Demian waved a hand in the air, as though dismissing their argument as nothing more than a petty annoyance. "The wood elves are here—as are you, representatives of Faerie—to resume payment of the tithe you owe me and mine."

The Wood Queen drummed her woody fingers on the table so hard that Donna thought they might splinter. She didn't look happy to have Demian telling everybody her business.

Taran gazed at Aliette, his blue eyes bright with curiosity and disdain. "Why would you be willing to pay the tithe again? Trying to ingratiate yourself with the demons so that you can return to Faerie?"

The Wood Queen turned away from the dark-haired knight, fixing her attention on one of the blood-stained paintings hanging from the wall.

Demian answered for her with questions of his own. "And why are *you* here, Taran? Why would Queen Isolde agree to send two of her knights to my gathering? Perhaps you should think on that. Perhaps you should think about what you *all* owe me."

The two men of Faerie exchanged a glance filled with foreboding, but before Donna could find out more, her mother put her cup down with a clatter.

"Enough of these riddles," she said. "We have not resolved the issue of the Stone. You have demanded something of the alchemists that is simply not possible."

Demian turned to face her. "You are telling me that the alchemists cannot make the Philosopher's Stone—and you expect me to believe that?"

Rachel shook her head. "You're turning the most complicated thing in the world into something simple."

He narrowed his eyes. "What good are you, if you cannot make the thing you were born to make?

"It's the *timing* that makes your demand truly impossible," Rachel sighed. "Nobody can make the Stone in a matter of days. It can't even be done in weeks. You need to give us more time, at the very least."

Demian's expression didn't change. "You have received all the time I am willing to give: no more and no less. I believe Donna Underwood is capable of greater things than your limited human minds can comprehend."

Donna shifted in her seat and stared at him, trying to match his steady gaze. "While I am … interested to learn that you have such faith in me, Your Majesty, I don't know how to create the Philosopher's Stone. Let alone how to do it in forty-eight hours."

"Ah, you have so little belief in yourself. In your *power*. I can see it from here, shining inside you. Do you understand what you're capable of? You could—"

Simon cut him off. "This girl is untrained. Untested. She's a danger to us all!"

Demian made a slashing motion with his hand, and although Simon's lips continued to move, no sound came out. The demon smiled. "Much better."

Miranda half-rose from her seat. "This is a neutral space. You cannot harm us here."

Demian seemed genuinely puzzled. "I didn't harm him. I merely rendered him less … bothersome."

Donna swallowed a trickle of slightly crazed laughter. She shouldn't find anything the Demon King did funny, but it was hard not to enjoy the fact that someone had the ability to shut Simon up so effectively. And she was so filled with a numbing sense of terror, it helped to grab hold of any passing emotions just to ground herself.

Simon, meanwhile, realized what Demian had done and had stopped even attempting to speak. His face was stark white with impotent rage. Donna smirked.

Her mother caught the expression and frowned at her.

Miranda had taken her seat again. The two faery knights appeared bemused by the disturbance. Aliette simply looked bored.

Demian leaned back in his chair, entirely in control and at ease. "Now," he said. "As I was saying, there is a precedent for creating the Philosopher's Stone very quickly. I believe there is even a known method for it."

Miranda spoke, her voice calm. "Yes, but that's assuming we can get all the ingredients that are needed. Is that why you have invited representatives from the fey courts here? So that we—"

"This is irrelevant," Demian snapped. "I asked about the method, not the ingredients. We will get to that."

Rachel clenched her hands before her on the table. "I know the method you're talking about, Your Majesty, but the Blackening is very dangerous, even for the most experienced alchemist. Donna is seventeen years old—an Initiate who has only just begun her training. If she creates the Philosopher's Stone outright and enters the Blackening, I can't even begin to imagine what would happen—"

"But *I* can," the demon replied. "I can imagine it very well. Perhaps that is your problem, alchemist. A lack of imagination."

Rachel's cheeks flushed, but she didn't back down. "It's impossible," she said, her voice final.

Donna sat quietly for a moment, letting them argue about her. She felt one step removed, as though she were inside one of her dreams and couldn't quite participate in what was going on around her. The Blackening? That was an alchemical term she knew very little about. It had something to do with the power wielded by one who could create the Philosopher's Stone—once the Stone was in their possession—but at this stage in her education, she didn't know what that actually meant. As with most things, she still had a lot to learn.

Demian was still speaking, equally as determined as her mother. "It *is* possible. Especially for someone who already possesses the most crucial element. Most alchemists would need to produce the first matter before they could even begin, which is the most difficult part of the procedure—but Donna already has the first matter inside her."

Rachel shook her head. "But—"

Miranda rested a hand on her arm. "I don't think he's going to change his mind."

Rachel took a deep breath, continuing in more level tones. "I will not allow my daughter to risk her life."

Demian laughed. "And how exactly do you plan to stop me?"

Donna pushed back her chair and stood. "Okay, have you all finished arguing about me while I'm right here? If it's possible that I can help create a new Stone—and if that will save the lives of millions of people—shouldn't I try?"

Millions of people. Just saying it made Donna feel dizzy, and she regretted doing the dramatic-standing-up thing quite so quickly. She grabbed the edge of the table to stop herself from swaying. But she was sick of being pushed around like one of Quentin's alchemical chess pieces. This wasn't an entertaining little diversion, no matter how much beings such as Demian enjoyed playing their screwed-up little games. Human beings weren't chess pieces.

"Sit down, Donna," Rachel said.

"Mom ... " Donna stayed on her feet, trying to make her mother see that things had changed now. *She* had changed during the decade of Rachel's illness.

Miranda spoke up. "If you won't listen to your mother, perhaps you'll listen to me. I am your mentor. You are my apprentice, Donna. Please sit down again and let's try to come to some kind of agreement. We cannot give that kind of power to the demons—would you have them re-grow their ranks so soon? You cannot trust anything the Demon King says, surely you know this."

Donna pursed her lips but did as Miranda asked. She took her seat, but perched on the very edge. Just in case. She pressed on regardless. "Aren't we talking about saving a lot of lives if we can give Demian what he wants?"

Miranda placed a cool hand on Donna's shoulder. "And who is to say whether he'll keep his word and stay away from our world if we *do* make a new Stone? Even if it were possible."

Taran spoke up. "This is all fascinating, I'm sure, but what does the creation of the Philosopher's Stone have to do with Faerie? We have no interest in such things. What care we for the fate of humans—or for the alchemists?"

Demian's black eyes narrowed. "It was your queen I wanted here, but as you have been sent in her place I suppose I have no choice but to speak with you. I dislike not having choices." The threat in his beautiful voice was clear.

Taran's face paled. "My queen is—"

"Unwell," finished Demian. "So you said. As is the Archmaster of the Order of the Dragon. Perhaps there is a mysterious illness in existence that can affect both faeries and alchemists. Most interesting."

Cathal pushed his goblet away from him and sat up straighter in his seat. "I too would like to know what both Faerie and the Elflands have to do with a disagreement between demons and alchemists. The Philosopher's Stone is of no interest to us."

Aliette turned her head toward Demian, looking truly engaged in the proceedings for the first time.

Demian smiled. "Isn't it obvious? You all possess one of the crucial ingredients needed to create the Philosopher's Stone. You each hold one of the sacred objects. I want you to give them to Donna Underwood so that she can complete her task."

Taran scowled. "And of course you need our cooperation in this matter."

Donna stared at him. "What do you mean?"

It was Cathal, the golden-skinned knight, who replied. "Each of the four races was given one artifact—one ingredient—to take care of, ensuring that the balance of power between races was maintained. Even the Demon King cannot take them from us. There are protected by a combination of demonic, fey, and alchemical magic."

"Who arranged for *that*?" Donna asked.

"A very wise man," her mother muttered.

Donna turned to look at her enquiringly.

Rachel smiled, clearly having already forgiven Donna for arguing with her earlier.

Donna frowned. "You're not talking about *him*." She nodded in Simon's direction, grateful that he'd been forced into silence for so long.

Her mother shook her head. "No, of course not. *Maker* split the artifacts between the races and came up with the plan."

"Oh." Donna thought about that for a moment. "But... that must have been a long time ago."

"Yes," Rachel replied. "A very long time ago."

Just how many "immortal" men were hiding out in the Order of the Dragon? Donna wondered. And she considered it interesting that they are all men. As usual, when it came to alchemy, women were second-class citizens. At least in her experience.

Leaning back in his chair at the head of the table, Demian crossed his legs in a human gesture that was both ordinary and unsettling. "Now that you have the history settled to your approval, am I to understand that you will all deliver the artifacts to Donna?"

Aliette tilted her head, her leafy hair rustling. "You know that each object must be freely given."

Taran nodded his agreement. "Or fairly bargained for."

Donna frowned. "Whatever these ingredients are, why would you even consider giving them to us?"

"Or bargaining for them," Cathal reminded her.

She waved her hand. "Okay, yeah. As I see it, the king of the demons is free again, threatening humanity. If he doesn't get the Stone he'll start destroying us, city by city, country by country... most likely until he does get what he wants. Right?"

Miranda, sitting beside her pale but composed, nodded.

Donna took a deep breath and continued. "The faeries have something we need to prevent that from happening. As do the wood elves." Here her gaze met Aliette's. "And Demian is just expecting them to help us?"

Demian smiled. It was a slow smile that spread across his face like the threat of knives. Or something worse.

Donna glared at him, anger winning over fear. "Why are you smiling like that?"

"Like what?" the demon asked, still smiling that awful smile.

"Like you're crazy. Or like you've already won. Or both."

Aliette Winterthorn pushed back her chair and stood up. "I suspect, Iron Witch, that the king of the demons is celebrating the fact that your humiliation is complete. I will take my leave of you all." Her elves chattered with each other as they gathered close. "Good luck with your quest to create the Stone."

Donna wanted to hit her, if only because she looked so smug.

Taran, too, rose to join Aliette, flipping his plait over his shoulder as though it was totally fine for everyone to just leave. "You'll never get the blade from my queen, Donna Underwood. I can't imagine what you could possibly have that would be worth the bargaining."

Cathal stood at the more senior knight's side, watching her, but he said nothing.

Blade? Donna needed to find out what these so-called objects—artifacts—*ingredients* were.

The steward stepped forward from behind his master's chair. "Majesty, what would you have me do?"

The Demon King's face was thoughtful. "Let them leave. They have served their purpose—for now."

The goat-faced creature bowed low, then turned to the blank wall and sketched a door with one hand. The door opened and he indicated that Aliette, her wood elves, and the two faerie knights should leave through the magically created exit.

"You will find your way to your homes through this gate." He gave the Wood Queen a look of warning. "You can only enter your *own* world from this door."

In other words, Donna realized, there would be no sneaking into Faerie for Aliette and her people.

Taran sniffed pompously. "It matters not. That one cannot walk in our realm without the permission of our queen."

Cathal nodded in agreement. "Queen Isolde may have chosen to unlock the door to Faerie for this meeting, but it is still well guarded." He met Aliette's black gaze. "*Very* well guarded."

The golden-haired knight was the last to leave, and Donna could have sworn he glanced at her before stepping through the door. The moment passed so quickly, though, that she wondered if she'd imagined it.

She felt hope sliding away like condensation on glass. "We can't just let them go!" she cried. "We need those ingredients."

Demian laughed.

She swung around to face him. "*Don't* laugh at me."

Her mother reached out to touch her arm. "Don't let him antagonize you."

"But I don't understand how he expects us to do this at all, let alone in *two days*," Donna said. "It's obvious that we're unlikely to get these ingredients—whatever they are—from either Faerie or the Elflands."

Demian nodded. He was no longer smiling. "Not to mention the ingredient you need to collect from *my* realm."

"What?!" Donna slammed her hand down on the table so hard it actually shook.

"We'll talk about it later," Rachel told her, with an expression on her face that communicated more than she seemed ready to say. "Okay?"

Trying to control her breathing, Donna nodded. "Okay." But she didn't stop thinking and planning. She couldn't stop wondering crazy things like, *How am I going to reach the Underworld without dying? What could be down there that Demian can't just give to us if he wants the Stone so much?*

"So, what do the alchemists hold?" Donna asked. "What's our crucial ingredient?"

Miranda and Rachel exchanged a glance. It was Miranda who spoke. "Each Order's library contains a copy of the Silent Book."

Donna nodded. The *Mutus Liber* was something she was familiar with. It was an instruction manual that contained no words—just a pictorial representation of how to make the Stone. Still, that didn't make much sense.

"But if we all have that, how is that something individual? I thought each race guards a unique ingredient or object..."

Demian's black eyes flashed. "The *Mutus Liber* is not the ingredient. What your fellow alchemists are trying to keep from you is that the most important element in the process— even more important than the fruit, the blade, and the cup— is the ingredient that binds all the rest. The ingredient that pulls all the others together and lights the match, so to speak."

"Which is?"

"You, Donna Underwood."

Her stomach clenched like a fist. "What do you mean, 'me'?"

"The *prima materia*, of course. That which lives inside you."

Donna immediately turned to her mother. "I'm an *ingredient*? So this is what you've all been trying to protect me from?"

Rachel nodded, although she wouldn't quite meet her daughter's eyes. "It is."

"When were you going to talk to me about how, exactly, this might work?"

"Again, I was hoping we wouldn't need to discuss it until we'd gotten home."

"Home?" Donna snorted. "Which one? Does the potential end-of-the-world scenario mean I get to go back to Ironbridge?" She was acting casual about it, but her heart had begun to beat faster and she held her breath.

Rachel glanced at Miranda and then nodded firmly. "It does."

Donna's heart soared. "Really?" *I'll get to see Navin again*, she thought. *And Xan!* "I can go home?"

Simon, who could unfortunately speak again, glared at all three of them. "Are you forgetting that Initiate Underwood's place is in London now, with Miranda and the Order of the Crow?"

Her mother returned his hostile expression with a challenge of her own. "And are *you* forgetting who the Archmaster is? Quentin told me that, if events from this meeting warranted it, Donna could return to Ironbridge with us while we figure out what our next move is."

The Magus looked away, and Donna wondered if he'd known about that. She liked the idea of Quentin using his authority—the way he *should*—to put Simon in his place. It didn't happen often enough, in her opinion, and she tried to wipe the victorious grin off her face.

Rachel raised her eyebrows. "You'll have to go back to London eventually, Donna. You understand that, don't you? When things get back to normal, I mean."

"Sure," Donna replied, not smiling anymore. She thought her mom was being a little too optimistic that they'd somehow overcome the massive odds against them and all go back to "normal."

Demian clapped his hands together, making her jump. "It seems we have come to an agreement. Excellent!"

She scowled at him. "How can you say that? Nobody has agreed on anything."

"You have agreed to my terms, I believe … "

"Only because we don't have a choice," she snapped.

Demian stood up with inhuman speed and grace. "I will see you again shortly, Donna Underwood."

Donna stood and faced him across the table. She ignored Miranda's restraining hand on her arm. "Nobody is going to give us their ingredients. You knew that all along, didn't you?"

He didn't reply, but that awful smile twitched at the corner of his hard mouth.

She frowned, trying to understand him. "Do you *want* us to fail—so that you can watch us struggle and try to save ourselves before you destroy us anyway? Is that it?"

Demian's head tilted to one side and he examined her with an intensity that made her feel angry and uncomfortable, all at the same time. "Why would I want you to fail, young alchemist? I want the Philosopher's Stone so that I can rebuild my own realm, and you will deliver it to me."

"But you can't even get me into the Underworld without killing me!" she shouted, suddenly furious. "You're expecting us to solve an impossible riddle in forty-eight hours."

Demian glanced at the expensive-looking watch she hadn't even noticed he was wearing. "Not even that many," he said, his voice both silky and threatening. "You'd better get started, hadn't you?"

She sat down quietly while Demian made arrangements to transport everyone back to their own worlds, and wondered just how much longer they all had left to live. The sand was slipping through the glass, and she didn't know how to stop it.

Nine

Xan knocked on the heavy door of Maker's workshop and waited, shivering in the freezing early morning air. February had not been kind to their little corner of Massachusetts.

He reached out a hesitant hand, wondering whether he should knock again or—

The door opened and the alchemist stood on the other side, leaning on his cane. He looked fairly good, given his advanced years and the fact that he often needed to use his personally designed wheelchair when his legs wouldn't hold him.

"Well, don't just stand there, come in," Maker said, then suddenly glared at Xan. "And put that damn thing out before you do!"

Xan hastily dropped his cigarette to the ground and stubbed it out, making sure to kick it as far away from the door as he could. He watched the old man's back as he retreated into the workshop. He hesitated. If he went through with this, nothing would ever be the same again. He thought about Donna—and what she would say if she knew that he intended to do this.

Well, he was at least considering it. That was all it was. No guarantees, that's what Maker had said to him.

Xan was used to a life with "no guarantees."

He took a deep breath and followed the alchemist inside.

Donna found herself sitting once again in the familiar surroundings of the Frost Estate, less than a month after leaving Ironbridge. She couldn't believe she was back, curled up in one of the richly upholstered armchairs in the Blue Room—Quentin's favorite library—with the comforting sound of his polished grandfather clock ticking in the background, soothing her nerves. Even knowing that the clock hid the entrance to Simon Gaunt's creepy laboratory couldn't spoil the fact that she was here.

Everything had happened so fast: they'd walked through the door that Demian and his demon shadows had opened in Halfway, and found themselves on the grounds of the Frost Estate. If anybody had seen their arrival, it would have looked like the strange group appeared quite literally out of thin air, the winter trees behind them and the mansion ahead. They'd still been dressed in their masquerade finery, which made it all the weirder.

Luckily, the only possible witnesses to this materialization would have been the Estate groundspeople. But since it was still pretty early in the morning, even they weren't out and about yet, and there were no awkward questions to answer. Oddly, Donna felt like she'd caught a few hours of sleep, too—she wasn't sure if that was due to demon magic or the change in time zones, but she wasn't complaining.

Even Miranda had accompanied them back to Ironbridge, leaving Robert as her liaison in London. Donna sympathized with how mad Robert had been when Miranda called him—he saw it as a point of honor (or something similarly British) that he should be part of the "war council" in Ironbridge. Donna, meanwhile, had put in quick calls to Navin and Xan. Navin's phone went to voicemail after numerous rings, so she left him a cryptic message. Xan seemed to have his cell switched off. No answer at the Grayson house, either. It was disappointing, but she was hoping to surprise them later. Sure, the world might be ending, but she was back in Ironbridge and she wanted to let them know.

It was good to be home.

Yet it wasn't possible to enjoy it fully while surrounded by arguing alchemists. Actually it was her mom and Simon doing most of the arguing, while Miranda watched intently and Quentin sat quietly, a pained expression on his lined face, in the chair next to her.

Donna glanced at the golden mask where it lay discarded on the upholstered arm of her chair. *Masquerade.* She resisted the urge to toss the stupid thing across the room. It had all been a charade. The whole situation was messed up, but as usual there was nothing to do but keep moving forward. Less than two days to save two cities. *Two days to save the world!* It sounded like the title of a particularly bad summer blockbuster, which made her grimace and wish she could share the joke with Navin.

She reached over and touched the back of Quentin's age-spotted hand. "Are you okay, Archmaster?"

He nodded, flashing a smile at her and looking more like himself. Well, except for the fact that he'd shaved off his beard and she could see how thin his face had gotten since she'd seen last seen him. He was still dressed impeccably, though, with his head held high and his eyes alert as they took everything in.

"I am quite well." He moved so that he could take her gloved hand in his. "It's lovely to see you again, my dear."

"Where's Maker?"

"At his workshop, where else?" The old alchemist rolled his eyes. "We have sent someone to pick him up."

Maker always refused to have a telephone or computer of any kind installed at his workshop, and he wouldn't be caught dead carrying a cell phone. There was no way around this major inconvenience—nobody could argue with him, not even Quentin.

Donna didn't really want to ask the next question, but she forced it out. She had to know. "And…Aunt Paige?"

His eyes twinkled. "Who do you think I asked to collect Maker?"

She smiled, but there was no joy in her heart. Not when it came to her aunt. The woman had been a surrogate mother to her for a decade—for all those years while Mom was sick—and just last month, Donna had found out that Paige had betrayed them all. First, she'd betrayed Donna's parents to Simon, revealing their plans to run away with their seven-year-old daughter to protect her from Simon's manipulation of her manifesting powers. And when Patrick—Aunt Paige's own *brother*—was killed in the Ironwood by the Skriker during the escape attempt, and Rachel was left in a state of magically induced psychosis, Paige had kept silent about her role in what happened while taking the badly injured Donna into her care.

But there had been one other shattering discovery: Aunt Paige had instructed Maker to bind Donna's growing powers at the same time that he healed her physical injuries—with the iron tattoos. On the one hand, the alchemists had probably saved her life, but on the other, they'd hidden who she really was—even from Donna herself. Paige had taken something fundamental away from her, not allowing Donna the option to choose for herself and take control of her own life.

As always, when it came to the Order of the Dragon, secrets were piled upon secrets. Too many lies to forgive.

One of the housekeepers came into the library with refreshments, and when they regrouped, Quentin declared that they needed to begin their battle preparations immediately. War was a terrifying but very real possibility. What had become clear, during their heated debate, was that nobody really wanted to give the Stone to Demian even if they *could* create it in two days. Or rather, if Donna could create it— since she was the person who would have to bring all the ingredients together and enter the process called "the Blackening." So the alchemists put the issue of the Philosopher's Stone on the back burner for a moment; their immediate concern was to come up with a plan to defeat Demian in battle.

The Demon King wanted them to deliver the Stone to him in the Ironwood. So, they would meet him in the Ironwood. It seemed as appropriate a place as any to go to war.

War. Donna's stomach cramped just thinking about it as she forced a sandwich down. She needed to find Navin and Xan, tell them what was happening. Warn them as soon as possible. Part of her wanted them safely out of the way when the shit hit the fan—which it was absolutely bound to, because this was her life and they were dealing with a *demon*, after all—but she also knew there was no way they'd leave her to face things alone.

Then again, as much as she hated to even think it, she might need their help as she tried to create the Stone. With the various alchemical Orders trying to make plans across continents, she was pretty much on her own. Robert Lee wouldn't be able to arrive until Imbolc; other alchemists would join them when they could, but their numbers were severely diminished in these modern times—and too many of them were elderly and unfit for battle. Yet despite the long odds of winning a battle with the demons, the alchemists had given up on trying to create the Stone before they'd even started. They figured that it was impossible.

But Donna had a lot of experience with the "impossible," and she wasn't giving up any time soon. Not while there was still a chance to save two cities filled with millions of people. Not while she was still breathing.

She looked around at the gathered alchemists. There was still no sign of Aunt Paige or Maker. As soon as the others paused for breath, she spoke up. "To return to the topic of the Stone for a moment... tell me more about these artifacts that we need and who has what. There are four ingredients total, right?"

Rachel shook her head. "Five, actually—it's complicated. The fifth ingredient is a problem."

"Well, what is it?" Donna waited.

Quentin cleared his throat. "Let's start with the more straightforward items. The Ouroboros Blade is in Faerie. Queen Isolde holds it safely."

Donna stared at him. That was "straightforward"?

Miranda continued. "And the wood elves are the keepers of the Cup of Hermes. The Philosopher's Stone is made from a liquid that needs to be drunk from that cup."

Donna's mind was already working, trying to figure out how she could possibly bargain these things away from the fey.

Simon wouldn't meet her eyes when he spoke. "The Underworld protects the Gallows Tree. On that tree grows a silver pear, the only one of its kind—a single piece of fruit untouched by time. The Gallows Tree stands in the Grove of Thorns, which is the one place in Hell that no demon can enter. Even a king. Only one piece of fruit grows at a time, and without it the Philosopher's Stone can't be created."

"So Demian *can't* actually get us the fruit himself," Donna mused. "Convenient."

Rachel spoke up. "There are legends—different versions, so nobody really knows the true story—as to *why* the Grove is a sacred space. I don't think the reasons matter right now. If we even attempt to create the Stone, we'll need that pear. Yet there's no easy way to enter a place of death."

"Not without dying," Simon muttered. It was a totally unnecessary thing to say, but also totally a Simon thing to say.

Everybody glared at the Magus.

Donna ignored him and counted the items off on her fingers. "We need the blade, the cup, the gallows fruit, and I have the first matter already—the spark that binds it all together."

Quentin nodded. "The *prima materia* guides whomever holds it. If you follow your intuition, you should be able to create the Stone on instinct alone. However, the Silent Book also holds the instructions for *how* to create the Stone—the method for the recipe, if you like. Our copy is right here in the library. You'd better take a look at it, if you're determined to follow this course of action. You've seen it before during your studies. It also has a map of the Ironwood that shows where the most powerful ley line is located."

"Ley line?"

"You'd need to be standing as close to it as possible when you activate your powers and make the Philosopher's Stone. The two energies combined trigger the Blackening," Simon said.

Donna took a steadying breath. It all seemed so far away, almost unreal. She tried to focus on one thing at a time. It was like a math problem. Okay, so she hated math, but she could get by if she concentrated.

"So, just what is the fifth ingredient?" she asked. *And how much more complicated could things get?* That was the question she really wanted to ask.

Quentin fixed Donna with a serious expression. "The fifth ingredient will prove the most ... challenging."

She laughed, but the sound came out angry rather than amused. "I already have to go to Hell to get the Gallows Fruit. You're saying there's something more difficult than going to Hell?"

Miranda joined in, nodding. "The fifth ingredient is a mystery. That's the point. No living creature knows what it is—every copy of the Silent Book has a blank space where that item should be listed."

"Or," Rachel put in, "perhaps it's been blurred or erased with magic. No alchemist in modern times has been able to figure out what this ingredient is. It's believed that only the spirits of the dead have the information, and of course not all of them. Only those who reside in the Otherworld, Demian's realm."

Miranda pulled her briefcase onto her lap and began to open it. "Which could be where this comes in." She produced what looked like a lump of polished black stone. It was flat, and roughly circular in shape, lying in her hands like something innocuous yet potentially filled with dangerous power.

The object looked remarkably like John Dee's scrying mirror, which Donna had seen photographs of on the British Museum's website.

"I thought that was destroyed in the fire along with everything else!" She couldn't keep the excitement out of her voice.

Miranda's lips twisted into a smile. "You don't really think that the Order of the Crow would leave original alchemical artifacts unprotected in a public museum, do you? Dr. Dee's work was certainly controversial, but it was also important. We keep his true grimoires safe—along with this."

Donna nodded. "His scrying mirror."

Quentin and Simon exchanged glances. It was the Archmaster who spoke. "Donna, it will have to be you who uses the mirror to contact the Otherworld spirits. Since you hold the *prima materia*, it will make the communication that much easier. None of us here are mediums."

Donna remembered that John Dee had to work with a medium named Edward Kelley in order to contact the "angels" and spirits whom he sought alchemical knowledge from. Some stories said that Kelley was a fake, nothing more than a charlatan, while others seemed to indicate he was very much the real deal. Donna also recalled reading a theory that while Dee and his medium thought they were contacting angels, they were in fact speaking with demons.

Of course, she had to go and think about something like that right now. She sighed, gazing at the glossy black surface of the scrying mirror where it rested on Miranda's lap.

Her mentor tucked her blonde hair behind her ears and fixed Donna with a serious expression. "This is a powerful artifact, but only as powerful as the seer who wields it."

Donna shook her head. "I'm no seer."

"Although I hate to agree with the Demon King on anything," Miranda replied with a smile, "I think you're going to discover that you are capable of far more than you believe."

Quentin nodded agreement, although his face was filled with concern.

"Okay, hand it over," Donna said. "I'll try communicating with the dead while you guys continue your war council."

The Archmaster pushed himself painfully to his feet, shaking off Simon's supporting hand. "I'll get you set up in my study, then leave you some privacy. Spirits are often more inclined to speak when they don't have an audience."

"What about all those public séances you see on TV?" Donna asked.

He raised his eyebrows. "What do you think?"

"Ah … " She joined him at the door.

Quentin turned back to the room's occupants. "When I return, I suggest we move upstairs, to a larger space. Other alchemists will be arriving soon."

There was a murmur of agreement behind her, and the sound of people gathering their things together as Donna followed the Archmaster.

This is my life now, Donna thought. She hated it, but maybe if they could get though this—impossible as it seemed—she could finally be free.

She gripped Dr. Dee's scrying mirror in her hands, feeling its surprising weight, and let Quentin lead her to a room suitable for a one-girl séance.

Ten

Xan waited in one of the back rooms of Maker's work-shop. The old guy had insisted he hide while he got Paige Underwood to go away. She'd apparently come to collect Maker for a meeting—a meeting he said he couldn't attend until later. Xan hadn't exactly wanted to be sneaking around back here, but at the same time ... who was he to argue? He didn't give a crap about Donna's aunt. Not after everything she'd done to the girl he cared about.

His thoughts were all over the place, contemplating the future ... and the potential consequences of his choices. *Is this what it was like for Donna, during the days leading up to the procedure that added the magical iron to her flesh and bones?*

But no. Donna's experience was entirely different than his. She'd been a child, near death, in danger of losing her hands even if she did survive. She probably didn't even remember much of her time with Maker—not in the beginning, at least. And "choice" hadn't exactly come into it.

"You can come back in now, young man," Maker called.

Xan saw that the old alchemist was fussing with schematic drawings spread out across a huge table. He was muttering to himself and rubbing gnarled fingers across two-day-old stubble on his chin. Xan tried to push back the doubt that was gnawing at him like a pack of hungry rats. Could this man really do the kind of magic Donna spoke of with such reverence? Was it even *possible*? Xan had seen a lot of things in his life so far, things that had left him full of pain, nightmares, and shadowy memories of events that might or might not have really happened. Torture. Cruelty. But this? A human who could make metal come alive?

Despite his reservations, he knew he had to try. His world had been empty for so long. And although he was grateful for Donna's friendship—more than friendship, he hoped— the breathtaking, soul-deep yearning he lived with every day refused to ease up, even when it made him act in ways that cost him Donna's trust. Xan had tried to stop wanting, but he wasn't sure it would ever be possible.

How can you give up the very thing that keeps you alive?

In Xan's case, the dream that he might one day fly.

Sometimes, especially during the summer, he would lie on the grass and stare hard enough at the sky that the sun's afterimage was still imprinted on his vision hours later. Sometimes he thought the sun might blind him, but he didn't let that stop him. He couldn't seem to stop gazing at that blue expanse of freedom, beautiful and cruel in its perfection.

He'd been born to have wings. It sounded like pure fantasy, admitting it to himself, but his scars and fractured memories offered a kind of proof that he found hard to toss aside.

Maker was rapping his knuckles on the counter and brandishing some very ordinary-looking measuring tape. "Are you ready? I need to check my calculations."

"Again?"

"We can't afford any mistakes, lad." The old man's voice was gruff but not unkind. "We need the prototype to be right. It'll be ready soon enough."

Xan's throat tightened. It had been years since he'd revealed his scars to anyone—and now he'd been regularly showing the second person in as many months. Revealing that part of himself to Donna, when they'd met, had seemed surprisingly natural. But showing evidence of his fey heritage to Maker still filled him with dread. He used to be so careful about sharing anything this personal. So potentially devastating. Yet Xan felt that there had never been any other choice. His scars ... the murmur of power that still ran through his veins—weak, yes, but still *there* ... always having to back away from people because they couldn't possibly understand.

And then he'd met Donna, and his inbuilt sense of self-preservation just ... melted away. Or maybe he'd just gotten tired of all the secrecy.

Maybe, just maybe, he believed that this man could really help him.

Taking a deep breath that caught in his throat, Xan turned his back and pulled off his coat before he could change his mind.

Stripping off his sweater and shirt, he stood waiting for Maker's assessment. There was a long moment of silence. To Xan, it seemed to stretch out into minutes, even hours. His spine tingled and there was a slow, painful pulse beating at the base of his skull. Something cold touched his back, and he realized that Maker was taking the measurements. The plastic coating of the tape was smooth across his shoulder blades.

The cold contact stopped and Xan listened as the alchemist shuffled away. He cautiously turned his head. "Are you done?"

"Yes, yes, of course," Maker replied. "Don't stand there half-naked. You'll catch your death in here." He continued to mumble under this breath, but Xan could make out enough of it to understand the basics—something about "young people today" and "hopeless."

Xan bit his lip to keep from smiling, but at least he felt a little better. He was immensely relieved to be able to cover up again as he gratefully pulled his clothes back on. If Maker could really help him—if this wasn't all some sort of elaborate plan against him, considering his faery heritage and the group the old man was a member of—he would be willing to keep his mouth shut for as long as it took. Maker had warned him that there would be consequences, but he hadn't exactly gone into specifics. Not yet. Xan had told him they could discuss the small print later; he'd only wanted to move forward as quickly as possible, before anything could happen to get in the way.

Xan sat quietly and watched the old alchemist's gnarled fingers dance across metal that shone with pure iron. He thought about costs, and whether the price could be too high. How much was he willing to go through in order to fly again—to regain his birthright?

How much pain could one man take? As he asked himself that question, Xan was no longer afraid. He knew all about pain.

Eleven

Donna sat at Quentin's desk, glad to have some time alone and relieved that she had an excuse for avoiding her aunt. They'd met Aunt Paige in the hallway while walking to the study, and Donna sent up a silent thanks that she would not have to be in the same room with her. Part of her knew she should at least try to be the better person and give her aunt another chance. At the very least, couldn't she be civil? But she couldn't help feeling resentment. She just wanted to shout at the woman who'd let her down so badly, and maybe use some of Robert's cool fighting techniques to throw her aunt around. Just a little.

Oh, and Aunt Paige had arrived at the Frost Estate alone: still no Maker. Donna had overheard her aunt tell the others that Maker was acting very strangely, saying that he couldn't leave a delicate experiment unattended and would call a cab when he could.

There was no moving the man when he refused to oblige. Even though Maker was supposedly part of the Order, and therefore answerable to its hierarchy, he was also ... not. Donna had never been able to figure this out before, but from what Quentin had told her about Maker's role in assigning the various artifacts to the races, the old alchemist apparently had powers she'd never dreamed of. This made his absence at their war council seem especially strange. The world was potentially ending—at the very least, Ironbridge could actually be destroyed in a matter of hours—and Maker was too busy with his latest pet project to come help out?

Unless whatever he was doing *was* helping. Perhaps he would save the day with an amazing contraption that repelled demons.

Donna took a deep breath and decided there was no more putting off the inevitable. She'd come in here to do a job—converse with the dead about the mysterious fifth ingredient—and that's what needed to be done. She felt vaguely comforted by the smell of old books and incense, and the eloquent silence of the familiar house. Closing the impenetrable text that Quentin had given her to look through, *Communicating with the Otherworld*, she placed it to one side. The only useful thing she'd gotten out of it was a page that contained a short list entitled "Instructions on How to Talk to Spirits." That had seemed clear enough, and it was at least written in a recognizable language—English—rather than Latin. Donna had never done well with Latin.

The scrying mirror was cold and heavy where it rested on her lap. About the size of both her hands cupped together, it was made of highly polished obsidian—a kind of volcanic glass. All she could do was stare at the surface and try to reach out from that now-familiar focal point of power in the region of her chest. Miranda had instructed her to keep her breathing slow and steady while concentrating on her desire to make contact with another world. She said that there were always spirits willing to talk, but that it might take some time.

Donna had no idea how long it took, but the minutes slipped by peacefully until something happened. The smooth surface of the scrying stone was opaque to begin with, but the more she focused the more that changed. She blinked as the inky depths cleared.

A strange-looking girl smiled at her from the mist in the mirror. "Hello," the girl said.

Donna was so surprised that she just sat there for a minute with her mouth hanging open. She hadn't known what to expect, but it certainly wasn't *this*. And it had happened so easily, too. The others had told her that the first matter made her a seer, but she wasn't sure she'd believed it. Until now.

The girl's voice turned mildly petulant. "Are you still there?"

"Yes." Donna shifted the scrying mirror to a more comfortable position on her lap. "I'm here. What's your name?"

"Miya. Who are you? Why did you call me?"

Donna licked her lips, glancing nervously at the door. She absolutely couldn't afford for anyone to come in and mess this up. Interruptions could ruin everything and too much was at stake.

"I'm Paige." It was the first thing that jumped into her head. *Don't give them your true name*, that's what the book about contacting spirits had said. "I'm looking for something."

Miya's face floated closer to the surface of the glass. "Someone called."

Donna frowned. "I used the scrying mirror. That's what called you, I think."

The girl narrowed her eyes. She no longer looked quite so pretty—or benign. "I don't know what you're talking about. What mirror? What do you want?" It sounded like she didn't fully understand where they were in relation to one another, or how they were communicating, and there was a hollow quality to her voice that sent shivers up Donna's spine.

She tried not to think about it. She couldn't worry about the *how* of the situation, she just had to use the resource in front of her and figure out whether or not to follow any information she got later.

"I'm sorry if I've confused you," Donna began. She forced a smile. "Do you mind telling me where you are?" The "Instructions on How to Talk to Spirits" came to mind: *Always be polite to unknown spirits.*

"I'm in the Otherworld," came the reply.

Of course you are, Donna thought. The demon realm. Hell. She tried to remember to breathe.

Miya pressed against the glassy surface almost eagerly. "Where are *you*?" she asked.

Give information in return, but not too much. Nothing that could lead a spirit to you later.

"I'm in … Massachusetts."

"Is that your home?"

Donna only hesitated for a moment. "Yes. It is."

"Oh." The girl seemed to think about that for a moment. Donna could tell she wanted to ask more, but perhaps she wasn't allowed to.

"I need to know something important," Donna continued. "I've been told that only someone very knowledgeable will have this information. You look like you might be the right person for that."

Use flattery.

Miya visibly preened. Her eyes shone. "I can help you! I know many things."

Donna bit back a smile. "I need to know what the fifth ingredient for making the Philosopher's Stone is—the one that is kept secret from all but … those such as yourself." She didn't know if she should actually use the word "dead." Maybe that was an insult.

"Oh," Miya said, delight practically radiating off her. "You're an alchemist."

"Yes."

"You seem young to be an alchemist."

"I'm still training," Donna admitted.

"And yet you're trying to make the Stone? Already?" Miya's expression turned sly. "You're just a girl, like me."

"That's true, but why should that mean we can't seek power?"

Appeal to its desire to be more than it is. Many spirits want to be human. Some used to be human.

Donna pulled herself up straight. Her back was aching and she felt so tired, but she couldn't stop now. Her eyes felt full of grit and a heavy pounding had started in her temples. Its slow beat seemed to match the pulse of power buried in her chest.

Miya seemed to be considering. She tapped her finger against the glass, and it was almost as though Donna could feel the vibration in her palms. It took her by surprise and she only just managed to keep hold of the obsidian mirror.

"If I tell you," the girl said, speaking slowly, weighing her words, "what will you give me in return?"

"What do you want?"

Be prepared to bargain. Be prepared to give more than you want to, but less than you can afford.

"I want to be able to see the human world again—I'll never play again, not the way I used to. I've been asleep for so long." She bowed her head. "So very long."

Donna swallowed a sudden tightness in her throat. She realized that the girl could be manipulating her emotions, playing for sympathy—she probably was—but that didn't mean Miya was any less sincere in her desire for freedom. For *life*. That, at least, was something that Donna understood.

"How would you do that?" she asked the spirit-girl.

Eagerly, Miya pressed herself against the glass. "Using this! The scrying stone. I could watch the children in the park. In your home of ... *Massachusetts*." She suddenly hesitated, looking uncertain. "There are still parks, aren't there?"

"Yes," Donna said, a slight smile touching her lips. "Things don't change all that much."

"Ah," Miya replied, "but at least they *do* change."

"You'll only watch? You won't try to escape or do anything to hurt people?"

The girl's eyes widened. They were huge and filled with innocence—and guile. "I only want to see, that's all. Not blood. No, no, no. Miya would be a *good* girl."

"How long would you want to ... watch?"

"A day. Twenty-four of your human hours."

"You don't need twenty-four hours to watch some kids play in a park," Donna said, her voice sharp. Suspicions started to rise once more.

Take control during the negotiations. Don't let the spirit order you around. You'll lose.

Miya crossed her arms across her chest and floated away a little. "Maybe just twelve hours, then. That would be enough."

Donna shook her head. "One." She didn't doubt for a minute that Miya would use her "watching" time to try figuring out a way to escape. If that was even possible.

"Six."

"One, or nothing."

Miya's face contorted into sudden rage. Her eyes grew too big for her face and her mouth seemed to stretch until it was almost touching her ears. Long teeth appeared and glittered like razors.

"That is not enough," she hissed. "I've waited so long!"

"It's all I can offer. And it's not up for negotiation."

"Two hours?" Miya begged, her face returning to normal.

Donna turned her heart to stone. "One."

"Only one? One hour for Miya to see again, to watch the world that she misses so much?"

Donna kept silent.

The girl sighed. "One hour. It will do."

"Do we have a deal?"

"Yes," she said, sulkily. "You're not very nice."

"Maybe not," Donna replied, "but you're still getting what you want."

Miya pouted for a bit longer before speaking again. "So you have the other four ingredients?"

"Not all of them."

"But you know how to get them? You know about the Cup of Hermes?"

"Yes." Donna thought about the Elflands and put a wall up around her fear.

"Do you have it?"

"Not yet," she admitted.

"The Ouroboros Blade? That one will be difficult to retrieve. The faeries are even meaner than you are."

"I can get it."

Her eyes narrowed. "The Gallows Fruit?"

"I know I need it," Donna said, trying to hold back a sigh. Just talking about this was exhausting. Terrifying. "I'll get it. Somehow."

"The *prima materia*?" Miya seemed to be holding her breath.

"Yes. That one I most definitely have."

"How did you get it? I must know!"

Donna licked her lips and thought for a moment. She still didn't trust this strange creature. "How about I tell you that, instead of letting you watch the world? We could renegotiate..."

"No." Miya shook her head. "No, I won't give that up."

"Well, those are the four ingredients listed in the Silent Book," Donna said. "What's the fifth, the one that seems to have been erased?"

The girl smiled, showing her tiny white teeth. Perfectly human. As if. "Even if I tell, you'll never get it."

"Let me be the judge of that. We made a deal, so just tell me."

The floating girl remained silent, as though building up the tension.

Wow, Donna thought, *spirits sure do know all about drama.* Even the seemingly young ones liked to string you along and squeeze the most emotion they could out of a single moment.

Refusing to play the game, Donna waited. Her heart was thumping so hard she wouldn't be surprised if Miya could hear it all the way across the ether.

Miya sighed. "You're really no fun."

"Probably not," Donna said. "I'm on sort of a tight schedule here. What's the mysterious ingredient?"

"You need a tear from a demon."

Donna stared into the mirror, wondering if she'd heard the spirit-girl correctly. A demon tear? "That can't be right. Are you sure?"

"Of course I'm sure." Miya's expression was indignant. "That's the fifth ingredient. It needs to go into the cup."

Oh, I am so screwed. Really and truly.

Miya's voice broke into her panicked thoughts. "Shall I tell you a secret?"

"Okay."

"Demons don't cry."

Yep, Donna thought. *Totally screwed.*

Twelve

Navin screeched to a halt on his bike, nodding with satisfaction as he admired the path he'd gouged in his father's newly laid gravel driveway. *That's me*, he thought. *Navin Sharma: rebel without a flaw.*

He glanced over at Donna's house next door. Her *aunt's* house, actually. He couldn't help checking for signs of a miraculous return, even though he had already promised himself to stop looking and hoping. It was instinctive where Underwood was concerned. She was his best friend. What was a dude to do?

Nisha came out of their own house looking severely pissed off. But his little sister was always moaning at him about something. She was fifteen. Wasn't that her job? It wasn't like she had much else to do with her time...

"Why do you always have to destroy everything with your stupid bike?"

"Hey, sis! Great to see you too. I'm very well, thanks." Navin tried to hug her. "And you?"

Nisha ducked out of his arms. "Ew, gross! Stop it or I'll tell Dad."

"Dad's not home," Navin said, grinning. "And how can you say a hug from your stunningly handsome big brother is gross? Do you have any idea how many of your friends would *die* to have these arms wrapped around them?"

"I have a pretty good idea," she replied. "Zero."

"Face it, I'm a love machine. You just can't handle how much of a stud I am."

"No, I just can't handle how much of a *loser* you are." Nisha rolled her eyes and handed him something that looked remarkably like his cell phone. "You left this at home today, loser."

"Thanks, dork," he said. "What are you doing here, anyway? Skipping?"

Nisha looked genuinely offended. "I never skip. Study day."

"Right." But he wasn't listening to his sister anymore, because he saw he had a missed call and voicemail from Donna.

He shoved Nisha back inside the house and closed the door on her, ignoring her squawks of outrage while he listened to Donna's message. Then called his best friend, heart racing.

"Don! You're home!"

"Hey, Nav. Thanks for calling back."

"Sure, dude. It's awesome to hear your voice," he said. Because it was.

"You too. I've missed you, and to show you just how much I've missed you, I'm going to request a crazy favor. It's pretty crazy, okay? Sort of insane. So if you want to say 'no' I'd totally understand. In fact, you probably should say no because this could get you in trouble. It could, at the very least, cause you a major headache when you hear what I want you to...um...collect for me."

She paused, and Navin was about to start asking questions, but Donna was on a roll. "You'll need help with it. I've been trying to get hold of Xan, too, but I have no idea where he is. I mean, it's not like I'm asking you to do something that'll get you hurt, or killed, but you could most definitely—"

"Wait," Navin said. "Just stop talking for a minute. *Please?*"

Donna immediately went quiet.

The silence stretched out for several seconds. Navin grinned.

"Um," Donna said. "What's going on? Why did I have to stop talking?"

"No reason. I just wanted to see if you'd actually do it without asking questions." He cracked up.

Normally, Donna would be laughing right along with him, and the fact that she wasn't made him stop.

"What's wrong?" he asked. "I thought you liked it when I made a funny."

"I love it when you make a funny," Donna replied. "It's just that…I don't have much time. *We* don't have much time."

"Whoa, hold on there, cowgirl. What do you mean, 'we don't have much time'? What's going on?"

Donna rushed into an explanation and he listened. He listened for what felt like a long time, and when he disconnected, he knew what he had to do.

᠊ᢒᢓ᠊

Xan sat at Maker's work counter and watched as the alchemist scribbled notes and made amendments to the complex geometrical plans spread out before him. Maker had assured him that he would have the prototype finished within a matter of hours. Xan wasn't exactly sure what a "prototype" involved, but it certainly meant progress: the kind of progress he'd previously only dreamed about. They weren't quite at the organically-attached-wings stage, but the alchemist was developing something that looked promising. The first step of a long journey.

Perhaps he should go out for a while. It looked as though the old man was all caught up in his work, even blowing off a big meeting at the Frost Estate so he could finish what he was doing, and—

Xan's phone chimed in his pocket, making him jump and earning him a reproving look from Maker. He glanced at the display and frowned. He didn't recognize the number. He also noticed he had missed calls from Donna, and realized that he'd left his phone on silent earlier in the day. *Shit.*

"Hello?"

"Hey," said Navin Sharma. "I think I need your help."

"What? Why are you whispering? You're breaking up. You sound like you're in—"

"A bathroom. Yeah, that's because I am."

"Why are you calling me from a bathroom? Are you naked?"

"Relax, Grayson. Not everybody falls at your feet in adoration. It's the only place I can get any damn privacy around here."

"You sound really strange, man. Are you suffering from some kind of post-traumatic thing?"

"Stop talking and leave the humor to me," Nav whisper-shouted. "You need to come pick me up, like ... now."

Xan couldn't shut down the flash of irritation. Who was *Navin* to order him around? "What the hell for? Dude, I'm in the middle of something important. I can't just—"

"Do you care about Donna?"

"What sort of a dumb question is that?" Xan glanced up and realized that Maker was watching him. He gave the alchemist an apologetic look and slid off his stool, taking the phone to the far end of the workshop. "What's all this about?"

"It's about the fact that if we don't get our butts to the Frost Estate in the next half hour, I'll have lost the chance to get her what she needs. If I have do this on my own, I'll probably end up getting turned into a frog. Or something. Not that you're gonna be so worried about that part—"

"Not particularly, no."

"But the part about Donna? Come on, Xan, you've been way out of touch. She needs us. *Both* of us."

Xan sighed. Of course he would help—Navin knew that already. He'd just been so excited about watching Maker's progress it was hard to think about straying too far from the workshop. Still, it would take a couple more hours to finish the prototype, right? Donna came first.

"I'm on my way."

Thirteen

Donna walked through Ironbridge Common, thankful to once again be wearing a pair of jeans and sneakers that she'd found in an old pile of her stuff at the Frost Estate. She increased her pace, trying to shake the feeling that she was losing the battle before it had even started. The afternoon was already growing short and they only had the rest of this day and early tomorrow to make the Philosopher's Stone. Correction: *she* only had that amount of time left to create the Stone. Alchemists from the four Orders were currently very busy examining detailed schematics of the Ironwood and planning their campaign of magical mayhem and violence. It was seriously messed up.

She'd left the others to it, slipping away after her phone call with Navin. It would still be light for another hour at least, and the demon shadows seemed to prefer the night. She didn't doubt that Demian would be watching her, but it was unlikely he would cause her harm at this point—even if he did randomly appear and say creepy, suggestive things. What was he going to do? *Talk* her to death? The worst he seemed capable of, where she was concerned, was making her head hurt with cryptic pronouncements. She figured she was safe enough as long as he still needed her to make the Stone.

It had been a relief to connect with Navin. But what if he couldn't find Xan? She really didn't want Nav going after the demon tear on his own. Which is how she found herself power-walking across Ironbridge Common in hopes of finding the elusive Mr. Grayson at home. Okay, so she really wanted to see Xan, too. She wasn't going to lie about that. But this was serious—things were moving so fast, and they were running out of time. It always came down to those sands slipping through the glass. Like in her dream.

Blowing out a breath, she tried to take in her surroundings and quell the panic that kept rising inside her like a fountain. The Common was all frozen and picture-postcard pretty, but it was difficult to focus too much on that while her mind was constantly whirring with plans and possibilities.

She glanced at a family walking along the path, seeing how happy they were and having to drag her gaze away. A mother and father with their chestnut-haired daughter running ahead, laughing. Donna ducked her head and changed direction, dodging a cyclist on her way to the lake. A pair of joggers passed her, not wearing enough for the cold weather and trailing frozen clouds like dragon's breath.

It was all so ordinary, so human, it almost broke her heart.

As soon as she left the path and took the familiar shortcut—happy, for another fleeting moment, that she was back in Ironbridge and actually able to *take* the familiar shortcut—she knew that she'd made a mistake. Most of the walkers and joggers were suddenly out of sight, further back on the open parts of the Common. Donna was walking among the trees where it was quieter, and she also had to slow her pace.

She heard something behind her. It sounded like something heavy landing on hard earth and fallen leaves.

Donna spun, preparing to fight, and then stopped with her mouth hanging open.

Cathal—the blond knight who'd represented Queen Isolde at Demian's negotiations—was standing there. He'd clearly jumped down from one of the tallest trees. He must have been watching for her—or watching for something. Waiting.

She stared at the tall knight as he approached. Today, his shining armor was gone; instead, he wore dark leggings and a silver-gray tunic embroidered with green. The sword still hung at his waist, though. She wondered if he'd walked through the more populated area of the Common like that, or whether there was a door to Faerie nearby. That was probably too much to hope for . . . but she couldn't help a burst of anticipation as she thought of the Ouroboros Blade.

"Forgive me," Cathal said. "I would speak with you a moment, Initiate Underwood."

Her eyes widened. She hoped it didn't seem rude to be staring, but up close the faery was one of the most beautiful creatures she'd ever seen. He sort of rivaled Demian on that level. His face was a perfect blend of smooth golden skin, full lips, and angular masculinity. His hair was the color of spun gold, with the top part secured away from his face with a piece of green twine. His eyes were viridian bright, breathtaking in their intensity. They marked him as *other*, just as Xan's eyes betrayed *his* fey heritage…

Donna gasped, unable to stop herself. She knew who this man was, and why he had requested to accompany Taran to the masquerade; perhaps even why he was here today, talking to her.

Cathal bowed his head, as though he had read her mind. "I was hoping to see my son when I journeyed Halfway, to the Demon King's council. I am given to understand that you are friends."

Holy shit. Holy *shit*. This freakishly gorgeous guy was Xan's father. He looked way too young to have a grown son, but that was the way things worked with the fey. Age weighed upon them far less heavily than it did on mortals.

Donna closed her eyes for a moment, feeling terrible that Xan wasn't here with her. But he could be! He didn't live so far away, though she figured he probably wasn't home. He still hadn't responded to the messages she'd left him, and maybe Navin had tracked him down already.

"Your son," she said, trying to speak past the lump in her throat. "You mean Xan?"

"Yes, that is his human name." Cathal's voice was deep and melodious, all at the same time. "I have not seen him since the night he was born."

Since the night he was snatched from the hospital of his birth, taken by wood elves, and replaced with a changeling.

"How is … Xan?" Cathal asked, stumbling over the unfamiliar name.

"Why do you care?" Donna asked. Where had this guy been for the past twenty years, anyway? She knew she shouldn't speak to a man such as Cathal like this, but all her mixed-up feelings made her brave. Or stupid.

His eyes flashed, but that was the only sign of anger that Donna could see. "I deserve that, I suppose. I would prefer to speak with my son about such things—perhaps there will be an opportunity for that later."

"There might not be any 'later,'" Donna said. She wasn't trying to be a wiseass; it was simply a fact.

Cathal rested his hand on the sword hanging from his belt and sighed. "I will aid you on your quest, if you will accept my help."

Donna's gaze flickered to the sword. "Aid me with what? What exactly are you offering?"

"Help in securing what you need to stop the demon. Queen Isolde has the Ouroboros Blade. I cannot take it from her, but I can help you gain entry to Faerie. With the abilities you already possess, it should be possible."

"Why would you help me?" Donna asked. She couldn't help being so cynical. Too much betrayal—and she didn't even know this man.

"For my son," Cathal said, his voice low. "A son I never knew."

They stopped by the lake, and Donna immediately wished she had some food for the ducks and swans. She smiled at herself for thinking about something so trivial, given that she was heading into Faerie to make a deal for a blade she'd only seen sketched in the Silent Book. But it really was beautiful on the Common, and surprisingly quiet. Sure, there were people walking by the lake, but it didn't seem too crowded—which was probably a good thing.

Cathal pointed at a grove of jagged-looking trees just beyond a small hill. "There," he said. "That will do."

"Those trees aren't evergreens, and there are still some people around," Donna said, stating the obvious but wondering what Cathal had in mind in such a public space. "Not enough cover."

"The people are few," he replied. "I will glamour us to be unseen."

She held up her hands. "What about these?"

Confusion crossed Cathal's face, and then cleared as he realized what she meant. "The tattoos will not matter. We only need to be camouflaged, not entirely invisible. Your iron will look like sunlight through the trees."

Donna shrugged. It sounded poetic, but what mattered was that they wouldn't be seen. "Fine. What should I do?"

He told her, and it seemed to be mostly the same process as she'd used to open the door to Hell. It scared her to think of doing something like that again, especially after the way that experience had ended, but she was running out of options. And time.

She repeated his instructions back, just to check that she had it right. She was hardly an expert when it came to manipulating the first matter, and her lessons with Robert and Maker had been unceremoniously cut short.

When Cathal nodded, satisfied, they said their goodbyes. "I cannot appear in Faerie at your side," he told her. "My queen cannot know I have spoken with you. I must take another path."

"What should I do about the guards?" Donna remembered the knights talking about that, when it had looked like Aliette might be getting ideas about sneaking into Faerie. "The door is guarded, I know that."

"I will distract them," Cathal said.

"Thank you."

"Be strong," Cathal replied. "Good luck."

I think I'm going to need it, Donna thought as she walked toward the grove. She could feel the thread of power inside her, warming her all the way through as it responded to her gentle probing.

She lay down on the winter-hard ground and prepared to travel across worlds.

Fourteen

Navin waited impatiently while Xan used the Magical Lockpick of Awesomeness that Maker had given them to open a back door into the Frost Estate's kitchens. Grayson had told him this was the door that he and Donna had used when they were looking for the elixir last fall, on their way to saving Navin from the Wood Queen.

Maker was waiting for them at the small cluster of trees on the Estate. There was no way his legs would do anything but slow them down, and he could hardly bring his wheelchair on a stealth mission. The thought of that made

Navin grin, although he wished he was sneaking around with Donna instead. He didn't really want to hang out with Xan any more than the wingless wonder wanted to hang out with him. Their ambivalence was very definitely mutual.

But they had one very special lady in common.

And Donna needed Newton—the demon who was trapped inside a bronze statue of an alchemist's head (for real)—so that she could find out how to get hold of a demon tear (for *really* real). This was all because she had to make the Philosopher's Stone and save the world. It was impossible to make this shit up, it really was.

Yes, it was all ridiculous and very possibly illegal. But what The Underwood wanted—if it was in Navin's power to get it for her—The Underwood would get. And if that meant he had to work with Xan as his wingman (no pun intended), then he figured it was a small price to pay.

Maybe Grayson would actually learn something from him. He tapped Xan on the shoulder.

"What?"

"How's it going?"

"It would go much better if you'd quit tapping me on the shoulder and asking stupid questions," Xan said. "I'm trying to concentrate."

Navin ignored him. "Thanks for helping me."

"I'm not helping you, I'm helping Donna."

"But I know, deep down, your love for me is deep and pure."

Xan snorted. "Whatever, man." The door sprung open. "Come on. And seriously, can you shut up until we've grabbed the statue? Maybe just... you know... shut up in general."

Navin placed his hand on his chest, taking a step back. "I'm offended. You think I don't know when to be quiet?"

Xan stared at him. "No. I don't."

"Let's go kidnap ourselves a demon," Navin said, rubbing his hands together.

His companion shook his head, a look of disgust on his face.

Navin smiled and walked through the door. He loved winding Xan up.

Donna's eyes felt heavy.

She didn't know why she'd come here, and right now she couldn't quite find it in herself to care. It was all so *pretty*. Maybe she should stay here.

Wherever "here" was.

She half expected to see a field of poppies, but then she remembered that she was going to Faerie, not Oz. She tried to fight the soporific effect of the thick air, but there was nothing she could do as her head fell back against the ground. The grass smelled sweet and fresh, and was so soft that she couldn't help but lay her cheek against it and take a deep breath of the fresh earth below. No sign of frost, which was strange. Ironbridge Common had been cold, just a few moments ago...

Sleep claimed her.

The last thing Donna remembered was cool hands touching her hair, and unfamiliar voices laughing as soft music chimed.

ॐ

When she opened her eyes again, it took Donna a few moments to remember where she was. Her eyes felt crusted together with sleep and the base of her skull pounded a steady, sickening beat.

She sat up, aware of the warm earth beneath her and the overwhelming perfume of spring flowers.

"You're awake," a female voice said. "Good."

Donna looked around, confused to see that she was no longer alone. A young woman was watching her—slender and pretty, with hair so red it was practically crimson. She was wearing a simple tunic the color of moss, and leggings that shone with a cool silvery light. Her golden feet were bare, the toes unnaturally long as they dug into the earth where she sat cross-legged across from Donna.

"Where did you come from?" Donna asked. Her voice came out husky.

The girl's lips quirked. "I have been watching you sleep, Iron Witch."

Donna's head whipped up at the casual use of that name. "Don't call me that."

The faery raised her eyebrows. "Then what should I call you?"

"Donna."

"Ah, you give your name too easily, alchemist. At least it is just one name. Don't most humans have two?"

Something tightened in Donna's chest. Had she made a mistake? But she'd only given her first name. She licked her lips, wondering what to say next. She didn't know enough about faeries. Her fey knowledge extended to the wood elves—and to Xan.

The fey girl laughed, the sound running up and down Donna's spine like someone was tickling her. "Don't look so scared, Donna no-last-name."

Donna pulled her knees up against her chest, wrapping her arms around them and trying to wake up. She still felt groggy. "What should I call *you*?"

"I am Etain." The faery ducked her head, for a moment looking shy and not at all like a threat.

But Donna knew enough to know not to trust appearances when it came to the fey. Especially not here, in the heart of their home. She took a deep breath, trying to quell a sudden stab of adrenaline as she realized that she'd done it. She'd made it into Faerie—successfully used her powers to open a doorway between realms and walk through to the other side safely. Well, with more than a little help from Cathal. She wondered if he would get into trouble for what he'd done.

"My queen will see you now, Iron ... Donna."

"Okay," Donna replied. "Take me to your leader." She wished Nav was here, so that he could laugh at her lame joke. But of course she was glad he wasn't here, really. He was safer back in Ironbridge, even if he *was* being forced to spend time with Newton. She was pretty sure he wouldn't let her hear the last of that particular task—if they succeeded in making the Stone and getting Demian out of all their lives, that is.

Etain led her from the hollow and across a wide field of grass that glittered like emeralds. The beauty of the setting took Donna's breath away. Ahead, a grand marquee stood like a giant glittering jewel, with smaller tents around it and canopies made of a gossamer material Donna had never seen before sweeping from trees. It seemed the royal court of Faerie was having some kind of gathering, and she was just lucky enough to walk into the middle of it.

Etain touched her arm, careful to do so as far away from Donna's tattoos as possible. "Behold, mortal. Queen Isolde's Court of Air."

Donna couldn't help being impressed, even while she knew she was here for a purpose. Not that she was guaranteed success . . . she was pretty sure that Isolde wouldn't just hand over the blade without some kind of terrible price. In fact, Donna wondered whether or not she would even be able to get out of here in one piece. She tried not to think about the fact that her next stop would have to be the Elflands. Aliette was going to be even more of a challenge than Isolde—she and Aliette had a history, after all.

Even though the faeries seemed more "human" and socialized on the surface than either the wood elves or the demons did, Donna knew they were just as inhuman. Fey morals were notoriously flexible—which was putting it kindly.

Queen Isolde was sitting on a throne made of tree roots. It rose up out of the ground and curved to form a seat, covered with golden cushions, below a high back that reached up toward the powder-blue sky. The gathered crowd murmured with anticipation and edged closer to the central dais.

As Donna moved toward the throne, she began to feel the faery queen's power pressing on the edge of her awareness, like cool fingers scooping inside her head and trying to pull out something important. The air around Isolde glowed and flickered with energy. She was far more powerful than Aliette, and that was enough to make Donna's knees shake. What was she even doing here? She was crazy. That had to be the explanation; it was the only one possible, really, considering the things she had done in the past twenty-four hours. The things she still had to do.

Donna stood before the queen and forced her shoulders back. She noticed Taran and Cathal, standing on either side of the throne. Taran stared straight ahead, his gaze not even flickering her way, but Cathal nodded his head at her. Donna squeezed her hands into fists. She hoped she had *one* ally here. Perhaps Cathal's wish to make amends with his son could help her get the blade. Okay, so he'd gotten her through the door, but surely there was something more he could do to help. Her mind raced as Isolde looked her over, slowly, from head to foot, her cool green gaze cataloguing and judging.

Etain curtsied and lowered her head, not looking directly at her queen. "Your Highness, I present Donna of the alchemists to you."

"The Iron Witch," Isolde said, her tone gently mocking. She raised her angular brows and smiled. "I would say that you are welcome in Faerie, but I am afraid that would be an untruth. As you probably know, faeries of pure blood cannot lie."

Donna swallowed. "Your Highness," she began, following Etain's lead with the faery queen's title. "I'm sorry for the way I just walked in here, but as you know I am trying to stop the demons from destroying my world."

"And you would risk your own life, in such an endeavor?"

"Why not? It's not like I have anything else to lose. If I don't at least try I'll be dead anyway."

Isolde's perfect lips tightened into a thin line. "You poison our home with cold iron, mortal. I can smell it on you." She looked around at her court. "I wonder," she said, tapping her chin with one long finger. "I wonder what sort of penalty should be given for such a liberty?"

As if on cue, some of the gathered faeries began to call out suggestions.

"Cut off all her hair and make her count each strand!"

"Tie her to the tallest tree and let the Joint-Eaters have her."

"Put out her eyes and throw them in the Spider House!"

"Chop off her hands and melt them down!"

Shrieking and laughter surrounded her, getting louder as each suggestion grew worse and increasingly bloodthirsty. Donna bit her lip and dug her nails into her palms. She didn't dare move, but the urge to run filled her like hot needles.

Bodies pressed against her on all sides as the crowd of faeries tried to grab a piece of her; her gloves, her scarf, and especially her hair. Donna lost count of how many times small hands tugged at it, and she yelped when a particularly small faery, about the size of her hand, flew on gossamer wings up onto her shoulder and perched there so she could tie painful knots. When one of them bit her, she started to get angry. That was enough!

"Stop it!" Donna shouted, trying to shake the little creature off.

"Stop it," they mimicked. "*Stop it*!" The fey voices echoed her own voice back at her in mocking, high-pitched tones.

They weren't really hurting her, beyond the hair-pulling and a few pinches that couldn't do much through her winter clothes, but Donna was getting mad as each minute ticked by. She didn't have long to act as it was, and this nonsense was nothing but a waste of her precious time. She figured that was the whole point, but her anxiety levels were almost through the roof already.

None of the more human-sized fey were doing anything to help her, and the queen was no doubt highly amused by it all, so it looked like Donna needed to get rid of the little pests on her own. Fine. She could do that. She'd faced down the Wood Queen, the Skriker, and the king of the demons. She could handle a few pint-sized faeries.

She shook a brown-skinned boy with dragonfly wings off her arm and quickly pulled off her emerald glove.

"Oooh!" the female faery on her shoulder cried, gazing at the brightly colored velvet with wide eyes. "That's pretty." At least she'd stopped twisting and tangling Donna's hair for a moment.

The sun flashed against her swirling tattoos, and everyone suddenly realized that "pretty" could also be potentially deadly. Especially when you're allergic to cold iron. Donna didn't want to hurt anyone here, but she would if she had to. The fey who were bugging her seemed more of a nuisance than a genuine threat, but they still had very sharp teeth.

Carefully, making sure that they could all see what she was doing, she took off her other glove and waved her arms around.

The faeries scattered, shrieking.

Donna smiled to herself, then turned to face Queen Isolde.

Fifteen

Navin placed the bronze head on the dresser beside his bed. Newton didn't say a single word, but that probably had something to do with the fact that he—it—had been stuffed into Navin's backpack during the ride home.

Newton's face—perhaps a representation of a deceased alchemist—was hawklike and watchful, with a hooked nose and a chin that protruded just a bit too much. It was carved to look like it was wearing a strange sort of hat, like a skullcap. The eye sockets were hollow, but when the statue spoke—and it could speak—the eye sockets lit up, as though holographic eyes were being projected onto their surface.

When Navin and Xan had first presented Newton with the escape plan, Newton claimed that the whole process was "undignified." He'd stopped arguing when Navin told him his only other option was to forget being rescued and stay behind to rot in Simon's lab. Right on cue, Maker created a brief magical diversion so they could get out of the house. It had been close, but they'd made it out with Newton intact. On the ride back, Maker kept reminding Navin to take the statue-bound demon to Donna, but that wasn't exactly helpful when Donna seemed to have disappeared.

So Navin had brought the statue up to his room, all the time wondering if he was making a huge mistake. He could hear his sister downstairs, doing the dishes. It was her turn tonight, thankfully, so he hadn't needed to have that particular argument. Their father would be away at the conference until tomorrow, which was another huge relief.

The uncomfortable silence stretched out as Navin and Newton regarded one another.

Newton blinked.

"You blinked first," Navin said.

"On purpose," Newton replied. His bronze lips didn't move when he spoke, which Navin figured was a blessing.

"Uh-huh."

"What happens now?" Newton asked.

Navin sat on the bed and thought about it. "You told me that you could help me if I helped you," he finally said.

"I lied."

"What?" Navin's heart thudded. "Why would you do that?"

"Duh," Newton replied. "Hello? Demon?"

"I know demons lie," Navin snapped. "Xan told me that already. But … surely you don't just do it for fun. There has to be a reason behind the lie, right?"

"Lying for fun," the statue said, dryly. "Now there's an idea."

"Be serious. You said you'd help me get a demon tear for Donna if I rescued you from the Frost Estate." Navin glared at the lump of metal, wondering why this wasn't feeling more weird than it did. He was getting used to this level of crazy in his life, and he wasn't sure whether that was a good thing or not.

Newton made a sound like he was clearing his throat. "Okay, kid. A deal's a deal. You got me out, I'll get you your demon tear."

"Good," Navin said.

"Boo."

Nav frowned. "What?"

"Hoo," Newton said.

"That's totally unfunny, man." Navin didn't like this thing. It was probably the most annoying … *person* he had ever spoken to, and he would far rather be hanging out with Donna, watching a movie, and eating the incredibly bad popcorn she always made.

"Okay, okay," Newton said. "For real this time. Here it is … "

Navin crossed his arms and waited.

"All you have to do is lend me your body."

Navin let the silence stretch for almost a minute before he could trust himself to speak again. "Have you completely lost your mind? What kind of Kool-Aid has Simon been feeding you? There's no way I'm lending you my body. Whatever that even means."

The demon sniffed. "Suit yourself. Looks like you just got yourself a permanent roommate. Where will I be sleeping?"

Navin fixed his eyes on the wall and took a deep breath. Several of them.

"What's the matter?" Newton asked. "Was it something I said?"

"I'm taking you back to Simon's lab."

"Now, wait a minute, let's not be hasty—"

"I wonder what he'll do to you when he finds out you *forced* me to help you escape."

Newton made a spluttering sound. "I did nothing of the kind! *You* came to rescue *me*."

Navin crossed his arms. "No, I remember *exactly* what happened. You used your demon mojo to control me. I'm sure Xan will back me up."

For once, it seemed that Newton didn't have anything to say.

"Don't go anywhere for a minute," Nav said. "I'll just find the Frost Estate's phone number and give the Magus a call…"

"Oh, you have no sense of humor, boy."

Navin sat on the edge of the bed and stared into the statue's creepy eyes. "I have a great sense of humor. I am *famous* for my sense of humor. I'm Mr. Fucking Humor! But right now, comedy is the last thing on my mind. Understand?"

Newton muttered something that Nav didn't quite catch. Not that he cared to.

"Do. You. Understand?" he repeated.

The statue actually rolled its eyes, with a creepy clicking sound. "Yes. There's no need to get snippy."

"Just so long as we're clear."

"But you still need to let me use your body."

Navin sighed. "Not going to happen, Newton. Pick another option."

"How do you expect me to provide you with a demon tear if I don't have a body? I can't cry you a goddamn river while stuck in a bronze reproduction of an ugly-ass alchemist. A dead one, at that."

"You can move your eyes," Navin ventured. "And you're a demon. Can't you do some kind of demon magic and produce tears?"

"Demon magic? Have you been eating Ironwood mushrooms? Demons don't do magic. Demons *curse*. We tear apart reality and feed on the blood of innocents."

Navin shivered. "Stop being so dramatic. You're hardly in the position to tear apart reality. You'd have trouble tearing open a packet of potato chips right now."

Newton made a horrific snorting sound that might have been laughter. "Ah, dear boy. And you said you weren't interested in comedy. If only I could cry tears of laughter right now, we'd be peachy."

"Shut up a minute. I'm trying to think."

"I know. I can hear your two brain cells rubbing together."

Navin's hand shot out on pure instinct. He grabbed the bronze statue by its base and hurled it across the room—where it landed on the clothes piled on his desk chair.

Newton began to splutter, but Navin was sick of it. He was suddenly sick of all this craziness, all the secrets and manipulation and deal-making. Maybe he wasn't so used it after all. That must mean there was hope for him yet.

"No more games," he said. "You're going to help me or I'll take you back to Simon's lab myself and melt you down in that giant furnace."

The statue lay on its side on top of a *Star Wars* T-shirt, blinking his eyes. "You wouldn't dare!"

"I don't know," Navin said, leaning back against his pillows and forcing his voice to sound casual. "It looked like it could use all the scrap metal it could get."

"Even if you *did* manage to melt me, it wouldn't actually harm me. This lump of useless metal is just a shell. My essence would survive."

"But in what form? Like…as a ghost?" Navin took a guess. "I bet you can't just leap into another body on your own, otherwise you'd have done it a long time ago. You could be stuck forever, in a sort of limbo. Right?"

"Put me upright on the desk and we'll talk. I'll help you."

Navin raised an eyebrow. He didn't believe the demon for a minute, but what choice did he have? This was what Donna needed to make the Philosopher's Stone—and if she couldn't do it, who the hell knew what would happen.

Not just to her, but to the whole of Ironbridge. To Nisha and his dad.

He wondered where Donna was right now. He hoped she was okay.

"I said," Newton repeated, "that I will help you." The demon said it with a flourish, if that was even possible.

"How? I won't let you hurt anyone."

"There's a ritual you might be able to do, with my guidance. It will give me a temporary body—"

"I said I'm not doing anything that hurts another person," Navin declared. "Just because I'm not letting you use *my* body doesn't mean we can just use someone else's. Being human doesn't work that way, Newton."

Newton sighed. Loudly. "If you would actually hear me out rather than rudely interrupting me, you would realize that I don't intend to harm a single living being."

Navin frowned. "Meaning?"

"Meaning, dear boy, we'll try putting my consciousness into a *dead* body. Take me to the nearest cemetery—stat!"

Navin stared at the demon. "Will that even work?"

"Who knows? Let's give it the old college try, eh?"

Could things get any weirder? Navin suspected that he was about to find out.

Sixteen

Isolde was smiling as she watched Donna chase off the faeries.

"Enough," she said. "We have had our fun with our unwelcome guest. Now let us find out why she has invaded our lands in the first place."

Taran shook his dark hair away from his pale face and drew his sword. "The court of Faerie demands to know why you are here." His words were formal, as would be expected considering his role as the queen's chief advisor.

Donna swallowed, fear warring with frustration. Frustration won. "Taran, you know very well why I'm here. You were at that so-called 'negotiation' in the Halfway realm."

Isolde raised an eyebrow. "Insolent girl. You will answer the question."

"Your Highness," Donna said, ignoring the queen's knight and representative, "I apologize for arriving unannounced. To be honest, I wasn't sure I could even do it. I tried, because I had to, and it worked. And yes, now I'm here and I wasn't invited. But I need the Ouroboros Blade, and I'm not leaving without it."

Cold silence filled the beautiful meadow. Every faery present was watching Donna as though she were a tasty meal served up especially for them. She felt the weight of their hunger and fear, their curiosity and their hatred. But she forced herself to stand tall and withstand the terrible weight of their regard.

"You did not come alone," Isolde said. It was a statement rather than a question, so Donna didn't bother to answer. She didn't want to incriminate Cathal.

Taran took another step toward her. Bright white sunlight flashed from the blade of his sword. "Who aided you in this quest?"

Cathal stared straight ahead. His face was a golden mask.

Queen Isolde narrowed her eyes. They looked like chips of emerald. "Oh, we know who aided her, don't we, Cathal?"

"Your Highness," the golden knight said. He stepped before her and went down on one knee. "I wish to help my son survive in the human world."

The queen tilted her head and stared at him as though she could see inside his soul. *Perhaps she can*, Donna thought.

Taran's grip tightened on the hilt of his sword. "You have betrayed us, Cathal."

"I only showed the Iron Witch a weak spot—a way that might be exploited for entry into our lands. Her power did the rest." Xan's father smiled, ever so slightly. "Donna Underwood is powerful enough without my aid."

Queen Isolde waved them away. "This is of no importance. The Iron Witch is here now and we will hear her offer. We can deal with Cathal later."

Taran sheathed his sword, looking somewhat relieved. But the threat hung in the air, making Donna's stomach hurt. She pulled herself straight, refusing to show this icy woman a single drop of weakness.

"What would you give me in return for the Ouroboros Blade, Donna Underwood of the alchemists?"

Donna shivered as she felt the queen's power move across her skin. "What do you want, Your Highness?"

Isolde laughed. The sound was both beautiful and terrible. "You mean to tell me, girl, that you have come to my realm and yet have nothing with which to bargain?"

Donna smiled sweetly. "What could I possibly bring for the woman who has everything? Tucked away in your safe little world, not caring who lives and who dies, as long as *you* continue on."

Taran drew his sword again. "Watch your tongue, girl!"

Cathal's hand twitched at the pommel of his own blade, but he didn't draw the weapon. Donna wondered if that was because he wasn't supposed to, or because he didn't want to threaten his son's potential girlfriend. Or maybe he would protect her from Taran…

Isolde waved Taran away. "Be at ease, Taran. I admire the human's spirit."

Her knight glared halfheartedly at her, but he stood down.

The queen rose to her feet, giving Donna her first glimpse of just how tall she was. Isolde stood at least six feet, slender as a reed. Her bare feet poked out from below the hem of her gown. There were golden rings on each of her narrow toes.

Donna bowed her head, unable to continue staring at the ethereal radiance of the faery queen. Her throat was tight with an unnamed emotion.

Isolde walked carefully down the steps and approached her.

"The blade is not to be used lightly," she said.

Donna forced herself to meet the queen's eyes. "I know that. But I have to try."

"You are tired, child," Isolde said, her voice impossibly kind. A trick, of course. "Why take on so much? You should be in school with others of your age."

Donna wanted to fall against her, let the queen put those slender arms around her. Hold her and offer comfort. Take away all the pain and fear and responsibility. It was so tempting. She took a step forward. Isolde was so kind, so beautiful, so…

Donna shook her head, confused and then angry. The queen was using her magic. Her glamour.

The court of Faerie laughed at her confusion and embarrassment.

Isolde smiled indulgently. "Please forgive me. It is in our nature to play."

Donna narrowed her eyes. *Yeah, right.* Like she believed that. "I'm not a toy, Your Highness."

"No, of course not," Isolde replied, in a tone that clearly said she believed otherwise.

"So, you really have nothing to offer?" Isolde asked, all business again. "Remember that in order for any of us to give up an artifact that might help make the Stone, we must barter for a fair exchange. That is woven into the terms of the magic that binds us all together."

"Let me think," Donna said. "Maybe if you ask me for something, I could give it to you. Or ... I don't know ... find something for you. I'm pretty good at finding things."

"Did you hear that?" the queen asked, smiling at the giggling crowd of onlookers. "She is good at *finding things.*"

Everybody fell about laughing. Donna wasn't sure what was so funny, but she gritted her teeth and put up with being mocked. It could be worse, she figured. They could decide to chop off her hands, just like they'd threatened when they were "playing." There were enough swords around here, after all.

The faery queen looked thoughtful for a moment. "Would you give anything in return for the blade?"

Donna swallowed. *Be careful,* she told herself. Be very careful. "I cannot promise something before I know what it is that I'm promising."

"Of course not," Isolde said. "Wise. Very wise." She tapped a slender finger against her lips.

Donna wished the queen would get on with it, but time moved differently in Faerie—she knew that much from Xan. For all she knew, only moments had gone by in her own world. Or perhaps Demian's deadline had already passed, and London and Ironbridge lay beneath bones and rubble.

Desperation made her bold. "Your Highness, I think we have both had enough of this game. Make me an offer, set me a task, and then we'll see if it's something I can actually do."

"Very well," Isolde said. Her eyes were cruel, all the glamour and compassion drained out of her in an instant. "I would like your hands as trophies on my wall. We could use the Ouroboros Blade to remove them, and I will then let you leave my realm with the blade. What do you say to my first offer, Donna Underwood?"

Donna didn't know what to say—she could only hope that Navin was having more luck than her. At least nobody would be threatening to cut off any of his limbs. She hoped.

Swallowing her rising fear, Donna took a step back, still wondering if this was another of Queen Isolde's "games." But the faery's perfect face looked deadly serious. Cruelty didn't make her any less beautiful, though she did look a hell of a lot more terrifying. Especially considering the fact that she'd just suggested maiming her.

Reflexively, Donna squeezed her iron-clad hands into fists, wondering what she would do if anyone attacked her. Could she access her abilities quickly enough to get out of here? Open a doorway back to her own world? She doubted it. She still didn't understand enough about this power that she possessed. Even as she felt the first matter begin to stir, she knew that she couldn't reach those delicate threads in time. Moving between worlds felt more hit and miss than a precise science. And, if she were brutally honest with herself, it had mostly been "miss" so far. Apart from today, when she'd had Cathal to guide her.

The court's wicked laughter rang in her ears as Isolde waited for a reply.

Donna decided not to play into whatever trap was being laid for her. She kept silent and crossed her arms across her chest.

Isolde pouted. "Ah, your silence shows wisdom beyond your years, mortal. If you will not give me your hands, I wonder what you would be willing give up?"

Donna felt her tattoos shift against her skin, and she hoped nothing was going to happen that she couldn't control. She tried to ignore the familiar tingling at the edge of her mind.

"Your Highness, why must I give up something of my own? Maybe there's something I can *do* for you. A ... a quest of some kind?"

"You would accept a faery quest, alchemist?"

"If it means I get to keep my hands," Donna muttered.

Isolde's lips twitched in what looked like genuine amusement. "What about your friend, the boy you know as Alexander Grayson? Would you give up your claims to ownership and give him to me?"

Out the corner of her eye, Donna saw Cathal take a step forward. She ignored the faery knight and focused on the queen. "*Ownership?* He is not mine to give, Highness. He lives in the human world and therefore lives by our rules. No human belongs to another—not truly."

Isolde stretched out her hands. "That is not what I hear." Her voice was playful again, almost as if she was sharing secrets with a girlfriend.

But Donna didn't have girlfriends. She didn't care about boyfriend gossip because it was something so alien to her experience of life. "Xan is half human," she said. "What would you want with him?"

"Halflings are welcome in my court," Isolde replied. "His fey half is of particularly good lineage. Perhaps he would like to train with the sword, beside his father. Perhaps we can … heal him."

Here, her gaze flickered to Cathal. The knight had relaxed, Donna noticed. Maybe he liked the idea of having his son here, living and working alongside him. Just the thought of Xan being healed made Donna's heart pound with a powerful cocktail of emotions; she knew what that would mean to him. And, she thought, it would get him away from the alchemists. She swallowed her fear at the idea of losing him. There was no time for that now.

"Even if he wanted to come here, it wouldn't have anything to do with me," she said. "I can't tell another person what to do."

"Not even to save your little world?" The queen raised those perfectly angled brows again. "Not even to save everyone in it?"

Donna shook her head. This was hopeless. She needed to offer something—something that would tempt a queen. But what?

"I'm afraid it looks as though you will have to leave my court empty-handed," Isolde said, her voice heavy with fake regret. "I will have Taran escort you out in a less disruptive manner. I would not have you use your power in my realm again." She turned her head to the faeries gathered beside her on the dais. "We will secure all our doors, at least until Demian has finished reaping the destruction he so desires. Taran, remove the girl—"

"I'll fight for it!" Donna shouted, terrified to find herself being kicked out of Faerie with no way back in.

Isolde turned back to her, interest flickering in her eyes. "Fight? You mean to say that you're challenging my court?"

Donna closed her eyes for a moment. What was she doing? *What I have to do*, she told herself fiercely.

"If that's the only way, yes. I don't know how this works, but I challenge—"

"I will fight her," Cathal said, stepping forward and cutting her off before she could complete a formal challenge to Taran.

Was that better or worse? She couldn't fight a faery knight—she didn't have a hope of winning. But she was desperate, and she'd opened her stupid mouth without thinking.

Cathal was obviously trying to help her, drag her out of the hole she was busy digging for herself.

But Isolde wasn't buying. "Step down, Cathal. There will be no challenges today." She narrowed her eyes at Donna. "I do not know whether you are incredibly brave or incredibly foolish, Donna Underwood."

Donna knew the answer to that, but kept her mouth shut. *See?* she thought. *I can be sensible.*

The queen smiled. The expression was hard and bright, like glass. "I will send you back to your world, and I will ensure that no time has been lost on your quest to make a new Philosopher's Stone." She walked to the front of the dais and one of her attendants, a short man with horns of bone growing from his forehead, handed her an ornately carved wooden box.

When Isolde opened the catch and flipped open the lid, Donna couldn't hold back her gasp. The Ouroboros Blade. The wicked-sharp blade was pure black and the handle carved of ivory. Her fingers twitched. She wanted to hold it; to take it now and run. She was one step closer to saving everything she knew and loved. If she could just get her hands on that knife.

She forced herself to be still, to wait for the queen's terms.

"You may have the blade, as much good as it will do you when dealing with demons," Isolde said. "This is the bargain I offer you, and it will be a bargain sealed with the blood of those you love. You are too reckless. I do not trust any deal made in which your own life is wagered."

Donna bit her lip. Okay, so now the queen thought she had a death wish. It wasn't true, but she could hardly blame Isolde for drawing that conclusion, based on her actions so far.

"We will hold the life of Alexander Grayson, born of Cathal, as collateral. Should you fail in the task I set you, his life will be forfeit."

Donna felt sick. "I can't bargain with his life," she whispered. "That's not fair."

"Fair?" Isolde laughed, sharp and brittle. "You talk to me of *fair*?" She shook her head. "No, these are my terms—and they serve equally as punishment for Cathal. I will give you the Ouroboros Blade so that you may create your Stone. If you succeed in appeasing the demons, you must also kill the Magus, Simon Gaunt of the Dragon Order."

Donna took a step back. What? Kill Simon? Her chest hurt as she tried to catch her breath.

Isolde held out the box. "So you see, Donna. I am nothing if *not* fair. If Demian destroys all of you, you won't even need to complete your part of the bargain."

Cathal took Donna to the edge of a grove of pine trees. The scene was beautiful. The air was balmy and the sky was clear blue as it swept overhead. It should have been the sort of scene to bring peace, but Donna only felt dread. She clamped down on it, keeping everything under control until she got the hell out of this place.

The tall faery knight touched the trunk of a tree that didn't look any different from its neighbors. The wood shimmered and melted, forming a small doorway.

"Descend the stairs and you will reach a long corridor made of leaf and wood. Follow it to the end, and you will reach another door. That will take you to where you most need to be."

She stared into the darkness, then back at Cathal. "It's that easy?"

"This time, yes," he said. "There are many entrances into Faerie, but they move on a daily basis. We have not had need to monitor these doors for two human centuries."

"It must be weird for you to deal with us again, after all this time."

"Indeed. It is strange to meet with mortals again, but I find I enjoy it." Cathal's handsome face broke into a smile. "I always did."

Donna smiled in return, thinking about Xan's human birth mother, but her expression felt forced. She couldn't stop her mind turning over everything that still lay ahead of her—not least of which was to find a way into Hell, of all freaking places. And now she had to kill a magus. Murder. Could she do that? It wasn't like she hadn't contemplated it before, like where Demian was concerned. But thinking about it in a flash of anger was one thing...

She pushed the thought away. She'd worry about it later. Her grip tightened on the box that held the Ouroboros Blade. It wouldn't matter, anyway, if she couldn't fulfill

Demian's terms. Nothing would matter, because the Demon King would begin tearing apart the world that she knew.

Cathal touched her shoulder. "I wish I could help you further, but my place is here. With my queen."

"Sure. I know that. You've already done enough—I didn't expect you to help me as much as you did. Thank you."

"For my son, I will do what I can. I hope to have the chance to make amends to him one day—even more so now that his mortal life is at stake."

Donna turned her back on the dangerous beauty of Faerie and walked through the doorway in the tree, *into* its trunk. Her feet found steps in the darkness and she used the rough-hewn walls to guide her as she descended a helter-skelter staircase. Round and round she walked, until she hit the bottom and made for the door that Cathal had described.

It will take you where you most need to be, he'd said.

Donna saw the night sky and stars as she pushed through, back into her own world. She could only hope she hadn't lost too much time.

Seventeen

Looking around, desperately trying to get her bearings, Donna felt disoriented, like Dorothy after the tornado deposited her in Oz. She hugged herself against the cold and wished she had better night vision. At least it didn't take too long to figure out that she was in the Ironwood.

It was dark and frosty. Donna gazed into the sky and was relieved to see a familiar stretch of bruised purple clouds. The smell of pine filled the air and frost crunched beneath her sneakers as she took a tentative step forward.

She had no idea where she was in relation to any of the exits from the Ironwood. Sure, what remained of the forest was hardly sprawling, but it covered a big enough space that, were you to find yourself dumped in the middle of it at random, you didn't have much hope of finding your way out. At least, not any time soon.

Twilight made the winter trees look bleak and sinister. Even the evergreens seemed to loom dark and threatening as she turned around, trying to get her bearings. She looked up at the sky again, wondering if there were any hints up there. But of course she didn't have a clue what she was doing when it came to stargazing.

I'm truly lost, Donna decided. Though maybe that was a good thing—she might somehow wander into the Elflands, whose main point of entry was in the Ironwood. But the only way to gain access to Aliette's realm was to locate an Old Path—the pathways of the wood elves—and use fey magic to request entry.

Donna had never thought this would be something she'd *want* to do, but right now she was willing to take all the lucky breaks she could get. Since Xan wasn't with her, she didn't have much chance of searching out the Elflands on her own, and she'd never been a very good navigator when map-reading for Aunt Paige as a kid. But she couldn't avoid the fact that getting the Cup of Hermes from Aliette was the next logical step—the next thing she must do if she had any hope of creating the Philosopher's Stone by dawn on Imbolc.

She picked a direction and started walking, shivering in the night air and hoping she would hit a path she recognized sooner rather than later.

A sharp screech made Donna jump, and she had to touch the closest tree trunk to get her breath and balance. She was badly on edge, all her nerves felt raw and exposed, but given her memories of the Skriker—the monster she'd killed just a couple months ago—she could hardly blame herself. The sound she'd heard definitely wasn't the fey creature, though—she'd know that particular cry anywhere. Probably it had just been an owl, swooping for its prey.

Just as Donna convinced herself it was safe to continue, the bushes on either side of the path rustled. Four wood elves scuttled onto the path, blocking her way forward.

The clicking and scraping sounds they made in the backs of their throats made her shudder. Donna's tattoos stirred against her arms. She spun around, planning to run back the other way, but another group of elves already blocked her escape, their black eyes watching her with creepy intensity.

Donna knew she could try fighting them, but six wiry elves, no matter how weakened they might be, were too many for just one of her. She darted to the side and off the path, plunging into the undergrowth.

"*Stop!*" The shout came from somewhere back on the path, and Donna was so surprised that she actually did as commanded. Not because of the order itself, but because wood elves didn't speak human language. Their mouths and throats could not form the right syllables—at least, not in their true, unglamoured form.

She turned around slowly. There was only one person who that voice could belong to.

Aliette stood straight and tall on the path, her six elves gathered around like giant insects.

Donna glanced over her shoulder and then back up at the sky. It was completely dark now, and she didn't stand much chance in the Ironwood at night—not if she wasn't even sticking to the main paths. The Wood Queen regarded her calmly, waiting for her to come to the only sensible conclusion.

Donna picked her way around brambles and fallen branches, stepping back onto the path strewn with dead leaves and dried berries.

"Your Majesty," she said.

"Iron Witch," the queen replied. Donna could swear that Aliette was smiling, but it was difficult to tell in that strange, woody face of hers. "You stink of my cousin, Isolde."

Donna raised her brows. "You can *smell* her on me? That's ... pretty weird. No offense," she added quickly.

Aliette waved away her minions. "Walk with me."

"Where are we going?" Donna asked. "I've already been in Faerie today—I'm not sure I want to cross realms again. Can't we talk here?"

"I will not take you into my lands tonight, Donna Underwood. If we follow this path, it will show you the way out of the forest. I assume you are lost ... "

Donna's shoulders slumped. She was lost, tired, scared. All of that good stuff. "Why would you help me?"

Aliette laughed, a strange brittle sound accompanied by a rustling sound like dead leaves. "When have I *helped* you in the past, and why would I start now? No, young alchemist, I only ever act in the interests of my people."

Donna put her hands on her hips. "Oh, really? Is that what you call letting the demons out of Hell?"

A sly look crossed the Wood Queen's features. "I believe it was *you* who achieved that particular task. Remarkable power, indeed, in one so young."

Donna scowled. "I'm sick of games, your Majesty. What do you really want?"

"I would give you what you seek—the Cup of Hermes. An alchemical artifact carved from the bark of the oldest tree in the Elflands."

"Just like that?" Donna snorted. No way would Aliette, of all people, make it so easy for her. "Excuse me if I don't believe you."

"I care little for what you believe. I care only about saving my kin. Now, the only way I can do this is to have the Elflands accepted back into the realm of Faerie. And to do *that*, I must play by the Demon King's rules. Take the cup—what good it may do you—and make your precious Stone. With Demian back in power, we are obliged to pay the tithe to Hell once more. Perhaps we can then return to Faerie and my wood elves may yet survive."

Donna examined the queen's words, turning them every way in her mind, looking for the trick. The trap. There was always a catch when it came to the fey, and it wasn't like she didn't have personal experience of Aliette's sneaky nature.

The Wood Queen made a sharp clicking sound and held out her hand. An elf leapt down from the tree beside Donna, almost giving her a heart attack. She stepped back, tripped over a stone, and narrowly avoided falling on her ass.

The wood elf chattered at its mistress and handed her a package wrapped in leaves. Aliette nodded, dismissing the creature.

"Here," she said, turning back to Donna. "Take the cup. It has been in our care these past decades."

Donna hesitated for only a second. What did she have to lose? It was only a cup. A roughly carved wooden cup; nothing special to look at, with no indication of its importance. It wasn't like it could hurt her. And what could the Wood Queen possibly have planned? The only real risk was that the cup wasn't the real artifact. Of course, that would be bad, but no matter which way she looked at it, Donna was sure the queen had nothing to gain by deceiving her. Not this time.

If nothing else, Donna believed that Aliette *did* want to go back to Faerie. She wanted to save her people.

Sometimes you have to take a chance, no matter what the consequences are. Donna seemed to be doing a lot of that lately. First with the trip to Faerie, and now this—accepting something that seemed far too easy. To think that the Wood Queen wanted the same end result as she did was sort of crazy, but also … plausible. In this case.

Aliette had been watching her examine the cup. "I see your doubt, and while I understand it, it will not take you long to verify the authenticity of the artifact."

Donna placed the cup next to the Ouroboros Blade in her messenger bag. "Fine," she said. "Thank you, I guess."

"Do not thank me. I would end you, if I could. I would gladly end all alchemists in payment for the deaths they have dealt my kind over the centuries. That is the nature of war." Aliette smiled her wicked smile. "But I also know when it is time to retreat. An effective leader always understands that." She pointed along the path, behind Donna. "Take the left-hand fork and keep walking. You will eventually reach the human road."

Aliette swept away, her elves scuttling in her wake.

Donna wondered if she would ever see the Wood Queen again. She hoped not, but as Aliette herself had said, they were at war. All of them. You never knew who you might meet on the path to freedom.

Her phone vibrated in her pocket, jolting her out of her thoughts. She'd forgotten about such mundane things as cell phones. She was surprised it still worked, after its trip to Faerie. Digging it out of her jeans, Donna stared at the caller display... and smiled. She hit the "answer" button.

"Navin?"

"Hey, Don." His voice was distorted through the crackle of a bad connection. "Um... I hate to play damsel in distress here, but I need your help."

"Where are you?"

He told her and Donna didn't hesitate. If he was in trouble, it was her fault. She grabbed the edge of her power and began unraveling it, wrapping herself in the glowing strands. Leaning against a wide tree trunk, she dug deep into her soul and *pulled*.

Eighteen

Donna was on the other side of town, in a cemetery.
But which one? There were plenty in Ironbridge. And
where was Navin? She'd focused on him as hard as she could.
If her teleporting power had worked the way it usually did,
Navin should be here.

She turned a slow circle, straining her ears for any sign
of life, but the whole graveyard was quiet.

Donna buttoned her coat and shivered in the cold air.
She spotted tall iron railings and a sign. It seemed she was

close to the exit. She took a step in that direction, fighting a vague feeling of nausea after the strange trip.

A loud groan stopped her in her tracks.

The tiny hairs on the back of her neck stood on end. She whirled, trying to pinpoint exactly where the sound was coming from. Now someone coughed—and kept coughing. It didn't sound healthy.

"Nav?" she whisper-shouted.

Was Demian tricking her? She didn't trust him not to be following her around, and half expected demon shadows to jump out of the real shadows.

"Help me," called the voice, followed by another round of staccato coughs.

She froze, searching the darkness of the cemetery as her eyes adjusted. There was no moon—or if there *was*, it was completely blanketed in cloud—and the burial ground didn't have any kind of nighttime lighting. The gates would undoubtedly be locked, and she'd have to climb to get out if things did go bad.

She took a quick breath and ran toward whoever was in pain. Was it Navin? Maybe Demian had hurt him. Or perhaps Simon had caught him sneaking around trying to get hold of Newton. She should never have asked him to help her!

Spotting a crumpled shape beside a freshly dug grave, Donna jogged over, slipping on the frosted grass.

Whoever it was, he was lying dangerously close to the edge of the grave. She stayed a few steps away, just in case, and crouched down beside the figure. It wasn't as though she couldn't defend herself if it turned out to be some kind of con.

And then her heart stuttered as she realized that the person on the ground was wearing a familiar red and black biker jacket. He rolled over, a lock of black hair falling across one eye as he squinted up at her.

"Donna?"

"Navin!" She scrambled forward. "Oh my god, Nav. Let me help you. It's okay, I'm here."

He frowned and licked his lips, as though trying to pick his words carefully. He seemed disoriented and even a little afraid. "How did you get here so fast? I only just called."

"It's a long story. Let's get you out of here first, okay?"

He focused on her for the first time. "I know you're super strong and everything, but please don't throw me over your shoulder. My manliness couldn't take it."

She choked on a sob, not sure whether she was laughing or crying. She was just so relieved to be with him again, and that he was okay.

"Donna?" Navin watched her with concern.

"Sorry, I just spaced for a minute. Seriously, let's get you on your feet and worry about everything later."

She wrapped her arms around him, using her strength to haul him into a sitting position. "Do you feel sick?" She checked his face anxiously. Maybe he'd hit his head. He might be concussed or dizzy or—

"You look beautiful," he whispered.

Donna froze. "What?"

"You heard me."

Okaaay. A concussion was starting to look like a very real possibility here.

Their faces were almost touching. She could see a cut on Navin's cheek, and his eyes didn't look quite right. Even in the near-dark he looked sort of stoned. His pupils were huge.

"Nav, I think you might be badly injured. Is your head hurting? I think—"

"I think you should stop talking," he said.

And then he kissed her.

It wasn't like when Xan kissed her. Those kisses were hot and wild and tasted of sunlight. Navin's lips were gentle, uncertain. It was as if he was testing her—testing them— wondering if this was really happening.

At least, that's what *she* was wondering. Donna was so surprised she stayed completely still, allowing the kiss if not entirely participating in it. She closed her eyes and leaned into him, just a little. Just for a moment.

Just to see . . .

His hand was cold on the back of her neck and he tasted vaguely of cloves.

She pulled away, cheeks flushed. Confused.

"Nav . . ."

What should she say? Should she say something about the kiss? Maybe she could pretend it hadn't happened. That might be best all round.

"Yes!" Navin shouted. He raised both hands in the air. "First base, baby!" He jumped to his feet. "Woo!"

Donna sat back on her heels and stared.

Navin was dancing, gyrating his hips, thrusting and crotch-grabbing Michael Jackson-style. "*The girl is mine!*"

Donna narrowed her eyes. Her nausea had returned, sitting like a heavy weight in her stomach. She had a very bad feeling about this.

Navin stopped thrusting and laughed down at her. "Oh, Navin," he simpered in a high-pitched voice, "you're so handsome. I never knew you cared. Oh Navin, your lips are so *soft*."

Donna pulled herself to her feet, stumbling as the blade and the cup shifted inside the messenger bag. "Demian?"

"*Bzzt!*" crowed Navin. "Wrong answer, princess."

She backed away from this crazy person wearing her best friend's face. She touched her lips with her gloved fingers, wondering how she could have let him kiss her like that. She should have known it wasn't even real. How had Demian fooled her? She was such an idiot.

"If this is your idea of a joke…" Her voice trailed off. Actually, she didn't think this *was* the Demon King's idea of a joke. She didn't honestly believe that Demian was capable of something as human as… humor.

Could it be a wood elf, wearing a glamour? They'd done that before, with Navin, but surely it wouldn't have quite so much *personality*.

The being wearing Navin's form did a slow circle, head tilted back as he scanned the sky and took a deep breath of frigid air.

"It's good to be alive, little alchemist," he said.

Donna paused for a stunned second. "Newton," she whispered.

"*Ding-ding-ding*! You have won a *prize*," the demon declared, opening his arms wide and grinning at her. "It is I, Newton: summoned by the Dragon Magus, entrapped by sheer bloody fluke on his part—appallingly bad luck I was having that day, I might add."

Donna thought she was going to throw up. She swallowed and rubbed her hand across her mouth, only half aware of what she was doing.

Newton-Navin raised an eyebrow. "What's the matter, princess? Didn't you like my moves? Should I have gone with some tongue? I wondered about that, but you seemed to like the whole shy, romantic shtick..."

"Shut up!" Donna gritted her teeth against a scream of frustration, of rage, and felt a visceral urge to punch something. "How *dare* you!"

"Oh, I'm sorry," Newton said, not sounding even remotely apologetic. "Did I hurt your feelings? Did you wish it really was sappy Navin delivering the kiss of your dreams? Did—"

"I said, Shut. Up." Donna fixed him with a murderous expression. "What did you do to my friend?"

Newton/Navin made a big show of looking all around. "What friend? Where?" He pulled the waistband of his jeans away from his slim belly and looked down them. "Nope, not much here."

She just stared at him, willing reality to change and for Navin to be there with her. Where he belonged. She remembered the kiss and pushed the still-vivid feeling away. It had just been one of those things. A crazy moment of relief.

And it hadn't even been Navin.

Newton touched his toes a couple of times, twisting his body from side to side and then started jogging on the spot.

"What are you *doing*?"

"What does it look like I'm doing? What *are* they teaching children these days? I'm exercising, *duh*. You have no idea what it's been like all these years. Trapped. Inanimate. In constant agony." He sounded out of breath, but he kept jogging. "Wow, this is tough. Does Sharma actually do any exercise? He's kind of filled out lately, now I come to think about it, so maybe he's been *working out*."

"You can't stay in his body," Donna said, her voice shaking.

Newton-Navin put his hands on his hips and stared at her as though *she* were the one who'd lost her mind. "Why not?"

"You just can't!"

"That ain't no good reason, baby," he said. "I was Simon Gaunt's bitch, and now I'm not."

Donna let out an angry breath. "I realize that must have been hard for you. But taking someone else's body isn't—"

"You realize *nothing*," Newton snapped. He stopped moving and glared at her from Navin's eyes—only they weren't Nav's eyes. She'd known there had been something wrong. She should have trusted her instincts. Instead she'd allowed him to kiss her and now, here they were, in a cemetery in

Ironbridge. Navin was ... who knows where, and a demon was running around (literally) in his body.

Her whole world was falling apart.

"Newton," she said, trying to get his attention. "You have to give him back. Please. I'm asking you. *Begging* you. Let him go and I'll help you find another body. I'll help you find your *own* body—wherever it is." She frowned. "If you have one. *Do* you have a body of your own?"

He ignored her, jogging a few steps and then throwing what was presumably meant to be an invisible ball. "*Howzat!*"

Donna buried her face in her hands. Could this get any worse? She peeked between her fingers at the person who used to be her best friend.

"Newton ... "

"It's alive!" he yelled to the skies, delight radiating from him. "Aliiive!"

"*Newton!*"

"No, no, no. Don't call me that anymore."

"You're going to tell me your real name?"

"No. I changed my name. You can call me the Artist Formally Known As Navin. Get it?"

Donna suspected that Nav was still in there somewhere, what with the wacky humor and all. She simply had to hang on to the hope that he was okay—but that hope was a slippery thing, and it was fading fast.

As she stood shivering in the chill air, and the moon seemed to wink at her from between a gap in the clouds, she watched the figure of Navin Sharma raise his hands above his head.

"I'm the king of the world!"

Donna was so busy watching what was left of her friend, and wondering how the hell she was going to fix it, that she didn't notice the huge shape swooping down on her until it was too late.

Nineteen

Strong hands hooked beneath her arms and lifted her up—then kept on lifting. Her whole body rose into the air. Donna froze, holding herself rigid for several moments before her instincts kicked in. She shrieked and thrashed wildly, watching in horror as the cold earth became more and more distant. Newton-Navin seemed very far away, and it had all happened so quickly she could hardly even begin to process it.

"Stop struggling," a familiar voice said in her ear. "I've got you."

Xan?

"But . . . *how?*" She could barely speak as the wind rushed past her face and froze her cheeks. Her mind seemed stretched too tight, almost as though it might snap. She honestly believed she was good at handling crazy shit, but this could be one step too far. One giant crazy leap too far, even for her.

Her legs swung out and hit tree branches, and she gasped.

"Hold still. I'm not very good at this yet."

"Xan, what happened to you?" Her teeth hurt in the cold air each time she opened her mouth, but she couldn't help it. Xan was flying!

"What do you think?" he asked.

"I . . . I don't know. I can't see you." She tried to twist in his arms, but it was impossible.

"Just turn your head to the side."

Donna glanced left and then right, very carefully, trying not to break Xan's concentration. She could see the arc and swoop of wings as they gained altitude, moonlight flashing on the metallic edges and razor-sharp tips.

They looked beautiful. But they also looked deadly, like weapons.

Xan wrapped his arms more firmly around her. She could feel the warmth of his chest pressing into her back.

His voice was filled with joy. "I'm flying!"

Confusion made her head spin, adding to the sense of unreality that already had her off-balance. Not to mention the fact that she was *flying* above Ironbridge. "How did Maker do something like this so quickly?" It didn't make sense; her own operations had taken weeks. Even months.

Xan held her more tightly. "They're not real, not yet. This is just a prototype that Maker's working on. They're not organically attached or anything, it's just a harness—but it's a step in the right direction."

Donna knew she should feel happy for him, but she'd just lost Navin and there was still so much to do.

"Where to, my lady?" he asked.

"Take me to the Frost Estate," she said. That was where she could confront Simon—and hopefully find a way to get Newton out of Nav's body. After all, he was the Magus' pet demon. Surely he'd know what to do.

"Your wish is my command," Xan said.

She gritted her teeth against the cold air rushing at them. She would *make* Simon free Navin.

They began to fly lower, heading back into the tops of the wintering trees. Donna's heart lifted even as their altitude dropped.

"Thank you," she breathed, thinking that Xan wouldn't hear her.

"You're welcome," he replied, his lips so close to her ear that she felt the warmth of his breath.

She could hear the smile in his voice. This was just so incredibly … wild. She couldn't comprehend it. How could she? They were holding a freaking conversation while flying over the Frost Estate.

❧

They landed after what seemed like only minutes, and Donna wished they could have flown forever. This was one of those times when she knew it was totally inappropriate to be focusing on how romantic something was—what with the fate of world hanging in the balance and all—but, honestly, how could it *not* be considered romantic?

Xan had literally swept her off her feet. Swooped in at the last moment and whisked her out of harm's way. Not that she'd really needed rescuing. For one thing, she believed she could take care of herself. For another, she didn't truly think that Newton would have hurt her. It wasn't just that the demon was wearing Navin's face, or the hope that Nav could influence Newton's actions in some way. Donna just had a feeling that, for all his bluster and bravado, the demon wasn't all bad.

For a demon.

Xan took her hand and they knocked on the door of the mansion. Donna knew that everybody would still be there, preparing for war, but she had a plan. A plan which she hadn't exactly thought through and that could have potentially fatal consequences. But she already had almost all of the ingredients she needed to make the Philosopher's Stone, and she wasn't going to fail now.

One more night before dawn—before Imbolc and Demian's deadline.

Rachel opened the door, but the expression on her face wasn't one of happy greeting. Her mouth was set in a grim line as she pulled them inside.

"Where have you been? The Demon King is here."

Donna's heart thudded. "He's early. We still have time."

"I know," her mother replied. "I think he's just playing with us, but he's been asking for you."

Xan tried to restrain her, fear clouding his eyes.

Donna touched his face with one gloved hand. "He won't hurt me," she said. "Let's just get this over with."

A voice called out from behind them. "Did you forget something?"

She stopped in her tracks, then turned around. Very slowly.

"Newton. What a pleasant surprise this is."

Nav's face reflected the demon's displeasure. "You left me behind."

Donna smiled. "I do believe you're pouting."

Newton leaned against the door jamb. "I never pout. Luckily, I know how to travel fast—even in this clumsy body." He hooked his (Navin's) thumbs into the pockets of Nav's familiar red and black biker jacket. "Nice jacket, though. Maybe I'll keep it after everybody dies."

Demian entered the hallway from one of the rooms off to the side. "Lovely place you alchemists have here," he said, his tone conversational. "Ah, Newton. How good to see you again."

"And you, Majesty," Newton-Navin said. He didn't sound all that sincere to Donna.

The Demon King raised his eyebrows and waved them all inside. "Shall we?"

❧

Donna stood in the center of the Blue Room and stared at the gathered alchemists: at her family, her friends (even if one of them was currently possessed by a slightly unhinged demon), and finally at Demian's cruel beauty. She'd had enough. War was almost upon them, and there were only a few hours left before the Demon King's deadline.

Quentin Frost stood beside Simon, watching her with concern. Maker had finally joined them and was sitting in his wheelchair, looking old and tired. Aunt Paige's face was white as bone, as if she believed the end of the world was pretty much upon them right that very second. And her mother... Rachel actually seemed calm. Her gray eyes were also filled with pride. Miranda stood further back, with a small group of alchemists whom Donna didn't know.

Newton-Navin was watching her with a predatory, almost feral gaze. "What are you thinking, little alchemist?"

Donna laughed bitterly. "Even though you're not really Nav, you seem to know me the best."

Newton raised Navin's eyebrow. "He's still in here, princess. I'm just not letting him speak. He really is quite upset..."

"He's not the only one. I *had* hoped that Simon could undo at least one crappy thing he was responsible for."

The Magus scowled. "I am not responsible for the Sharma boy breaking into my laboratory—again—and actually letting a demon, of all creatures, take over his body. You're on your own."

Demian took a step forward. "Newton will be home soon enough."

Xan caught her gaze, steering her away from Simon, Demian, and from all the others in the room. "Donna, there must be a way around this. You always find a way."

"I used to think I could do anything if I put my mind to it," Donna replied in a low voice. "Now? I'm not so sure. I need to get into the Otherworld to find the Gallows Tree, otherwise everything I've done so far will be for nothing."

"If you give up, what kind of message does that send?" Xan nodded in Demian's direction. "To *him*, I mean."

"Who said anything about giving up?" Donna ignored everybody else and stepped into Xan's arms. She reached up and kissed him, holding him close and tracing the curve of his lips with hers. His temporary wings closed around her, shielding them from the room full of people.

Donna wondered if he knew she might be saying goodbye.

Xan's mouth opened against hers. He tasted of tobacco and mints. He tasted of the sun, and she pressed herself closer, trying to lose herself in his warmth, wanting to shut out the rest of the world if only for a moment. His hands cupped her face and he made a sound in the back of his throat. Donna wanted to hear him make it again so she kissed him harder, put more of herself into it and tried to tell him everything she wanted to say with a single kiss. This was her moment with Xan, just in case. Just in case her plan didn't work.

Yeah, it was a reckless plan, but wasn't that what Queen Isolde had said about her? Something about how Donna was unpredictable. Chaotic. Something about a death wish. *Fine*, she thought. *Let me hold tightly to all of that and use it.*

She pulled away from Xan and looked once more into his now-glowing eyes. Their inhuman inner light shone viridian-bright and she tried to smile. Turning her back on him, Donna walked to the center of the room.

Xan looked ready for action, but she refused to involve anyone else in this hopeless quest. Not any more. She was still missing two of the ingredients needed to make the Stone, and it was time to do something about it. She knew what she had to do. Of course, knowing it and *doing* it were completely different things, but she had to try. There wasn't anything else left.

She was done playing nice. Now she was playing for keeps.

Donna felt something new shift inside her. It was like a creature unfolding its wings in her heart, testing them for strength before venturing into the sky. A little like Xan and *his* quest for wings ... but maybe she could find her own somewhere deep within.

Her fingers curled around the hilt of the Ouroboros Blade, where she had slipped it inside her coat pocket. She was glad for her gloves. Glad that she didn't have to feel the tug on her soul as her fingers gripped the cold, carved bone.

Maker tried to get out of his chair.

Demian moved toward her as she whipped out the blade, but he was too late. They all were.

Donna wrapped her other hand around the hilt, lacing her fingers together for a better grip, and plunged the wicked black blade deep into her gut. A gasp of surprise escaped her lips as she fell to her knees.

If she had to die to save the world, then that's what she would do. She could only hoped that she survived it.

The first thing she felt was pain.

And then there was nothing.

Twenty

D onna fell.
A rush of air cold enough to make my teeth hurt.

The sound of wings.

A kaleidoscope of color circling around me like a halo.

She tried to process all these things as the world moved—
or perhaps she was the one moving—and she arrived back on
solid ground.

Here, at the entrance to the Otherworld, everything was
blanketed by a blue-gray mist that wound around and above

the jagged treetops. The smell of sulphur hit her hard, along with a spicy mixture of decay and burnt flesh.

This was no special effect. This was real.

Donna lay on the hard earth beneath twisted trees. Every muscle in her body hurt. How could she be so tired? She looked up at the few remaining dead trees that trailed jagged branches above her face. She took an experimental breath, wondering if it was still necessary to breathe in the Underworld.

"Aren't I dead?" she wondered aloud.

"You're not dead yet, little alchemist," an amused voice replied.

Donna rolled onto her side, her heart pounding. "Newton?"

Newton stepped forward, still in Nav's body, and offered her his hand. Donna didn't hesitate, allowing him to help her up onto her feet.

She frowned. Something wasn't right. Well, apart from the fact that she was in the Otherworld. Then she realized what it was.

"My hands hurt." She automatically went to pull off her gloves, but realized that she wasn't wearing them any more. "Oh." Donna frowned, watching her tattoos glittering in the sickly yellow light. She swallowed. "What's wrong with the sky?"

Newton shrugged. "Nothing. It's the sun making it look like this."

"Hell has a sun?"

"The Otherworld sun is made of iron," he replied, as though it should be obvious.

"How can the sun be made out of iron?" Donna turned around, trying to take in her surroundings.

"The Demon King manifests a vision of Hell that he finds the most...comfortable. Demian has always been fascinated by the Aztecs. He probably stole the iron sun from them. You don't expect demons to be *original*, do you?" Newton leaned toward her, lowering his voice to a conspiratorial whisper. "Our lord and master has always lacked imagination, you know."

Donna shook her head. It was crazy. She was in Hell, talking to a demon walking around in the body of her best friend. She touched her stomach, for the first time remembering that she'd stabbed herself.

There was no wound. Her clothes weren't even ripped. But she could still remember the sensation as the blade sliced through flesh.

"How can you say I'm not dead?" she demanded. "I'm not even injured. This can't be my true body."

Newton smiled benevolently. "You have much to learn."

"What kind of an answer is that?"

"The only one you're going to get."

She glared at him. "Fine. Why are you even here?"

And then her heart sort of jumped and her gut clenched with sudden fear. Not for herself—she was way beyond being scared for herself.

"You're really here? In Navin's body?" Blood pounded in her ears.

Newton held his arms out on either side. "As you see."

"You brought my best friend into Hell?! What are you doing?" She advanced on him. "How *could* you?"

Newton stood his ground, though his expression turned wary. It was the same look Navin got whenever Donna started talking about magic or elves or demons. "Quite easily, thank you very much. I have every right to go home. I've been a prisoner long enough."

"But . . . what about Navin?"

"You can hit me if it would make you feel better," Newton said.

Oh, how she wanted to. But, of course, she couldn't hit the demon without hurting Nav.

"How did you get here?" she asked. "I thought you couldn't get home?"

"I clicked my heels together and said—"

"Stop it! Stop acting like this is all a big joke. I just stabbed myself. I'm in Hell to find a piece of *fruit*. And you dragged my best friend down here with us." She stopped, trying to calm her breathing. "Just answer the question. For once. Please?"

Newton narrowed his eyes, which looked wrong because it just wasn't a Nav expression.

"Very well, Miss Grumpy Pants. I followed you. When you killed yourself—" He gave Donna a fierce look to stop her from interjecting. "Yes, you did kill yourself, but you're not quite dead. Not yet."

"So, when I . . . did that, what did *you* do?"

"I followed. It was simple because Demian was too busy watching you to notice little old me, and by stabbing yourself with the Ouroboros Blade—nice move, by the way, didn't think you had it in you…" He stopped speaking and raised his hand for a high five.

Donna ignored his hand and waited for him to continue explaining.

"Oh, be like that." Newton rolled "his" eyes. "When you stabbed yourself, you opened a door to the Otherworld and pitched yourself through it. I followed. Shame you had to land us so far away from where you *want* to be. Top marks for entry, not so good on positioning. Know what I mean?"

"I'm getting the picture," she said.

"There are so many more interesting places we could be right now," he complained. "The Wailing Bridge, the Plain of Sorrows. You practically dumped us in the middle of nowhere."

Donna glared at him. "I hardly did it on purpose. Anyway, why are you still in a human body? In Navin's body? Shouldn't you have turned back into … I don't know … your true self once you came home?"

Newton glanced away, looking almost embarrassed. "Yes, well. I have to admit that I thought I'd leave this body as soon as I stepped through the door you'd opened. I did everything right. Of course, I didn't know quite what would happen for sure, but it seemed a pretty good theory." His expression turned mournful. "Maybe my own body is lost…"

Donna had had enough. She picked a direction and began following the line of blasted trees, heading toward what looked like open space and walking away from Newton. He would either come with her or he wouldn't. She secretly hoped he *would* follow, what with the tiny issue of him still wearing her best friend's face, but she was just so tired. And scared.

And, now she came to think of it, pretty hungry too. Dying was hard work.

Newton immediately caught up to her and kept talking. "I thought you wanted me to explain?"

"You're taking too long." Donna kept walking.

He huffed slightly beside her. "This body is quite unfit, you know," he said again.

She almost smiled, but quickly stopped herself. She would not be disloyal to Nav and laugh at any of this creep's jokes.

"Donna," Newton said, sounding slightly plaintive.

"What?"

"I can help you."

"*Really?*" Her voice dripped sarcasm. She hoped he got the message. "Maybe you should concentrate on helping yourself, considering that you're now stuck in Hell, in a human body that you shouldn't even be in now that we're supposed to be dead."

"You're here, aren't you?"

"Because I'm dead."

"Nope. You're only a little bit dead. Doesn't count."

"Okay, because I used the blade?"

"Very good! That is the *correct* answer."

Donna sighed, but she slowed her pace and picked her way across the stony banks of a trickling stream. The water looked like it could easily be blood, and it smelled like a dead pigeon (she knew what those smelled like because she and Navin had found one in his attic, once upon a time).

"Why would you even offer to help me? Not that I believe, for one minute, that you'll actually do anything useful."

"I'm insulted! I am mortally wounded. Offended. Upset."

"Oh, please ... " Donna muttered.

"Hurt."

Donna stopped walking and swung around. She grabbed the front of Newton-Navin's T-shirt and pulled him toward her.

"Quit. Screwing. Around. Or, so help me, I will do every-thing in my power to make you regret it."

Newton tried to twist out of her grip, but Donna just shook him until he stopped squirming.

"Oooh, you're so strong!" he said. "You're so masterful. Take me now! I already know you're a good kisser."

She glared at him some more.

"I *am* here to help you, you know. Consider me your own personal psychopomp. I can guide you through the domains of the Otherworld."

Donna released him and spun away, pissed beyond all measure. She pressed the heel of her hand above her right eye and took a deep breath. She could feel a headache starting.

Please don't tell me I'm going to be stuck with Newton for all eternity, she thought.

Now that really *was* her idea of Hell. And she wanted her friend back. Like, right now.

She tried to take in some of her surroundings as they walked. All around them, colors shifted and breathed into new forms; the air heated and cooled and then burned again. She walked through an ornate, gothic-styled doorway that had appeared out of nowhere—with nothing but wide open space, like a multicolored desert, on either side of it—and touched the gargoyle sitting on its crumbling post as she went by. The gargoyle's stone head turned to watch her and blinked its eyes.

Donna gulped and kept walking.

Everything changed and yet stayed the same, but the sun in the sky was constant. Burning silver-bright, casting that strange half-light over the Otherworld. Until they came to a point in the alien landscape where her companion suddenly stopped.

"I can't go any further with you," Newton said.

"What? I thought you were my own personal *psycho*?"

"Psycho*pomp*," he said, looking offended.

Donna didn't exactly want him around, but she wasn't enthusiastic about being left alone either. At least with Newton in Navin's body, she got to see Nav's face—no matter how twisted the whole situation was. She was also worried that if she let the body-snatching demon out of her sight, she would lose Navin for good.

Newton grimaced. "I'll show you why I can't go any further, shall I?"

"Go ahead, then. Astound me," Donna said.

Newton reached out with both hands. His palms appeared to press against some kind of invisible barrier, like he was standing behind a pane of glass.

"You're trapped?"

Newton nodded, downcast. "The Demon King knows I'm here. Damn it all to Hell!" He made the sign of the cross, then winked at her.

He continued to search the air in front of him with his hands, doing a good impression of one of the old-fashioned mimes that Donna sometimes saw outside Ironbridge's Central Mall. It was surreal.

Newton punched the barrier. Hard. "You'd best go on. Demian will be waiting for you."

He hit it again.

Donna swallowed against the sudden dryness in her throat. "Don't keep doing that. Remember whose body you're using."

Newton examined his knuckles. "Good point. Oooh … pretty bruise, wanna see?"

"No," she snapped. She took a deep breath, scared to leave Navin behind but not really having a whole lot of choice. What was that famous Winston Churchill quote that Robert liked? "If you're going through Hell … keep going."

Donna figured that she'd better keep going.

She trudged up the side of the hill, trying not to think about what would happen at the top.

The higher Donna climbed, the darker it became, as though somebody with a giant eraser was rubbing out the sun. It was a strange sun, with that jaundiced light, but at least it had provided *some* kind of illumination on the earlier part of her journey. She stopped for a moment and rested against a jagged boulder. The mountainside was scattered with them, as though a giant's teeth had fallen out. She tugged off her coat and left it behind, spread out on one of the rocks, then tied her hair back into a loose ponytail. Despite the receding light, she was getting hotter rather than colder. She checked the contents of her messenger bag and was surprised to see everything remained intact. Being "dead," at least in her case, obviously didn't mean you moved on to the next realm without your worldly possessions.

Finally, after what felt like hours, Donna staggered to the summit and walked onto a mercifully flat shelf of land. There were tufts of blackened grass sticking out at intervals, but other than that it was made up mostly of red-tinged earth. Dust gathered around her and made it difficult to see as she walked forward, slowly, taking care so as not to fall off the edge of the world.

She was so busy watching where she placed her feet that she only realized she had company when he was directly in front of her.

Demian smiled benevolently. "You made it."

Donna pushed her damp fringe out of her eyes. "I did."

"I am ... glad."

"Was this some kind of a test?"

His silver brows rose. "Test? No. How could it be? I did not know you planned on killing yourself."

"Got you with that one, did I?"

"It was not something I'd predicted." He regarded her with his coal-black eyes. "You are a surprising creature, for a human."

Donna was too busy catching her breath to reply. She tried to look over the demon's shoulder, but the cloud of red dust was too thick.

Demian held out his hand to her. "Come, let me show you my kingdom."

Donna almost laughed. "A guided tour of Hell? I don't think so, Your *Majesty*. I'm here to find the Grove of Thorns."

He inclined his head. "And you need to pass through the city to reach it. Why not let me escort you? You will reach your destination unharmed—I give you my word."

Donna nibbled her lower lip and considered his words. She had to admit that, for a demon, he did seem more honest than she'd been led to believe. Newton was all about games and trickery, but Demian was almost straightforward in his dealings. She tested his words in her mind, looking for the hidden clause that would allow him to harm her.

Demian's hand was still extended, never once wavering.

She said, "You won't hurt me, in any way?"

"As I keep telling you, I have no desire to cause you harm." His eyes turned sly. "You are almost dead, anyway, so I wonder why you would worry so much."

"I don't want to end up all the way dead," she replied. "Not if I can help it."

He seemed to think about this for a moment. "If you don't give me a reason to cause you injury, then you really have nothing to worry about."

Donna shook her head. "And there's the catch. How do I know what would drive you to change your motivation toward me?"

"I swear, on my kingdom, that while you are in the Otherworld with me on *this* occasion, I will not harm you in any way—no matter what—nor will I allow harm to come to you by way of any of my subjects. How does that sound?"

"Pretty good," she admitted. "What about the Gallows Tree? Will you help me reach that?"

"Ah," he said. "That I cannot do."

"But you want the Philosopher's Stone as much as anyone else."

"That is undoubtedly true, but you must remember that I am forbidden to enter the grove, so I won't be able to help you beyond escorting you there."

Donna blew out a breath. "That's good enough."

He bowed, a mocking smile on his face. "I am glad the agreement meets with your approval."

"Any advice for me?" She hadn't expected a reply, so was surprised when he took her question seriously.

"Enter the grove alone. You'll never find the Gallows Tree otherwise."

Donna narrowed her eyes. "Who would I take in with me? I *am* alone."

"For now," he replied.

Nav, she thought. He's talking about Navin. Hope gripped her heart and she tried not to hold on to it too hard.

"Will I be able to get home, afterwards?"

Demian turned away so that she could no longer see his expression. "We'll have to see, won't we?"

She shot him an irritated look. "You talk in riddles just to annoy me."

His shoulders stiffened. "You are mistaken. Everything I do is not about eliciting a reaction from you. Some things simply just … are."

She shook her head. He really wasn't helping. She was starting to wish that Newton was still here.

Demian continued walking. "I wouldn't expect you to understand, but that doesn't mean—"

"I wish people would stop treating me like a child," Donna said, interrupting him. "'You wouldn't understand,' they say. 'It's for your own good,' they tell me. And you're doing exactly the same thing."

Demian stopped suddenly, forcing Donna to stop with him. "Now you really *do* misunderstand me." His head tilted to one side as he examined her. "It is true that I said that you don't understand my ways, but I was about to say that I would like it, very much, if you learned. Just because someone doesn't understand something, doesn't mean they can't *gain* an understanding. Given time."

Time? Donna didn't intend to spend any more time with Demian than she was forced to. And she certainly didn't want to "understand" him. He was so very alien to her. *Other* didn't even begin to describe the way he somehow felt when she spoke to him. Even dealing with the fey didn't have the disconcerting sense of *wrongness*.

"Here," he said.

Slowly, the mist cleared to reveal how high up they were. The Otherworld sky was now filled with crimson clouds, covering the iron sun, but a thousand lights like fallen stars glittered far below.

Donna took a tentative step toward the edge of the cliff. She looked down and gasped.

Twenty-one

L ook upon the Sunless City," said the demon. He made a sweeping gesture with his hand.

The city spread out far below, buildings and streets and alleyways like a living, three-dimensional map. All the light came from a variety of scattered structures. There was no order to anything—at least, not one that Donna could recognize. There were small buildings next to large. Narrow streets that opened into huge, red-streaked highways. A river the color of dull iron wound snakelike through the center, and towers that almost touched the sky seemed to grow from the very ground itself.

There were no people. No living things scurrying about their business on the streets below. No birds flying through the dusty air. But then, Donna thought, why would there be? They were in the Otherworld. The *Under*world: a land of the dead.

Demian watched her taking in the terrible beauty of his world. She could feel his eyes on her, burning into her with an intensity that made her want to hide.

"Come," he said. "I will take you where you need to go. Time grows short."

He extended his hand, palm up, waiting for her with all the patience of a centuries-old tree waiting for rain.

She took his hand. It was cool and dry, his skin even paler than hers. He tugged her toward him, so that she was forced to take an extra step. She found herself in the circle of his arms, looking up into those strange eyes.

Donna held her breath—one hand in his, her other touching his chest to keep him at a distance. Here she was, dying in another world under a strange sun with the king of the demons. Life as a daughter of the alchemists had seemed pretty extreme . . . wood elves and half-fey boys, magic and changeling girls . . . it all pushed the boundaries of what she believed was possible. The emergence of her own power, bound for a decade by people she'd once trusted, was yet another step into the unknown.

But this . . . this was something else. She felt lightheaded, and wondered if their altitude was affecting her. Or perhaps it was the crimson dust that tickled her nostrils and made her feel like she constantly needed to clear her throat.

Demian didn't move. He didn't attempt to pull her closer, but he also didn't release her. The cool mask of his face cracked and the corners of his mouth raised, just slightly. It was the first smile Donna had seen that didn't seem touched by cruelty.

"Donna Underwood," he said. "I would have you for my queen."

"Your *queen*?!" Donna pulled her arm back, but the demon held her with a grip of iron to rival her own.

"Think about it: you are deeply unhappy in your world. I know this is true. Together, we could rule. Not just this realm, but all the realms that stretch throughout eternity. With my strength of will and your ability to access other realms, we could rule not just one race—but all of them."

Horror crawled through Donna's chest like a living thing, making it difficult to breathe. "Let me go."

She tried to jerk her hand free, but Demian simply drew her closer. His other arm clamped her to his body, and it was like being pressed against the cool weight of stone. His silver hair stirred in a sudden breeze.

"I want you." It wasn't a statement. It was a declaration of intent.

A demand.

Is this what he'd meant when he'd appeared to her that night on a quiet London street? The Demon King's eyes were glittering, just like they had then.

"I am well accustomed to getting what I want," he added.

"Too bad," Donna said, trying to catch her breath in the vice of his arms.

"I will have you," he said. His expression was impossibly arrogant.

"You don't want *me*," Donna said, as panic fluttered in her stomach. "You only want my power."

"Semantics," he said. "You hold the power, therefore I want you."

"Want? *You* want? What about what *I* want?"

Everything felt too intense, too *real*.

But if it felt real to her, hopefully that meant it felt just as real to Demian. She wouldn't let him take what he wanted without a fight. She was way better than that.

The Demon King loosened his hold on her. Just a little. "Perhaps I am not only talking about your power. Perhaps I speak of something ... more."

"Like what? *Love*?" The temptation to laugh was rising dangerously. Donna swallowed it down and tasted bile in the back of her throat.

"If that is a word that means something to you," Demian said.

She met his inhuman eyes. "You wouldn't know the first thing about love."

"And you, child, don't know the first thing about me."

"'Child'? Right. A child. So ... you want to *be* with this 'child,' do you? Sounds kind of twisted to me."

His eyes narrowed and his hand tightened on the back of her neck. "It is just a word. You are much younger than I, therefore you seem childlike to one such as me."

"Exactly. So why not go find someone your own age?"

His lips twisted. "What you don't realize, Donna Underwood, is that the very thing that gives you your power—that sliver of first matter that resides in your soul—is older even than I am."

That little revelation hit Donna like a slap in the face. What did it mean? Was it true?

Demian moved one of his hands so that he could touch her face. "I see ages-old wisdom in your eyes. Not *your* wisdom, of course, but the ghost of something ancient that lives in this human shell. With you by my side, I would be truly immortal."

"See? It's not about me at all. And, for the record, I will never stand by your side."

His lips curved. "Never?"

Donna ignored the hunger in his eyes. "Never."

"Never is a very long time," he replied, his voice suddenly deadly serious.

"So you might as well give up now."

"I am a patient man," he said. "I waited for my freedom for two centuries."

Donna shivered. "I'm sorry to disappoint you, but I'll be long gone by then."

"Perhaps."

"Let me give you a tip, Your Majesty. If you want to get the girl, you might try not grabbing her and forcing her to do your bidding."

"I grow tired of your arguments."

"And I'm sick and tired of everybody in my life treating me as some kind of weapon. Now I can't even *die* in peace—I have the King of Hell trying to use me."

Demian's eyes narrowed to onyx slits. "Don't pretend you wanted to die. You knew that the blade would not truly kill you. You were like Inanna, beating at the very gates of Hell and demanding we grant you entrance."

Donna didn't know who this Inanna was, but she liked the sound of her. "I didn't know, not for sure. I had a feeling."

"And what do you think gave you that … feeling?"

She met his gaze, trying not to shake under its heat. "My female intuition?"

"The *prima materia* guides you, and even now you try to deny it. You make jokes rather than face the reality of your power."

Donna slipped her right arm out of his embrace, hauled back, and punched him as hard as she could. In the face.

Even with all the iron covering her human flesh and bone, she felt as though her whole fist had just shattered. And the result of her punch was sort of comical: Demian took a single step back while she fell to her knees, tears of pain filling her eyes.

"Shit," she whispered, glancing down to check that her hand was still intact.

The king of the demons touched his jaw, gazing at her with something that looked suspiciously like wonder. Donna's mind flashed back to the joke Robert made about how Demian would probably like it if she hit him.

She swallowed, still clutching her injured hand, resolutely pushing those thoughts away.

"I should punish you for that," the demon said. But it sounded like he was only really saying it out of habit.

"Punish me? Like this isn't already punishment enough. What the hell is your jaw made of, anyway?" Donna stumbled to her feet and shook out her hand. "Don't answer that." She glared at him. "Listen, all I want is to find the grove, get the fruit, and see if there's any way out of this nightmare."

"You stabbed yourself with the Ouroboros Blade. Your life is forfeit! Only *I* have the power to release you from death."

"Well, good for you. You got me. I'm in your power. I bet that really gets you off, doesn't it?"

Demian advanced on her. "You are treading on very thin ground, girl…"

"Oh, really? And what are you going to do to me? Kill me?" Donna laughed in his face, knowing that she sounded slightly deranged but not even caring. She wasn't a pawn. She would not be a weapon—least of all for a petulant demon who didn't know the first thing about common decency.

Demian looked down, his perfectly unmarked jaw clenched. Unchecked emotion passed over his face like a storm. It was the most expressive Donna had even seen him.

She swallowed, terrified. Waiting.

She was still expecting some kind of attack, so the fact that the Demon King wasn't doing anything at all shocked her more than whatever he might have done.

He turned away. "I will take you to the Grove of Thorns. You will need all your remaining strength for that. The Philosopher's Stone is more important to me than your lack of respect."

Raising her eyebrows, Donna wondered if she could call this round hers.

Demian transported them instantly to the city below, and they walked side by side through what looked like a low-budget movie set for a western. Donna half expected Clint Eastwood to appear at the other end of the dusty street. She wished Navin—the real Navin—was here to make a silly comment about tumbleweed and awkward silences. These were the slums of the Otherworld. The closer they got to the Gallows Tree, the less activity there seemed to be.

Apart from telling her where they were, Demian was quiet, contemplative. She wondered what he was thinking about. Was he angry with her after her outburst? He didn't seem to be. What did a demon king have to occupy his thoughts? Revenge? Perhaps. Did he think about Simon and the alchemists? Maybe he was planning his attack, figuring out how he would redecorate the world once he was in charge.

Donna was distracted from her own thoughts by a sudden movement she saw out the corner of her eye, but each time she turned her head, whatever might have been there had already disappeared. After this had happened several times, she grew increasingly frustrated and stopped walking.

Demian stopped beside her. "What is wrong?"

"Are we being followed?"

"No."

"Watched?"

The corners of his thin mouth curved. Very slightly. "Possibly."

She searched the dark windows of the nearest wooden structure. "From inside?"

He nodded. "Many call the Otherworld their home."

Home. What a strange word to call ... Hell. Donna shivered.

"Who is watching us?"

"Here?" Demian clasped his hands loosely behind his back. "Scavengers, mostly."

"But what about—?"

"You ask too many questions. It will soon be night here, and you need to enter the grove before darkness falls."

She narrowed her eyes. "Fine. Let's go."

❧

The Grove of Thorns was exactly what Donna had expected— only twice the size and ten times more unwelcoming. She shielded her eyes against the disorienting half-light and swirling dust, looking across a wide expanse to her final destination. Everything was so desolate here. The grove was entirely surrounded by rose bushes, but even they didn't help improve how bleak everything was. They were black roses, after all. At least now she knew where Demian got his seemingly endless supply of the stupid flowers.

Somewhere in the middle of all that twisted vegetation was the Gallows Tree. But before she could even think about going into the grove and finding it, there was a slight problem to be dealt with. She swung around and faced Demian.

"You didn't say anything about a river."

He shrugged. "Should I have?"

"Some kind of a warning might have been nice," she muttered.

The river was wide and black as coal, glittering and swirling in a way that made her stomach twist in response. It looked cold.

"Warnings are unimportant," Demian said. "You must cross the river one way or the other. Knowing about it in advance does not change that fact."

Donna crossed her arms. "Easy for you to say. You're not the one who has to get wet." She glanced at him hopefully. "Unless there's a bridge? Newton said something about a Wailing Bridge…"

Thinking of Newton made her think of Nav, and fresh panic bloomed in her stomach. She still had to find him, make sure he was safe. And she still had to, somehow, get her hands on the tear of a demon. *One thing at a time, Underwood*, she told herself. One thing at a damn time.

A muscle flickered in Demian's jaw. "Newton talks too much. The River of Memory and Forgetting does have a bridge, but it is not that which he named. That one is in the main part of the city."

"Figures. So I have to swim." Donna's shoulders slumped. "I'm not a very good swimmer."

"No," Demian said. "There *is* a choice. You can enter the water and relive a forgotten memory, or you can walk across the Bridge of Lies."

Donna searched the river bank, gazing longingly at the grove beyond it. "There's no bridge. What are you talking about?"

"Look again." He pointed, and as she followed the line of his pale hand she saw a crumbling bridge rising out of the water like a black spider.

She shivered. "What happens on the Bridge of Lies?"

"I cannot tell you. It is different for each person who crosses."

"Will it hurt me?"

The corner of Demian's mouth lifted. "Not many survive it."

"But I'm dead anyway," she said, trying to control her fear. "So I suppose it doesn't really matter, does it?"

His smile widened, almost imperceptibly, but he didn't reply.

"What about the river? How safe is that?"

"If you don't swallow any water, you might yet live."

"Fine." Donna sat down and began unlacing her sneakers. "I was just thinking that it looks like a nice day for a swim."

Twenty-two

Her feet were the first part of her to hit the shifting black waters of the River of Memory and Forgetting. She didn't even look back at the Demon King—she just acted. Now was the time to rely on instinct. Time might operate differently down here, but she didn't want to waste any of it. What if she did manage to get out? Who knew what time—what *day*, even—it would be back in her own world? All along, Donna had been determined to make amends for past mistakes. This was her chance, and there was no going back now.

As the waves crashed over her head and she became fully submerged, she held her breath and kept her eyes as tightly shut as physically possible … until everything faded away. The blackness of the water seemed to fill her, and Donna found herself able to open her eyes and look around. Not that there was much to see.

She was suspended in a vast space, cold and wet and tired—she was vaguely aware of those sensations, on some level of consciousness—and yet it also felt like this might be the closest thing to death she had yet experienced. She felt faint and dizzy, especially when she realized that she'd begun to breathe again without even meaning to. Despite being underwater, breathing was the most natural thing in the world. Keeping her mouth tightly shut, she tried to force her eyes to see something in those dark depths. A direction to swim in. A sign. A spark of light … *something*.

Her consciousness began to fade, but then a voice from her past forced her back to full awareness. Her father's words echoed in her mind, strong and true:

"Run, Donna! Don't look back! Whatever you hear, promise me you won't look back."

The last thing Donna remembered was the water tugging at her, the river taking her into its cold embrace and dragging her down, down into its shadowed depths, deep into the heart of the Otherworld.

Into the heart of Memory and Forgetting.

She watched the little girl with her father, surrounded by swaying trees and blowing leaves with the huge dark sky overhead. The memory caught in her chest, like her heart had snagged on something sharp and was slowly unraveling.

The night closed in as the images sharpened. Donna—grown-up Donna—pressed herself against a tree and watched from a short distance. She didn't think anyone could see her. She didn't think she was really here. And yet she still felt the urge to hide, to duck back against the shelter of the solid trunk. Even if this was some kind of dark Otherworld magic, she knew it could all just be more demon lies. A ruse to make her vulnerable and steal the fight from her.

Or maybe it was real. The truth of the life she'd spent so many years repressing. After all, she'd chosen memories when she'd chosen the river. The Bridge of Lies had seemed far too easy.

Just as the scene from her past in the heart of the Iron-wood became sharper, it also became far more painful. Donna watched her younger self and squeezed her fingers against the rough bark, wishing that the scrape of splinters would somehow bring her back to herself and take her out of this, even if the only escape was into the Otherworld. Into death.

The little girl was pale but composed. "Where's Mommy?"

"I'm going to get her, darling, then we'll all leave together."

"I don't want you to leave me!"

"I'll be right back, I promise."

"But Daddy," Little Donna said, taking a step after her father, the desire to follow, to not be abandoned, written all over her young face. "What about our bags?"

She gestured at the small pile of luggage that Donna, watching from her hiding place, had only just noticed. Of course... she'd forgotten this part. The part where the Underwoods—Patrick, Rachel, and Donna—had packed a few belongings and left in the middle of the night, attempting to flee the Order of the Dragon; Simon had planned to take Donna away and use her developing powers to enter the Elflands, so that the alchemists could exterminate their sworn enemies, the wood elves. She might even have been their ticket to conquering Faerie itself, eventually, if a way through Faerie's many wards and protections could be found. With her ability to open doors, Donna was like a walking, talking key.

And, beyond that, there was something else sleeping inside of her that none of the alchemists but Maker had glimpsed. Something more powerful, which the Underwoods couldn't afford to reveal.

"Stay with the bags," Patrick said. "Just stay here. Don't move."

He ran back along the path, disappearing between trees that were just beginning to shed their leaves. It was a chilly fall night. A night that Donna remembered in her bones, in her dreams, if not in her waking memory. He was gone, for good this time. The little girl waited for him to come back for her, wondering whether he'd made a mistake and actually meant to take her with him on the path after all. But it remained silent, apart from the wind through the branches.

She watched herself scuff a foot along the earth and eye the baggage. "Move the bags," she whispered to her younger self.

Little Donna seemed to make a decision, and began dragging each bag to the edge of the pathway, hiding it as best she could behind the trunk of a tree even bigger than the one her future self currently hid behind. Donna smiled, despite her fear and confusion. She remembered this—she really did.

She remembered the feel of the bag strap against her small hand. Recalled how heavy her father's backpack had been and how difficult it was to pull it safely behind the tree. But eventually she managed. She had all the bags safely tucked away, not really visible from the path unless you were looking for them. Especially not in the darkness, with only a sliver of moon overhead.

Donna watched as the little girl sat on the largest bag and peeked around the tree trunk, watching and waiting. She remembered the beating of her heart and the pain in her throat. She remembered how thirsty she was, and how she wondered whether she dared open Mommy's bag and look for some water.

And then a howling, alien call shrieked through the entire forest, and Donna remembered what it was like, the first time she heard the cry of the Wood Monster. The terror, without even know what she was afraid of.

"Daddy?" she whispered, knowing that she wasn't supposed to make a sound.

The monster screamed again. It was getting closer.

Donna fell *into* the memory, and everything else slipped away.

Twenty-three

*S*he waits for her father to return. She knows he'll come back for her. She knows he would never leave her behind—not forever. He was going back for Mommy and then he would come for her.

What had happened to Mommy? She tries to remember, pressing her small hands against her face and wishing she was home in bed where it is warm and safe. (Only it isn't safe any more. That's what Mommy had told her. That was why they were leaving.)

Mommy had stayed behind at the edge of the last clearing to do some of her magic. Donna remembered her words, spoken to her father, not to her: "My wards are stronger. I'll set them here and here." A pause. "And one over there."

Daddy had argued. He said they should stay together, but she had insisted that "keeping Donna safe" was the most important thing.

"Go on," she'd said to her father. "I'll be right behind you. Keep my little girl safe."

He always listened to Mommy.

And now, Donna is alone, sitting on an overstuffed backpack and waiting for someone to come back for her. There had been a scream, and it sounded like Mommy. Her father had told her not to worry, that it was probably nothing—just a bird—except Donna knew there weren't birds in the Ironwood at night. The only things in the Ironwood at night were the wood elves, and they didn't sound like a woman's sharp scream cut off too quickly.

Tears threaten as she waits, and she has a horrible urge to go to the bathroom. She even considers relieving herself behind the next tree, so she can still see the bags and the path, but she's afraid to move. Especially after she heard that terrible sound. The trumpeting howl of some kind of beast—a monster, the kind of thing you only read about in fairy tales. And, even then, the monster is always defeated by the princess. That's the way her daddy tells the stories.

Donna jiggles her legs and fiddles with her jacket. Her hands are cold.

And then the noise comes again. Not the one Daddy had tried to say was a bird. But the long howl that makes her bones shake.

Donna stands up and creeps to the path. The fear is bad enough that she feels all numb with it, all across the top of her head, and her ears make a funny noise. But she has to see what is making the noise.

She has to see that her parents are safe.

The air shimmers between the trees and there is her father, running toward her, his face white and stricken in a way she's never seen it before, not even when they set out from the house and she knew he was worried about being seen. He had been tense but in control.

The expression on her father's face is so much more terrifying. Not that he looks afraid, though perhaps he is, but it is as though he is trying to keep some sort of terrible emotion from escaping.

He grabs her from the path, scooping her into his arms and turning around and around. Searching for something…

"The bags!" He looks into her face. "Where are they?"

"I hid them," she whispers. "I'm sorry, did I make a mistake?"

"No darling, you did great," he says. He squeezes her so tightly against him that she can't breathe properly. "Show me."

They reach the bags and he places his daughter on the ground. He opens the heavy backpack, the one Donna had so much trouble moving, and pulls out a small axe. The blade flashes with magic.

Her eyes widen as he hefts it in one hand and grabs her shoulder with the other.

"Donna, if I tell you to run, you'll run. You will listen to me. You—"

"Where's Mommy?" she wails, unable to keep the tears from filling her eyes.

Her father closes his eyes for a moment. A bleak expression crosses his face as he opens them again. "She'll be here in a moment. She's right behind me." His voice breaks. "Just listen to me, okay?"

"No she isn't," Donna says, knowing that he's lying to her. Something he has never done before. "Did the monster eat her?"

He removes his spectacles and tucks them inside his coat. "Not the monster you're talking about," he says grimly.

"I don't—"

"Get behind me, Donna," he shouts as the Wood Monster bursts onto the path. Blue flames surround its dark muzzle and its eyes glow like two fiery embers.

Donna bites back a scream, hanging onto her father's hand, trying not to let him push her back. She wants to hold onto him, and if he insists on her staying behind she won't be able to feel his hand in hers. "Daddy, don't leave me!" she wants to say, but the words won't come. Her throat hurts and she grabs his leg.

But he shoves her back with ease and she has no choice but to watch as her father, Patrick Underwood—the man she idolized all the seven short years of her life—brandishes the shining axe and stares down the Wood Monster.

Donna broke from the water, choking as the blackness threatened to drag her down again. There was blood beneath the surface—she didn't want to go back, didn't want to see. All that blood from her memories, as wet as the river that surrounded her, and the look of agony on her father's face. She gasped, fighting the watery arms that threatened to drown her. It felt as though something in the water was alive, as if, even now, it was feeding on her memories. On her pain and terror.

She thrashed about with her arms and legs, wondering if she would sink to the bottom from all the iron in her body, testing her theory that she'd never been cut out for swimming. She'd hated it as a small child, anyway. Strange how she could remember so much about what life had been like before the age of seven.

Or maybe, not so strange at all.

The River of Memory and Forgetting flowed by and she managed to float on her back, letting it carry her along as she recovered from reliving such a memory. *Dad*, she thought, fighting tears. *Oh, Dad…*

She kicked her legs and tried to direct herself to the shore. The water was painfully cold; so icy that the shock of it was enough to bring her to full consciousness before she could sink. *Is it even possible to drown?* Donna wondered. *If I'm already dead, that must be pretty impossible.*

A pair of arms wrapped around her from behind.

She thrashed in the freezing water, not even knowing who or what had grabbed her. Not caring. "Get off me!"

"Stop struggling," a familiar voice said. "I'm trying to help you."

"I don't need your help, Newton. I've got this. Get your hands *off*!"

Navin's face was inches from hers. "It's me, Donna. It's Nav. I'm back!"

She almost swallowed a mouthful of water when she forgot to kick her legs for a moment. "I'm not that easy to fool a second time," she gasped. "Any excuse to cop a feel."

He looked genuinely shocked. If it really was still Newton, he was doing a good job of acting more like the real Nav. "What are you talking about? I wouldn't do that."

Donna put her hands on his shoulders and looked into his eyes. "Is it really you?"

"Yeah, but can you stop leaning on me like that? You're going to sink us both. Have you put on weight since you went to England?"

It was Navin. He was here, with her! Donna threw her arms around him, letting him do the work of keeping them afloat for a little longer. She pressed her cheek against his and almost cried with relief.

"I was so worried about you."

"About me? I was worried about *you*."

"I can take care of myself," she said. "Don't forget, I'm a powerful Iron Witch."

He laughed and almost sank them both, but managed to keep his head above the water. "Do you think we can talk once we're not in danger of drowning? Also," he added seriously, "if we stay in here for too long, you might start to rust."

When they were finally sitting on the banks of the River of Memory and Forgetting, with their clothes already drying under the brittle remains of the iron sun, Donna grabbed Navin's hand and held on as tightly as she dared. They swapped tired smiles.

She said, "I thought I'd never get you back."

"Hey, now," he replied, looking embarrassed and pleased at the same time.

She looked beyond him, examining the Grove of Thorns. This was where she would find the fruit that she needed to make the Philosopher's Stone. Navin followed her gaze. It seemed impossible that anything could grow in a place like this, but there they were: black roses spilling out and flowing across the ground. There were so many of them, it looked as though the ground was covered in a carpet of black satin.

"Oh, hey," Navin said, super casual. "I got something for you."

And he took a tiny crystal out of his still damp jeans pocket and pressed it into the palm of her hand.

"What is *this*?" Just for a second, Donna almost forgot their current situation. Almost.

"A parting gift from Newton. He said it's thanks to me that he's free again."

The demon tear was beautiful. Faultless. Like a shard of ice with all the colors of the rainbow inside it—and some colors she didn't even recognize. She gazed at it in wonder, holding her breath.

"Oh my God," she whispered. "Nav, you did it! Thank you."

He smiled. "I'm the best, right? Tell me I'm the best. You know you want to."

"You're the best," she said. "I can't argue this time."

He grinned.

Donna looked at the perfectly formed teardrop in the palm of her hand. "I can't believe Newton kept his word."

"I'm pretty sure he thinks we're buddies."

"That's ... weird."

Navin nodded. "I know. Totally weird. But, then again, now that I have a demon for a BFF, who knows where that could get me? It's sort of cool."

Donna stared at him for a moment. "No, it's really not."

"You're just jealous," he said, playfully punching her on the shoulder. "Don't worry, Don. You're still my Number One."

She fought back a smile, shaking her head.

"Either way," he said, "that's another ingredient down, right? How many does that make?"

This time Donna let the smile rip, as much in disbelief as anything else. "Four. Four out of five. One more to go."

"And then we can go home?" Navin's eyes shone.

"After the Gallows Tree." She swallowed. "I have to go in there, and I can't let you come with me. Demian said I have to go in alone or I'll never find the right tree. Some kind of twisted demon magic. Curse. Whatever."

"Maybe he was lying. I don't want to leave you alone—not when I just found you again."

"I don't think he was lying about this, Nav. We can't take the risk. Just wait for me, all right?"

He nodded, his jaw tight.

She thought of the silver pear at the center of the grove. It was the final ingredient she needed to make the Stone, but in the world above, preparations for war were already moving forward. Not to mention the tiny matter of her untimely death. She had the horrible suspicion that her resurrection would not be such an easy trick to pull off.

Donna forced herself to focus and plunged into the thicket.

Twenty-four

Navin waited by the exit from the Otherworld. He'd concluded that this was the way out because, quite helpfully, there was a huge sign marked *Exit*, which had appeared—along with an escalator—right after Donna had disappeared into the grove. Seriously, a freaking *escalator*.

He ran a tired hand through his damp hair and examined the moving stairway that supposedly led all the way up and out. It was long and smooth, shining with silver and chrome. It looked like something that belonged in a science fiction movie. Leaning against its shining metal sides, he slid down and sat on the dusty ground to wait.

He was always waiting for Donna. Not that he minded—she was his best friend, after all. That's what you did for the most important people in your life. She always came for him when he was in trouble, and he would do the same for her. They had literally walked through Hell together (even if he'd been taken over by a demon at the time).

Newton. He thought of the moment when Demian had ripped the demon from his body and set him free. Navin had seen Newton's true form, and it wasn't something he'd forget any time soon. He swallowed and tried not to think about it too hard. Newton had been grateful, requesting a private "chat" with him before Demian had dragged him off to reprimand him about . . . whatever it was that Newton was in trouble for. Probably getting himself summoned and captured by Simon Gaunt in the first place.

But Navin's heart was heavy. He had a suspicion—one that had been planted in his mind by Newton and growing with every moment that passed—that something was going to get in the way of a Happily Ever After.

Then Donna came bursting out of the grove, her hair wildly dishevelled and several scratches marking her face. The iron tattoos on her arms were whirling with desperate activity. She was breathless and wide-eyed, but the good news was that there was something clutched in one of her hands. Something that looked a lot like a silver pear.

Navin pulled himself out of his funk, forced a smile, and waved her over.

As she emerged from the thicket, Donna tried to get her bearings. Where was Navin? She could see the path that led down to the river, and the little town in the distance with its houses filled with watchful eyes, and then the magnificent Sunless City spread out beyond that. And yet now, at the end of the path, was a circular chamber and a high-tech escalator.

Donna felt like she had stepped from one film set to another. It was strange and disconcerting, but she could hardly say she was surprised.

Navin was waiting for her by the staircase. He looked sad, but as soon as he saw her he seemed brighter.

"Nav?" She couldn't help herself. She had to check that it was still him. "You're okay?"

"Sure, don't worry. Newton's really gone." He glanced down at her hand. "You got the fruit?"

"Right here."

She opened her palm and showed him the shining silver pear. Its skin shimmered beneath the spotlights that lined the walls of the escalator. It looked like one of those kitschy ornaments that people collect and keep in fruit bowls. She shoved it into her messenger back with the other artifacts, cringing as everything rattled together.

She looked at the grove one last time. Then she stood on tiptoe and scanned the surrounding roads. No sign of Demian. Were they really getting out of here? It seemed too easy. That always made her nervous.

It was quiet. Nothing stirred except her tattoos, shimmering along her arms and making her hands ache.

"What are we waiting for? We've got everything," Navin said, nodding at the escalator. "Come on, let's get out of here. I'll be right behind you."

"You should go first," she replied. "Just in case."

He smiled, but the expression didn't quite reach his eyes. "In case you need to protect me, you mean? We're home free."

"Navin..."

His voice sounded strangely hollow. "I don't want you to have to rescue me again. They can't keep using me against you."

Donna remembered the Wood Queen's bone blade against Navin's throat—back in the Ironwood, what seemed a lifetime ago. Her fingers clenched. "They don't care about what we want."

He swept her a clumsy bow. "Ladies first. I insist."

A tiny thread of worry slithered into her stomach, but Donna did as he asked. Surely it would be okay. What could be worse than Hell, right?

Her sneakered foot hit the bottom stair of the escalator and she began to ascend. She watched as Navin stepped on behind her. He was two stairs below her, and they looked into one another's eyes as they moved up, up, beyond the bright lights and into the dark unknown.

And then the escalator stopped moving, and Donna knew things weren't going to be as easy as she'd hoped after all. She should have trusted her gut. Not that there had been anything she could actually *do*. Not when she hadn't even known what was wrong in the first place.

Navin met her troubled eyes. "Uh-oh," he said.

"Yeah." She swallowed, looking below them and seeing how far they'd already traveled. They were high—impossibly high—and the escalator only went one way.

Well then, she thought. *We can just walk.*

"Come on," she said. "How far can it be … "

"Probably very, very far," Nav muttered. But he began to climb with her and they seemed to make progress, for a while.

The stairs made an ominous grinding sound, and then reversed direction. Sending them back down into the Otherworld. Fast.

"Shit!" Navin yelled, gripping the moving rail for balance as they plummeted downward.

Donna stumbled and sat down on a step. She didn't want to chance being thrown off entirely. Not that she figured much could really happen to you, once you were already sort-of dead.

Then the stairs stopped moving—and they were stuck again. The ground looked no closer than before, which of course made no sense at all.

Navin sat down beside her. He touched the back of her hand, and her tattoos swirled in response to his fingers.

"I think I know what might be wrong," he said. He looked away from her.

"What?" Donna's stomach hurt.

"It's something Newton said just after he left my body. I didn't want to think about it, not when I was just so grateful to be back to myself again, you know? I didn't want to worry you."

Donna grabbed his hand, wincing apologetically when she realized she was almost crushing him. "What did he say? You know you can't trust him, right?"

He shook his head sadly. "I know. But even though I don't trust him, I do believe him. On this one thing, I think I have to."

She wanted to shake him. "Spit it out, then!"

A grim smile touched his mouth. "As usual, Underwood, you've hit the proverbial nail on the head."

She just glared at him.

"'Spit it out.' That's just it. That's the problem—I didn't. You know..." He raised an eyebrow. "Spit."

Donna wished she could make some kind of crude joke so that they could move on to figuring out how to get the escalator moving again. But the expression on his face was too serious. It wasn't like Navin at all, and it scared her.

"The water, Don. In the River of Memory and Forgetting. I swallowed a whole bunch of it when I jumped in after you."

No, no, no.

"No," Donna said. This wasn't happening. It wasn't. *This isn't how it's supposed to go.* They were supposed to get out of here—together—and move on to the final stage of the plan. She had to make the Philosopher's Stone and she needed Navin with her. She couldn't do this without him.

She couldn't lose him, not again. This time it might be forever.

He shook his head, placed his fingers on her lips. "Don't," he said. "I knew it when it happened. He warned me. I just hoped…" He shrugged, unable to continue.

"You just hoped it wasn't true," she finished.

"Yeah. And when I got on the escalator and we started moving, I really allowed myself to think that I'd gotten away with it."

Horror dawned on Donna, filling her heart with ink-stained fear. "We'll figure something out. I'll—"

"No." Navin shook his head. He had visibly paled, but he seemed composed enough. "You have to take the ingredients out of here. You don't need me for that."

"But I do," she whispered, eyes burning.

They held hands for a long moment, and Donna counted the beats of her heart.

And then something else happened. Navin's stair started moving *down* while hers resumed its ascent. They were moving in opposite directions—on the same freaking escalator—and there was nothing either of them could do about it. She felt nauseated trying to make her brain process what was happening, the sheer impossibility of it.

"No!" Donna screamed, trying to run back down against the upward drive of the mechanism. But no matter how fast she moved, Navin continued to slip further and further away.

"I love you, Donna!" he called. "Take good care of yourself."

His final words were for her. He was so selfless, and this wasn't fair.

Donna glanced up, feeling desperate, and realized that she was approaching what could only be the top of the escalator. A summit that hadn't even existed until now. More demon tricks.

She clenched her fist and punched the moving handrail with every bit of the strength in her iron hands. She rarely cut loose like that, not completely. It was too dangerous.

The results should have been staggering. But her fist bounced off the rubber and metal and all she got for her effort was an agonizing shooting pain through her knuckles.

She screamed with frustration, then took a deep breath. Preparing herself. She gripped the silver rail and tried to stop the escalator's inexorable progress. She threw a wild glance over her shoulder, trying to catch sight of Nav, but he was nothing more than a pinprick at the very bottom.

Donna breathed deep and *pulled*.

The metal gave way with a rending, shrieking sound. She managed to tear the entire section of rail off its moorings—

But it was hopeless. The stairs were still moving, closer and closer to the top.

Then the escalator stopped. Her eyes widened. It had *stopped*! She could run down again, back to Navin.

Donna flew down the stairs, wondering how long it would take her to reach the bottom. She already felt exhausted, but she didn't care. Not many people would consider entering the Otherworld by choice, even once. But to do so twice? Probably she was crazy, which was fine by her. She was sure she'd go even *more* crazy knowing that Navin was stuck down there while she went about her business in the world above without him.

Her chest burned and her knees ached, but she kept going.

Until the stairs suddenly sprang into life once more, and they slid upwards faster than ever, taking her with them.

"Shit!" She kicked the side of the stairway. It didn't make her feel any better.

She sat down in despair and waited for the escalator to dump her at the top. She wasn't getting down; she knew that now. Navin wasn't getting out. He'd drunk water from the river and this was the price.

Opening her bag, Donna gazed at all the pieces of the puzzle. The Ouroboros Blade, something that had possibly already served its purpose by getting her here. The Cup of Hermes, the glittering demon tear, and now the shining pear, fruit of the Gallows Tree—all these things had brought her to this place. She squeezed her hands together. Was it worth it? Could creating the Philosopher's Stone be worth Navin's life?

Donna already knew the answer to that.

Biting back a sob, she jumped off at the top and ran out into cold darkness.

Twenty-five

Donna found herself running straight into the heart of the Ironwood. Of course—where else would an escalator from Hell drop her off? Somehow, everything came back to this place. It always did. It was night, and she wondered how long she had until dawn. She hoped she was in time.

The trees that circled the clearing began to bend in a wind that was gathering around her, a portent that didn't do her nerves any good. She stood in the center of it all and clutched the bag full of hope to her chest. What if she couldn't do this? She didn't know what came next. Okay, in *theory* she did, because she'd "read" the Silent Book and committed each diagram to memory—each stage in the creation of the Philosopher's Stone. But knowing it and doing it were two very different things.

Donna looked at the frosty ground and imagined Navin somewhere far below. She refused to let the tears fall. She'd find him again. Somehow.

"Donna," came a voice from between the trees. An old friend wheeled himself into the clearing.

"Maker! What are you doing here by yourself?" Donna ran to him, relief and joy surging through her.

He smiled through his beard and waved his hand to quiet her. "No time, no time. The others are coming. You need to make the Stone before Demian follows you. I knew you'd do it, Donna."

Maker stayed close beside her as she laid out the ingredients. Then he handed her a small vial of salt, indicating that she should cast a protective circle around them. She hoped Maker would help with this part—with his power supporting hers, the barrier she created would be far more likely to delay anyone who might try to interfere with their work. But Maker shook his head.

"No, it must be your power, and yours alone. The first matter you draw upon will hopefully be enough to hold off a demon—even one as powerful as Demian."

Donna didn't question him, just cast the circle and set to work crushing the fruit and the glittering tear into the Cup of Hermes. She used the hilt of the blade to help with the process, wondering if it was what she was supposed to do; that part hadn't been clear in the instructions, but it felt right. So she went with it, following her intuition and listening to the thread of power inside her like she'd been taught. Like Quentin and Maker had said to do.

Maker's eyes filled with pride as he watched her, nodding approval and pointing out things here and there that she'd forgotten.

Donna began to believe she might actually do this. That there was hope, and she could make something as impossible as this final bargaining chip to use against the demons. Against—

Demian materialized directly in front of them, on the outside of the circle of salt. His pale face was drawn into tight lines and his mouth was hard, his skin practically glowing in the darkness. He pressed his hand against the invisible barrier surrounding them.

Sparks flew, and there was the sound of lightning.

Donna glared at him. "I'm busy, go away."

"The Stone is mine."

"Give me a chance, I haven't finished yet," she said, trying to stop her hands from shaking. She turned away and bent over the Cup of Hermes, reestablishing her connection to the *prima materia* within her. Maker watched the king of the demons, his wrinkled hands clutching the arms of his chair.

The first matter throbbed in her chest, beating in time with her heart. Donna focused on shaping reality, on making something that didn't exist. She tapped into the power of creation and held her breath. Everything around her seemed to fade … Maker, trying to keep an eye on her and Demian at the same time, and the suspicious Demon King, waiting with his hands gripped tightly into fists.

She looked upward, into the sky, seeing the edges of the trees that vaulted above everything. Then she drank.

Darkness rushed into her, filled her, and then came light. Bright white light that cut her in half and made her scream. Her arms felt as though they might shatter, and her heart wanted to do the same. Wind stormed and howled like its own kind of demonic force, blasting back her hair, making her face hurt and her eyes stream. The trees tilted at strange angles and she heard the crack of branches.

Then the whole world went silent, and she realized she was lying on the ground.

Beside her, inside the circle, there it was. The Stone.

The Philosopher's Stone. She got to her knees and touched it, reverently, forgetting everything around her, just for a moment reveling in the feel of smooth stone beneath her fingers, the pulse of heat she could feel slowly spreading from its center. It was a warm shade of reddish-brown, and egg-shaped—it fitted perfectly in her palm. As though it were made for her. For her and nobody else.

Maker's eyes shone as he sat beside her.

Demian tried to cross the barrier, fury pouring off him in almost palpable waves. He hammered against the air with his fists, but Donna's circle held.

"Come out, alchemist," he screamed. "Come and out and face me!"

Donna's head jerked up. "You can huff and puff all you like, Your Majesty," she replied. "But if it's all the same to you, I'll stay right here."

"You can't stay in there forever, Donna," Demian said. "Nor you, old man."

Maker smiled a determined sort of smile. He wheeled his chair out of the circle. "I don't intend to, *demon*."

"No!" Donna ran to follow him, but stopped herself just in time as she reached the barrier.

Demian's coal-black eyes seemed to glow as he grabbed the ageing alchemist by the throat and lifted him, one-handed, from his chair.

"Open the circle," he demanded, his voice like thunder.

Maker was choking, his face growing red, but his eyes held triumph. "I can't. The circle is hers. How else do you think I could leave it without it breaking?"

"Let him go," Donna said, her voice quivering. Terror made it difficult to speak. She had the Philosopher's Stone, but what good was that doing now?

Maker turned his head toward her. "Use the Stone, Donna. Use it to—"

"Quiet, little man!" Demian roared, tossing the alchemist away like he was nothing but an oversized ragdoll. Maker bounced against a tree, and there was a sickening noise as he fell to the ground and lay still.

Donna screamed, facing the Demon King across the barrier.

Demian placed both palms against the transparent wall formed by her circle. His hands exploded with black light, the strength of it making her shield her eyes. Everything turned into a sort of photo-negative ... Demian was using his power to tear down her protective wards.

"Give me the Stone!" he bellowed.

"Never!" Donna shouted. Had he really thought that she'd just hand it over? Demian, Aliette—they were all the same. Blinded by their greed, their wants, so much so that they couldn't figure out that Donna Underwood wasn't about to follow their orders quite so easily. She'd learned a few things while training to be an alchemist, after all—and maybe the Stone was her greatest weapon. Why give it up now?

She licked her lips, wondering if it would work. Wondering if the demon's desire for the Stone would be enough to distract him for a few moments more. Now was the time to find out.

She took a step back, exiting out of the other side of the circle so that the wide ring of salt stood between them. Then she held the Philosopher's Stone up toward Demian as bait. His eyes widened in desire, and then in triumph, as he gazed at the prize. Eagerly, he stepped toward her—and into the circle.

The moment he did that, Donna crouched down, still clutching the Stone, and touched a small section of the salt. Her tattoos were moving so violently she thought she might throw up, but she managed to hold everything together as she remembered Robert Lee, surrounded by shadows, in this place in another time. She shouted, "*Lux!*"

White light poured upward from the salt circle, forming a whirling barrier around the Demon King. A king who was now trapped inside a solid ring of first matter energy. Donna wondered if it would be enough to hold him, at least temporarily.

Demian roared his fury. "What did you do to me?"

"Restrained you, Your Majesty," Donna replied, staggering to her feet but barely able to stay upright. "I think you'll find yourself unable to act quite so much like a petulant god now, running around destroying anything that makes you mad. Maybe you'll have to fight fair. I wonder how long it's been since you've actually had to do that?"

He reached for her, so fast it took her breath away. Too fast. His fist shot through the barrier and clamped in her hair. *Damn he's strong*, Donna thought, feeling a vague shock. His arm sticking out of the wall of light had been terrifying enough, but now Demian began dragging her toward him. All his smooth seduction had disappeared. He looked truly awful, like the King of Terror he was.

Donna yelped as some of her hair was pulled out at the root. She felt herself being dragged toward him—it was either that or lose a chunk of hair. The searing pain all along her scalp made her eyes water. *How had he broken through the ward?* Despite his power, Donna had believed the circle would hold him. It should have worked! Even if it hadn't contained him for very long, it should have held for more than a few seconds.

"Do you think your little prison can hold *me*?" Demian growled.

Donna struggled, in too much to pain to respond with anything coherent, but at least the Demon King wasn't actually free. Not yet. Maybe he'd had enough strength to thrust that one hand through the wall to grab her, but it didn't look like he could step all the way out. Strain showed on his face, as though breaching the barrier at all was almost too much for him.

Yet he kept hold of her. She was almost standing on the line of salt. If her foot touched it, even for a moment, the circle would collapse and the demon really *would* be free. Not to mention majorly pissed at her.

"I could tear you into pieces," he said. Their faces were almost touching, on either side of the wall of light. "I don't need to be able to destroy cities or worlds to be able to destroy *you*."

"You say the sweetest things," Donna said, the toes of her sneakers inching toward the barrier. She panted with pain, trying desperately to focus on the agony in her scalp so that she would stay conscious and be able to act. She pushed the thought of Maker's broken body from her mind—at least, for a few more moments.

"There will be no mercy in me if I have to take the Stone from you, Donna Underwood," the Demon King said. "Only pain. And perhaps death, eventually."

"And to think," she gasped, "you wanted me to be your queen at one time."

"You are unworthy," he spat. "Once I have the Philosopher's Stone, I will wipe the memory of every pathetic human from this world."

"You would have done that anyway."

"I look forward to crushing you beneath my heel, alchemist."

"I think you'll find it's too late for that, *Majesty*," Donna said, hope suddenly surging through her. "Look!"

Demian raised his head, keeping his brutal grip on her. One of his hands was firmly around her throat—maybe even preparing to snap her neck. Then the demon's eyes widened.

A shimmering door had opened on the horizon, and the glittering army of Faerie was riding out of the light. The alchemists' "war council" had clearly been a success; leave it to Quentin and her mother to convince the races to work together. Donna smiled through her pain.

Fey horses spilled out, looking almost as if they were riding the waves; their riders crouched low over their backs, inhuman eyes fixed straight ahead. White, black, chestnut—no matter their color, the steeds were tall and strong and impossibly swift, with shining armor around their fine heads. One of them even had wings, and Donna thought her heart actually skipped a beat as she watched its indigo wings curve up and down in majestic arcs. The faeries who rode the horses all brandished flashing swords and were clothed in the polished silver chainmail she was already growing familiar with. Donna saw that women rode alongside the men, and they were so fierce and beautiful that it hurt her eyes.

And then a new disturbance, on the other side of the clearing, drew Demian's gaze away from the approaching army. The Wood Queen was coming toward him as well, striding tall and straight and dressed in armor made of polished bark. Her helmet was wreathed with ivy, and, attached to her shoulders, there was a cloak made of leaves and moss. Dozens of elves spread out behind and beside her. They clicked and scraped as they lifted weapons made of wood and thorn, their teeth bared and their black eyes glittering with vicious intent. They bayed for blood, a sound Donna well remembered.

Queen Isolde had reached the edge of the clearing, flanked by her knights, Taran and Cathal. Donna gasped when she saw Xan flying overhead, in the mechanical harness that Maker had fashioned for him.

"No!" Demian cried, finally releasing Donna's hair. She fell to the ground and lay there, panting but mercifully out of reach. "You will *not* defeat me, you alchemists, with your arrogance and greed. Not again!"

Donna suddenly realized that there was a demon army gathering in the sky and on the ground. Shadows slid between the trees like silent death, and giant birds with razor-sharp beaks flew above the treetops.

Isolde and Aliette approached one another on the battlefield. Isolde's hair gleamed under a silver crown threaded with leaves. She wore no helmet, but her armor was so brightly polished that the pale moonlight reflected off it, making Donna squint.

"Cousin." The Queen of Faerie smiled.

Aliette clasped her cousin's hand. "Cousin. It has been too long."

"Yes," Isolde said. "When this is over, we will be glad to finally see our kin return to Faerie."

The Wood Queen's head tilted to one side. "If we survive."

Isolde's gaze was fierce. "We will."

Donna's heart filled when she saw that the alchemists, led by her mother and Quentin Frost, were taking up positions around the edges of the clearing. Aunt Paige and Simon Gaunt were with them, along with others that Donna was too tired even to register. She saw a few familiar faces—there was Alma Kensington, her tutor, wearing strange purple robes— but many of the alchemist warriors were unknown to her. They looked fierce and battle-ready, with magic crackling around their hands. Some of the men and women looked younger than she would have expected, probably belonging to the mysterious Order of the Lion.

She searched the crowd for Miranda and Robert, but if they were here she didn't see them.

All the alchemists raised their hands. Donna knew they were working together to encompass Ironwood Forest in a cloaking spell, which would hide the battle from mortal senses.

As Demian howled in his cage, human and fey joined together to fight the forces of the Underworld. Demons clashed with elves, and alchemists blasted jagged lightning bolts into demon shadows. Trees burned, and blood spattered the ground below.

Donna looked up into the sky, helpless as she watched Xan fight off a giant black owl with scarlet eyes and talons so long they could probably remove a human's head from its shoulders. She remembered reading about the demonic Strix and their child-eating ways, and prayed to nothing and nobody in particular that Xan would escape. He was waving a sword around like he knew what he was doing, but when had he had time to train? It was madness. Maybe he thought he was being brave, but Donna just wanted to scream at him to come down before he got himself killed.

Crawling further away from Demian and his fury as he pounded the walls of the circle, she wondered what she could possibly do to help. She felt utterly spent … used up and just about ready to collapse.

Fights were breaking out all around her and overhead. She saw Simon Gaunt firing some kind of glowing crossbow at the demon shadows. As each bolt found its mark, the creature collapsed in on itself and disappeared. Her eyes widened as she watched her mother and her aunt working together to surround more giant birds—those creepy owls, as well as golden eagles with bloodstained beaks—with a ring of silver energy. She finally caught sight of Miranda and Robert, pushing back another group of shadows with the combined force of their magic. Everything was chaos, and the Ironwood was filled with flames and screams and the clash of steel.

Donna watched it all, forcing herself to witness the bravery of her friends and allies. A lump filled her throat and she found her vision misted over with tears as the battle grew more fierce.

And then more shadows poured out of the ground, a seemingly endless supply of demonic warriors arriving from the Otherworld. Their numbers were overwhelming, and her eyes widened. Perhaps their king was trapped, but he could clearly still command them.

"Donna," called a frail voice. It was weak, barely audible over the ringing sounds of war, but she recognized it.

"Maker, you're alive!" She dragged herself across the clearing, still holding the Stone and dodging bolts of fire as she went. Demian raged behind her, but she refused to look back.

Maker had pulled himself up against the trunk of the twisted tree, his face so white that his lined flesh was almost translucent. "We can't win this battle—not even with Demian contained. There are simply too many demon warriors. You must unleash the dragon."

"What?" Donna shook her head, trying to understand what he was saying over the sound of fighting. "What are you talking about? I have to get you out of here."

"No, dear girl," Maker replied. He touched her cheek. "It is long past time for me to rest. It's up to you now."

"No." She trembled, no longer able to focus on anything except Maker. Interspecies politics, warfare, Faerie, and even the Underworld … it all faded into white noise. "Don't talk like that. You're going to be okay. I can—"

"Don't argue," Maker replied. His voice was strong, his eyes certain. "This is the work that only you can do. The Great Work—that's the name of true alchemy. You know this. The creation of the Philosopher's Stone is only the first step. Next comes the Blackening. Facing the dragon." He began to cough and blood ran down his chin, but he gripped her arm and forced himself to go on. "*Accepting* the dragon."

"And then unleashing the dragon," Donna whispered. "But that's just symbolic. It's all symbolic. The books talk about how the Order of the Dragon was named after the creature itself, but only as a *myth*."

The old man raised his eyebrows. "Since when did you stop believing in magic, young lady? Especially after what you've achieved here today?"

Donna swallowed, only vaguely aware of the smoke that burned the back of her throat. She rubbed her palm across her dirty face, probably smearing ash and making everything worse.

"Maker, you're not going to die."

"Of course not, not in the way you mean," he replied. He coughed, more blood flecking his lips. "But it's time to move on. Long past, actually. I'm quite looking forward to going home."

"Home? What are you talking about?"

"Never mind that now," the old man said, patting her shoulder. "Simon is not the man he once was, and Quentin's time at the head of the alchemists is over. The Order of the Dragon will pass into new hands—better hands."

"Who?" Donna shook her head, but she knew exactly what the old man was going to say even before he spoke.

"Rachel Underwood will make a very fine Archmaster." His lips quirked into a tiny smile. "*Archmistress*."

Donna thought of her mother and wondered if the alchemists would really accept a woman as their leader.

Maker shook his head. "We don't have time for me to explain everything now. You have to use what remains of the *prima materia*—along with the Philosopher's Stone—to tap into the ley line beneath the Ironwood. There you will encounter the dragon—that's where you'll find the power to defeat the demons and send them back where they belong."

Donna remembered the Silent Book, and specifically the image of a serpent breathing fire. The Blackening.

She took a shaky breath and patted Maker's shoulder. "I'll be back for you. Don't … don't go anywhere."

"Take the Stone." The old man smiled at her. "I'm proud of you, child. So very proud."

Donna covered him with the blanket from his wrecked wheelchair, trying her best to make him comfortable. He nodded his thanks and she forced herself to walk away. If she didn't do it now, she never would. Everything was crazy. Chaos was raining down on them all. The Ironwood was on fire, and the night sky was streaked with smoke and flames. The Strix flew overhead as Demian's army punished the alchemists and the fey for daring to join forces against him. The King of Terror might be trapped within her circle, but his power reached way beyond his cage. She might have weakened him, but perhaps he was strong enough to destroy everything anyway.

Maker was right. She needed to find a way to stop the war before Demian took everybody with him. She hated that it all rested on her shoulders. She hated that she was alone. Xan was out there, with this father, fighting a battle that they most likely couldn't win. And he'd never trained with that stupid sword. What if he was injured, even now? What if he was *killed*? She'd already lost Navin.

No. Donna forced her mind away from terrifying possibilities. If she even allowed herself to think that way, then Demian would have already won. She still had some strength left. She just hoped that it was enough.

She ducked a flying blast of energy and limped further into the Ironwood. The ley line was close, she knew that much. It had been marked in the Silent Book, and she was surprised to find that she could recall the hand-drawn map almost perfectly. She just had to find it, walk into it, and then ... activate her powers.

It sounded easy.

It was the hardest thing Donna had ever done.

Call the dragon? How did you even *do* something like that?

The Blackening, Donna thought, dizzy with pain and power. This was what her mother had feared, when she and Miranda had tried to protect her during the negotiations. The air around her burned, buffeting her as she held the Philosopher's Stone in both hands and focused all of her energy on it.

The sound of screaming forced her to her knees. She wondered if it was *her* screaming or something else. She didn't know. She didn't know anything anymore, only that she felt like she might be dying for real this time. Her chest hurt, she knew that much—almost as if she could feel the shining piece of first matter inside her soul pushing itself out like a living splinter.

Pressing her hands to her chest, Donna tried to hold back the pressure and pain. Terror threatened to take away her reason—whip it up and carry it away in the howling maelstrom that surrounded her.

"*Accept the dragon,*" Maker had said. But how was she supposed to do that? How did you accept something that hurt so much? She couldn't even *see* what she was supposed to be accepting.

She crawled through the fiery air, clutching the Philosopher's Stone tightly in one fist, until her other hand came to rest on the trunk of a tree, the feel of the bark rough against her palm.

It felt like... scales. Donna swung around and touched the tree with both hands. *Scales.* The bark of a tree felt just like scales. She looked at the ground—it was churned-up dried mud, as if giant claws had gouged out a path of their own. Lightning flashed in the sky—like the forked tongue of a great serpent—and the booming thunder sounded like a dragon's roar. The wind, perhaps, resulted from the flapping of monstrous leathery wings.

And Donna understood what all the alchemical texts had been trying to tell her, throughout her life—the dragon was in everything. Just as the first matter was everywhere and nowhere, so was the dragon.

Blackness filled her eyes and her mouth, and Donna collapsed onto the ground.

Twenty-six

The presence spoke, inside her head and all around her: *Donna Underwood of the Alchemists, Daughter of the Dragon, thank you for awakening me.*

Donna gasped, trying to push down the visceral urge to heave.

"Are you in pain?" asked the voice.

"It's..." She licked her lips, trying to form the words in her head but still having to whisper them aloud. "It feels like too much. Too... loud." She pressed her hands over her ears and crouched on the floor of a shadowy version of the

Ironwood, keeping as low as she could, somehow figuring that might protect her. It was pure instinct to make herself small against the sheer power of that voice. A voice that belonged to a creature as old as the stars.

"Is that better?"

The voice still vibrated through her body, making her bones ache, but her ears no longer felt like they were going to start bleeding.

She peeked out from behind her hair and gave a tentative thumbs-up. "Better."

The dragon—oh god, the *dragon*—took a gliding step toward her. It moved with the fluidity of water, its wings iridescent in the dawn light and its sinuous body reminding her of a giant snake. Where its tail flicked back and forth, trees fell and small animals ran for new cover. It was magnificent and just so, so *big*, its beautiful scales the color of silver and gold, each one as large as her hand.

The battle seemed to have disappeared, but Donna knew that wasn't possible. Somehow, her own power combined with that of the Philosopher's Stone had transported her into a pocket of existence one step removed from reality. Maybe they were somewhere like Halfway, although she could still recognize her surroundings. It was like a mirror image or something; the ley line had been a doorway of sorts. Despite the fact that she was talking to a freaking *dragon*, Donna had to admit that she preferred this absence of blood and thunder, away from the alchemists, demons, and fey clashing in the real Ironwood Forest.

Adrenaline made her heart race, and her vision narrowed until all she could see was the majestic creature in front of her. Donna concluded that she might really be losing it. She could handle almost anything: iron tattoos, alchemy, the existence of Faerie and all kinds of fey creatures, even demons. All of these things—and more—she could somehow adjust to. Her mind would stretch and stretch, like a rubber band put under the worst kind of pressure but which would eventually snap back into shape and let her move into her new understanding of reality. Each time that Donna's world became just a little bigger, she had *handled* it.

But this? A ... dragon?

She realized that she was sitting on mossy ground beside a stream. It was cold right where she had collapsed, but she didn't care. She wondered if splashing water on her face would help.

The dragon moved again, shifting its wings and bringing down another tree in the process.

"Stop!" Donna cried. "You're destroying things."

The massive head swung toward her, lowering until the giant black eyes were almost on the same level as hers. It blinked. Donna could count its eyelashes, and she had to squash a hysterical urge to reach out to touch them to see if they were real.

The dragon's snout puffed out a breath that blew Donna's hair away from her face. It was like being caught in a hurricane, and reminded her of what had happened when she'd created the Stone. She got a strong whiff of burning wood and held her breath. Fire flickered around the beast's cavernous nostrils. Donna thought she might pass out.

She figured that would be perfectly acceptable under the circumstances.

"You called me," the dragon rumbled. Its voice still came from directly inside Donna's head, taking her by surprise. "I am here."

"I...I..." She shook herself. *Get a grip, Underwood.*

"You called me." The tone brooked no argument.

"I'm sorry," Donna whispered. "I didn't mean to."

"I believe that you did." The dragon nodded its mighty head and waited.

What was it waiting for? In the part of her brain that hadn't quite lost the plot, Donna knew that this was part of the process—the Blackening—and yet she hadn't realized there would be an actual dragon.

Like, for real. She desperately wished that Xan and Navin could be here to share the moment, but she also realized that would be impossible. This was a moment for her, and her alone. Somehow she knew this was true.

Maybe it was some kind of vision, like the lucid dreams she had, when signs and portents seemed to flow through her the way the dragon's wings flowed with their own inner light.

She forced herself back to her feet, her knees trembling but just about holding her upright. Time to take control of the situation. She glanced at the immense creature before her and stifled a burst of hysterical laughter. *Control?*

The dragon settled back onto its mammoth hindquarters, folding its wings against its body and regarding her with an almost human expression of benevolence.

Donna cleared her throat. "*How* exactly did I call you?"

"You died. You came back."

"Dying means someone can summon dragons?"

There was an awful trumpeting sound. Snorting and snuffling followed by a spurt of fire, which ignited a bush on the far side of the stream.

Donna realized that the dragon was laughing. At her. She stood taller. "Hey, I'm new at all this."

"If you are so untrained, child, you should not be in possession of such power," the dragon rumbled.

"I'm just doing the best I can. That's all. Please...won't you explain?"

"The ability to call the dragon has been sleeping inside you since your birth. You knew that much, yes?"

"No...I didn't know anything about dragons. Not real ones, anyway."

"You have the dragon spark in your soul. Why do you think the Demon King wants you so badly?"

"Dragon spark? You mean, the first matter?"

If dragons could shrug, Donna was sure that's what it would have done. "If that is what you call it. The *prima materia*. Dragon spark. Names change. The nature of the power does not."

"Does this mean that you'll fight for us?" Donna asked, suddenly seeing things more clearly. "I think that's what Maker wanted."

"Maker?" the dragon mused. "So he still lives in this world, does he? I can't say that I am surprised."

She stared at the noble, ancient creature. "You know *Maker*?"

"Of course, child. All of the old ones know him."

Donna didn't know what to say. She wanted to ask more, to find out once and for all just who Maker really was. But there was a war to fight. That mystery could wait—at least until a little later. It would give her something to anticipate, if she survived.

She swallowed smoke and ashes. "What do I do now?"

"You have the Stone," the dragon replied, which was no reply at all. "Use it to command me. It is no more complicated than that. You are the Twice-Born Daughter of the Dragon."

"I…" She watched the magnificent beast's slowly blinking eyes, still trying to wrap her head around what was happening. Maybe this was a shamanic vision, like how she'd relived the past while in Demian's realm. Except for the part where the freaking dragon actually *knew* Maker. That sounded pretty real.

The dragon continued to wait. It had all the time in the world.

Donna shook her head, trying to clear it. "I've never commanded anything before."

"Does that mean you can't do so now?"

She frowned. "I don't know how. I'm not sure I like the idea of… controlling others. I get that done to me in my own life, you see."

If dragons could smile, Donna was pretty sure this one was doing just that. It was surreal and beautiful all at once. "You created the Philosopher's Stone. You found me beneath the Ironwood. All you have to do is tell me what you want of me, and it will be done. But only once, do you understand?"

"One command?"

"Yes. After that, every last drop of the dragon spark within you will be gone. That is the price you pay for commanding dragons."

Donna paused, wondering if that meant what she thought it must. Would she lose the first matter for good? Her heart lifted and she almost smiled. That was supposed to be a cost? She would gladly pay that price.

She took a tentative step forward and laid her hand against the great leg of the dragon. The scales rippled cool and smooth, hot and jagged, all at the same time. It was like touching the bark of a great tree, and yet it was nothing like that at all.

It was everything she had ever dreamed of.

It was magic.

Donna took a deep breath and steadied herself. This was it. What she said now would change reality. It would affect her life forever—assuming she survived.

She held tight to the Philosopher's Stone and commanded the dragon: "Help us end the war and send the demons back to where they belong."

The creature bowed its head, and Donna could almost swear that she saw a flash of pleasure in its bottomless gaze.

Reality shifted, and she heard the rush of giant wings. Darkness descended and then lifted. The real world returned to her like a wall of heat, quickly enough to knock the breath from her body as the sounds of battle resumed.

Then Donna got the hell out of the way, as her dragon took to the sky and the Ironwood burned to the ground.

Twenty-seven

The war was over.

Donna crawled toward the remains of the clearing, smoke in her eyes and clogging up her throat. It was like one of those thick fogs in a bad horror movie, or like too much dry ice pumped onto the stage during a play. She was still holding the Philosopher's Stone in her bare hand, but her tattoos had finally stopped moving. The place inside her chest— deep in her heart, where the first matter usually resided—was quiet at last.

Once she reached the edge of the clearing, she stopped and sat against the trunk of a tree. The circle that had once held a demon king was empty, and inside there was just a scorched patch of earth. Maker's wheelchair, lying forlornly on its side, was a reminder of that terrible loss, and she fought down the urge to assume the fetal position for the next few hours. Was Demian really back in his realm, locked away again? She hoped so. Another couple of centuries without him around wouldn't be such a bad thing.

She looked up at the sky, watching the dragon sweep the last of the demon shadows away. The sight was both terrifying and awe-inspiring. Her eyes blurred, no matter how much she rubbed them with her grubby hands.

Tears continued to pour down her cheeks as she looked around, and Donna realized that they were real tears—tears of grief and pain rather than simply the result of too much smoke. People had died here today. Navin was gone, presumably still trapped in the Otherworld. There was no way Demian would let him return, not after what she'd done to him. She hugged herself as she sat on the hard earth and sobbed, finally letting it all out.

Only a few trees remained. She tried to block out the last sounds of fighting—a few scavengers from the Otherworld had managed to stay behind when the gates were closed for the last time—but it was impossible to ignore the things that were still happening. Demons screamed, and the dragon roared in the distance.

She listened to the echo of her father's voice in her head—the voice she'd heard while dreaming in a river that had no beginning and no end—and he told her to stay strong. It's what he would have said if he were alive today. She knew that. But that didn't make it easy to do. She was tired of staying strong. Heroes in books and movies...it always seemed like everything came too easy to them. There was a bit of struggle, sure, but you knew they were going to win in the end.

How can I win, now? she thought. There was no winning when people she loved were injured—or worse. Her throat ached and she stayed in her position for what seemed like a thousand years, her forehead resting on her knees. She had nothing left in the tank. She was empty. Alone, in those moments, it felt like one of the worst trials she had ever faced.

"Hey," said a voice. "Did you miss me?"

She looked up so quickly that she almost gave herself whiplash, and found herself staring into Navin Sharma's shining eyes. He was undeniably dirty, and his jacket was badly ripped, but otherwise he seemed unharmed.

Donna leapt to her feet, finding the energy from somewhere, and threw herself into Navin's arms, bursting into a fresh round of tears. She hugged him so tightly she was probably hurting him. To his credit, he didn't complain.

"Navin," she whispered, over and over again. "Nav, you're here." Her voice was hoarse, unrecognizable, scrubbed raw by emotion. She pulled away and stared at him, honestly wondering if this time she really had died and he was a ghost. Or she was back in Demian's realm. Or—

"It's really me," he said. "I know what you're thinking, Underwood."

"But…how did you get out?" She wiped at the tears on her face.

"Newton." Nav shrugged, as though it were obvious.

"You mean you saw him as an actual demon?" Despite everything that had happened, and despite the proverbial shit hitting the fan right now, Donna couldn't help feeling a stab of curiosity.

"Yeah," Navin replied. "He looks…pretty fucking weird."

Donna gasped out a laugh. "Like, how?"

"I can't tell you."

"Can't? Um…well, what's his real name? It's obviously not Newton."

"I can't tell you that either."

"Sharma, what's going on?"

"Seriously, I promised. Apparently it's a binding deal."

"You made a deal with a *demon*? Have you completely lost what remains of your sanity?"

"Clearly," he said. "I'm friends with you, aren't I?"

Donna hit him gently on the shoulder. "Yeah, well. Whatever."

"Seriously, if I tell you I'll have to kill you."

"You mean Newton will have to kill *you*."

"Something like that." He grinned, but the expression fell just as quickly. "Demian came into the Underworld—appeared out of nowhere, totally covered in flames—and he couldn't get out again. Things looked pretty bad for a minute. I owe Newton for sure."

Donna nodded. She didn't like it, but Nav was here and that was all that mattered. He was safe. "As long as you're okay."

"Honestly, owing Newton a favor is a small price to pay for getting out of there."

She hugged him again. "I believe you."

Ironwood Forest was gone, the last remnants just debris on a battlefield. The surviving alchemists may have woven wards around the area to hide the truth from human eyes, but something would have to be done to explain the destruction in the future. Still, right now, there were more important concerns.

The casualties were heavy on all sides. Isolde lost her first knight, Taran, who had been slain while defending his queen against a horde of Strix. The faerie queen herself had been injured; a scar stood out against her ivory complexion. Donna was surprised to see her beauty marked in such a way. Was it possible that demon injuries were permanent, even for a being such as Isolde? It was as though the wound—what must have been a nasty gash in her cheek— had already healed and scarred in the space of minutes. But the scar itself was showing no sign of fading.

Isolde did not seem to care. She was mourning Taran's death; it turned out that Taran had also been her consort. Donna swallowed her own sadness. Immortality didn't matter if you could be killed by demons. The fey weren't strictly immortal, anyway. They could live for a very long time without aging or illness, but they could still be killed. It was complicated, but there had to be checks and balances in life and death, even for the most powerful races.

Donna was glad to see Cathal. The tall knight carried wounds of his own, already healing, but he too would be scarred. Something had tightened in her throat when the smoke first cleared and she'd caught sight of Cathal with his arm around Xan. Father and son had been reunited under the worst circumstances imaginable. Probably, had their meeting taken place under any other conditions, Xan would not have been so quick to accept the birth father he'd never known.

As it was, Xan leaned into his father, helping him to sit down so that his leg could be tended to. Amazingly, Xan's only injury was to his left arm. He'd broken it when a Strix had knocked him to the ground. Fey healers were already setting the bone and tying a sling made of an iridescent gossamer material around his neck.

Donna approached him. "Can't they just fix it with magic?"

Xan smiled. He looked tired. Older. "They wanted to, but I'd rather they saved their mojo for the people who really need it."

"I have to tell you something," she said. There were so many things to say, but this was the one that could hurt him the most. "It's about Maker."

How was she going to tell him? How could she say that his dream of wings was gone now that Maker had died? Well, Maker's body hadn't been found in the wreckage, and some of the alchemists were trying to tell Donna that it had probably burned up in the dragon's fire. This time, however, she wasn't buying it. All the other bodies had been recovered, so why not his? What exactly was it that Maker had said to her before she woke the dragon? *Something about how he was looking forward to going home…*

And the dragon itself—the dragon who had already melted back beneath the ground, back into its ley line—had known who Maker was, which made no sense at all.

She swallowed as Xan touched her face, surprising her. He wiped away some of the dried tears and ash smeared on her cheeks. "I know about Maker. It's okay. This isn't about me anymore. Maker's gone and … maybe that's the way it was meant to be."

"But what about your wings?" Tears shimmered in Donna's eyes, blurring her vision.

His smile was gentle. "What about them? It would have taken dozens of operations. It was never going to happen overnight, you know? And Donna…" His smile widened. "I've been up there, now. The prototype worked and I flew."

Donna swallowed past the huge lump in her throat. "You were magnificent."

He returned her smile, joy radiating from him like the slowly rising sun. "I was, wasn't I?"

They held each other for a long time, then Nav wandered over and told them to get a room. Donna blushed and hugged him, too. And then the two guys shook hands and Xan introduced Navin to his father.

It was a strange thing to witness, but it was also pretty awesome.

Later, she stood shoulder-to-shoulder with her mother, surveying the wreckage. Donna remembered how she'd thought that some parts of the Otherworld landscape looked bleak, but that was before seeing the after-effects of a battle.

Rachel was clearly drained, her face was almost black with smoke and ash, but she was all in one piece. That was the main thing. Donna took one look at her mother's expression and knew what was coming.

She asked the question anyway, because she had to. "Where's Aunt Paige?"

Rachel reached out to Donna, trying to draw her into an embrace.

Donna held up her hands, warding her off. "No. Not her as well."

"I'm sorry, darling. So sorry." Her mother's face crumbled, and Donna felt strangely shocked to see her cry for her sister-in-law. The woman who had betrayed her more than once. Patrick's sister—and Simon's puppet.

And that was it, wasn't it? Donna thought. They'd all been puppets. Aunt Paige with Simon. Quentin with Simon, too. The wood elves with the faeries. Even Isolde, dancing to Demian's tune. Everybody had had a master. She took a shuddering breath and finally allowed her mother to hold her. Rachel stroked her hair away from her face, kissed her forehead.

Donna looked up into her mom's eyes—soft gray eyes so like her own. "How did it happen?"

Rachel shook her head. "Does it matter right now?"

"I need to know."

"She was running from demon shadows. There were so many of them. Quentin was the closest. He tried to help, but there were just too many ... " Her voice trailed off.

Donna swallowed. What a terrible end. Nobody deserved that. *Nobody.* She had loved Paige very much at one time, even though it had all gone so wrong toward the end. Now there would be no opportunity to mend bridges with her aunt. No second chances.

No goodbyes.

Her mother drew back, holding Donna at arm's length and examining her for a long moment. "How does it feel?"

Donna frowned. "About Aunt Paige?"

"No, of course not." Rachel shook her head. "I meant ... how does it feel not having the first matter inside you anymore? Do you feel different?"

"Not really." Donna checked on that place in her chest, the place she focused on when trying to access her powers. It was empty. But not in a bad way. It felt okay.

"I feel fine," she said. And she did, at least physically. "How's Quentin holding up?"

Her mother smiled. "Very well, all things considered. He's incredible."

"Oh!" Donna's eyes widened. Everything had been so overwhelming that she'd almost forgotten about Quentin's unpleasant other half. "What happened to Simon? I haven't seen him. Did ... did something happen to him, too?"

It wasn't that she cared. She just needed to know where she stood, now that things had settled down enough to actually *think*. Now that her "pet dragon"—as Navin seemed fond of calling it—was back where it belonged, safely sleeping until someone else with the first matter in their soul died and came back to life, created the Philosopher's Stone, and then called it up to fight a war. ("That'll be next week, then," Nav had said with a grin.)

"Mom?" Donna prodded. "What about Simon?"

Rachel sighed, an unreadable expression on her face. "He died saving Quentin's life."

Ding-dong, the Magus is dead. She felt surprisingly calm. "At least he did something good. At the end, I mean."

"There's a first time for everything," her mother agreed.

Donna realized that the expression on Rachel's face was relief. She was *relieved* that Simon Gaunt was dead.

But Donna didn't feel anything about it, not really. It registered, vaguely, somewhere at the very back of her mind, that at least her bargain with Queen Isolde had been fulfilled. Indirectly. Apart from that, she could only think of Maker and Aunt Paige. The Magus didn't deserve her sympathy, though perhaps she should spare a thought for Quentin's loss . . .

Nope. Donna shook her head. She couldn't even do that. She honestly tried, but there was nothing left in her to give. No compassion for anything concerning Simon Gaunt's life or death. He had lived long past his allotted time on this planet, anyway, and at what cost to so many others?

"The thing is," Rachel continued, her face twisting into something resembling guilt, "I'm glad he's gone."

Donna nodded. This wasn't exactly news. "I know that, Mom. Me too."

"But it's not that simple. Simon and Quentin ... they were linked by Simon's magic. Without him, I honestly don't know how much longer our Archmaster can survive. So, although I'm *glad* that Simon Gaunt can no longer influence the Order of the Dragon, I just wonder if that freedom comes with too high a price."

Oh, Quentin, Donna thought, immediately fighting a rush of guilt about her feelings. She remembered Demian's conversation with Simon at the masquerade ball. So it was true—the Magus really had been keeping Quentin alive. Or, at the very least, keeping illness at bay. She took a deep breath, forcing herself to stay calm.

"Does that mean that Quentin will die?" *Yet another death*, she thought. Another part of her childhood drifting away.

"We all die, sweetheart," her mother replied.

Donna looked up sharply, remembering her dream. "That's the secret of life, right?"

Rachel gave her an odd look. "Well, yes. But I don't think we need to worry immediately. Quentin is strong. Stronger than Simon gave him credit for, I think."

Her mother drifted away, and the alchemists and the fey worked together to clear the bodies from the charred remains of the Ironwood. If the sight weren't so grim, it might have been incredible to think of the joint effort between two races historically at war with one another. Aliette was commanding her small band of wood elves, and they ran around like ants lugging debris. Once, her eyes met Donna's through the smoke, and she nodded. Her face was expressionless.

Donna turned away and watched the sun rise higher on the horizon. She had questioned, more than once in the past few days, whether she would ever see that beautiful sight again. Now she knew the answer. She felt sure she would find out more answers in the coming days, but right now she was just happy to know that she was alive—and that the world would survive.

At least for a little longer.

Navin came to stand beside her. "What are you doing, Underwood? Watching the sunrise and dreaming of Xan?"

She'd been so engrossed in her own thoughts that she hadn't heard him approach. "Hey, you," she said.

"That's what you're thinking about? 'Hey, you'? That's a new one."

Donna smiled softly. "I was just thinking about how it's all turned out."

"Yeah," Navin said. He looked at the blackened earth and the blasted trees. Fire and death still lingered in the air. "It turned out pretty crazy."

Donna nodded, glad he wasn't celebrating victory. What was there to celebrate? Demian's forces had been destroyed, or at least dramatically reduced. But the Demon King himself had survived.

We shut him away again, Donna reminded herself. *He's not getting out any time soon.* She shivered as an inky shadow passed across the sky. Just a crow. Not a demon.

Navin put his arm around her. "You gonna be okay, Don?"

"I don't know." She leaned against him and watched the sky. "But I'm looking forward to finding out."

EPILOGUE

Sitting on the roof terrace of the Grayson townhouse was both familiar and strange. It seemed so long since Donna had first met Xan, and yet it was only three months ago.

It felt like a lifetime.

Today, with the winter-bright sun peeking out from behind the clouds at regular intervals, Donna was starting to feel human again. It even looked like spring might come early this year.

Xan sat across from her, smiling. "I have the strangest feeling that we've been here before."

"Déjà vu? Really?" She smiled in return. "That's cool."

"You don't find this...*familiar*?" He raised an eyebrow and his green eyes sparkled.

She laughed. "Maybe you dreamed it."

"Maybe," he said quietly. "Maybe I did."

Donna leaned back against the wall and waited to feel the sun on her face. She smiled to herself, wondering about the future. Wondering about the choices that lay ahead of her. It was okay not to know what came next—it was a gift. Freedom didn't come without a price, and the price of her freedom hadn't come cheap. She intended to make the most of it. Honor the memory of those who had fallen. Make the most of her life, and do the best she could to always keep looking *forward*.

Starting with traveling, just like she'd always wanted.

It was too late to submit college applications this year anyway, which worked out fine because it was giving her a whole extra year to herself. A year to see what was out there, beyond the boundaries of the alchemists. Rachel Underwood's first act as the new Archmaster had been to give Donna her blessing for any and all plans—even those that didn't include alchemy. Quentin also gave his full approval for this course of action. The only people not happy with this decision were some of the older alchemists, especially from the Order of the Rose. Now that Quentin had officially handed over his title to Rachel, she had to complete a million tests in record time to keep the Council off her back, and the Rose alchemists were the ones overseeing that process.

Perhaps Donna would pay them a visit in Prague, just to keep them on their toes. She grinned, imagining the fuss that would cause.

Navin had deferred his own admission to college, much to Dr. Sharma's horror, and would be traveling with Donna during the summer and perhaps beyond. This made her happier than she could ever have imagined being. It was another gift from the Universe—that was how she chose to see it.

Maybe even a gift from a dragon.

Demian had made a mistake when he'd set the deadline for getting the Philosopher's Stone on Imbolc. Donna had looked up the holiday in one of Quentin's many books—alchemists were never short of books, that was for sure—and discovered that "Imbolc" meant "in the belly." Traditionally, it meant the time of year when life begins to stir in the belly of the earth. A time of new beginnings ... the spark of life ... *possibility* whispering in the cold air. Yes, frost might still lie on the ground, snow can still fall, but spring has its first glimmerings. Maybe it's not quite knocking at the door, but it's very definitely on the horizon. When the deepest day of winter passes, a time of cleansing begins.

Imbolc was the time of the dragon, and the dragon had awakened. The Demon King hadn't anticipated that. Perhaps he wasn't aware, when he'd chosen his "impossible" deadline, that a power even older than his own slept beneath the Ironwood.

Donna thanked the gods for boring alchemical texts, good friends, and being born different. All that reading while shelving for Miranda had been worthwhile in the end, as she'd slowly pieced together her plan to thwart Demian. She hadn't known that there was a plan to build—not even when the British Museum was reduced to rubble and Demian faced down the other three races at that charade of a masquerade. Things had seemed hopeless—which was what Demian had intended.

Robert—who had relished both his role in the battle and coordinating communications in the aftermath—had told Donna that the Philosopher's Stone was now being looked after by the Order of the Lion. It seemed appropriate that the most secret of all the secret Orders was safeguarding the most powerful artifact in the world. A new elixir could now be created, but nobody was rushing to complete the process. Maybe they never would. Rachel and the other alchemists had agreed on one thing: alchemy belonged to the past. The future involved new directions, and a whole new purpose. They just had to figure out where they fit in the modern world, and immortality wasn't something that humanity was ready for.

Taking a deep breath, Donna glanced at Xan. He'd decided to return to his birth father's home. It had been a ... *surprise* when he'd first told her about it. Donna had hugged him and nodded enthusiastically, but inside, her heart had broken just a little.

She leaned toward him now, with a sigh, and kissed his warm cheek. He moved to her side of their little nook and wrapped his arms around her, holding on tight.

They spoke about it again, up there on the roof: Xan's intention to spend some quality time in Faerie at Queen Isolde's personal invitation. Cathal was the queen's new first knight and would be needed there for the foreseeable future. Donna couldn't help feeling that they were saying goodbye forever, although she hoped that wasn't true. Forever was a long time.

"I'll visit," he said.

"I know."

"Probably not a good idea if *you* try to visit me."

Donna shook her head, a wry smile on her face to match his. "Probably not."

They sat quietly for another few minutes.

Donna snuggled in closer and leaned her head on his shoulder. "Do you think you'll come back here? To live permanently, I mean."

"I don't know," he said. "It's like... I've only just found myself. Where I'm from. Who I really am. I need to explore it—at least for a while. Beyond that? I honestly can't say. Not yet. I promise you though, Donna, you'll be the first to know. I won't keep any more secrets."

She nodded, trying not to focus on the sadness that stopped her from speaking. At least he was being honest.

"You won't miss me," he said, in a tone of voice that said he clearly hoped she would. "You'll be too busy traveling the world with Sharma."

"Oh, just shut up and kiss me," she told him.

Xan grinned and his green eyes flashed. "Your wish is my—"

Donna pressed her lips to his as the sun finally broke through the clouds.

It was going to be a beautiful day.

"So," she said as she pulled back, flushed and breathless.

"So." Xan's expression was difficult to read, but there was the ghost of a smile at the corner of his mouth. "Do you come here often?"

"Not often." She swallowed—why did saying goodbye have to be so difficult? "The guy who lives here is kind of a private person. He doesn't let people in easy, you know?"

"Yeah, I know the type. I know someone just like that, actually."

"You do?"

He nodded. "A beautiful girl. A beautiful young woman, I should say." His gaze met hers, and she was surprised to see the shimmer of tears. "She changed my life."

"That's funny," she said. "This guy? The one I told you about? He changed mine, too."

"Really? Coincidence, do you think?"

"I don't believe in coincidence."

"Then ... what?"

"Magic," she whispered, right before kissing him again. "I believe in that."

THE END

APPENDIX I

Extract from:
*A History of the
Dragon Alchemists*

....
Edited by
Quentin P. Frost

MAKER'S STORY

Once upon a time, there was a man who was born a god. He wasn't the most powerful god, nor was he the most well-liked, but he worked hard and did his duty and didn't upset the order of things.

At least, not in the beginning.

Let's call this god... Hephaestus. This may or may not be his true name, you understand, because as with all gods he had many titles. The Smith of Olympus. God of the Forge. Maker of Wonders. But Hephaestus will do for now, because he was good with his hands. He made things. He made many wonderful, magical things, and his skills were in great demand. He could have been rich, with all the commissions he was given, but he didn't charge for his work because he loved it so much. Gods—even those who had forsaken their godly homes—didn't need money.

Hephaestus wanted to be left alone on his island to build and make and invent. That's all he had ever wanted. Solitude was important to him. People irritated him, even when he was a young man, and he wondered how they lived together in such close proximity. Sometimes, his fellow gods would come to visit him and ask for something or other to be made, and he was always glad when they left. Sometimes humans would petition him for help with a project, and he never minded blowing the breath of invention into their work—so long as they put in adequate effort, too. So long as they put their heart into the thing. There was no point in their asking for his help if they expected miracles, or if they weren't willing to sacrifice something of themselves.

One day, a god and goddess came to his island together, but they weren't alone. They brought their children with them: two beautiful boys, who looked like the sun and moon. One shone brightly, with hair the color of pure sunlight; the other was dark, with hair like the wings of Hephaestus' pet ravens.

He looked at the children, and something in his heart broke open. He had never been lonely before, but now he thought about family and how he would probably live a very long time by himself. These were strange, unfamiliar feelings. They unsettled him and caused him to question many things about his existence.

As he worked on the small job the family had brought for him, Hephaestus stole glances at the boys' mother, the young goddess. She was beautiful and elegant, with smooth dark hair and skin the color of fresh honey.

After the family left, the two boys happy with the clockwork birds that Hephaestus had given them, he went into his workshop and locked the doors. He didn't come out for a very long time.

Twelve years passed.

Many people came and went in that time. Gods visited the island in hopes that he would invent something for their home or offer consultation on the latest technology. Human beings paid homage to him and burnt offerings, in hopes that he would create a new weapon for their latest war. But Hephaestus was getting old, and he was tired and wished they would all go away and leave him in peace. He was busy making something the likes of which he had never before attempted.

Finally, he was done. His latest masterpiece was complete, and Hephaestus opened the door to his workshop once again.

Everybody—both gods and mankind—breathed a sigh of relief and prepared to place their orders. Twelve years is a long time when there are worlds to rule and wars to be won.

The gods looked down upon the little island and raised their eyebrows. They looked at one another with barely concealed surprise, because Hephaestus was no longer alone. He had built twelve beautiful maidens, all with limbs of silver and gold. They shone beneath the sun as they danced and sang.

Now, whenever anybody came to the island to beseech Hephaestus for his skills, they were treated to the warm hospitality of his twelve metal maidens. Incredibly, they each had their own individual attributes—all distinct from one another. They lived on the island with the retired god and seemed happy.

But one of his creations was different. She became restless, and her personality changed and developed over time. She seemed more human than her sisters and liked to go for long walks with her maker. Hephaestus, for his part, began to fall in love for the first time in his long life. When he had built the maidens—each one created and shaped over the course of a year—he was simply trying something new. Those first pangs of loneliness had left him curious, and he wondered if it was possible for him to make his own companions. A family. He remembered the goddess with the two sons, and each of his twelve maidens was built in her image. Each subsequent attempt came ever closer to the original, until his twelfth and final creation was a perfect replica. Except for the limbs, which were of course made of silver and gold.

Her name was Twelve, and she was beautiful and kind and he loved her.

Hephaestus turned to the gods for help. He had helped them many times, and he felt certain that his own plea would not be ignored. He begged them to make Twelve human so that he could ask her to marry him. The gods were angry. They didn't want to lose their maker to something as trivial as love. They liked him better when he was living quietly on his island, making things they wanted and needed. This new turn of events was too unexpected. It was too chaotic. Too human.

They refused his request.

Years passed, and some of the maidens began to show signs of slowing down. Hephaestus tried to fix them, but nothing he did seemed to make any difference. One by one, the beautiful automatons froze until there were eleven shining statues scattered across his island.

Only Twelve remained, but even she was having more difficulty getting around. Her knees hurt and her arms were stiff. No matter how much oil he poured on her joints it didn't seem to help—at least, not for very long. Twelve never complained, although it was clear she was suffering. She wondered if this was what it was like to grow old, but Hephaestus couldn't tell her because he himself was immortal. Just because he had chosen to live separate from the gods, it didn't mean he wasn't still one of them. One day, he watched his beautiful Twelve struggle to cut a pear in half—her fingers couldn't grip the knife properly—and his heart shattered.

He went to the home of the gods and asked for their help. Unfortunately, he made his petition to the god whose wife had served as the template for the twelve metal maidens. This god was angry, and the only reply that Hephaestus received that day was to be lifted off his feet and physically thrown back down to the island.

It was a long way to fall, even for an immortal, and the impact was enough to break his legs. Twelve nursed him back to health, but Hephaestus never walked entirely unaided again. He had to use a cane, on rare good days, or a specially created chair on wheels. After his recovery, after he saw how tired Twelve still was, Hephaestus made a decision. Things couldn't go on like this.

He returned to the home of the gods and threw himself on their mercy.

"Please," he said. "I'll do anything you ask. I will pay any price. You have already crippled me, and still I return to you and beg for the life of the woman I love. Please don't take her from me. Make her human, that's all I ask. Just a human lifespan so that she may live and know what it is like to feel the sun on her face."

The gods decided to punish Hephaestus. They were cruel and selfish, and some of them were fed up with watching him live his hermit's life on the island. They agreed to grant his wish and make Twelve human, but the cost was high: they would only do so if Hephaestus gave up his own immortality and became mortal with her. The gods were sure he would never agree to such terms.

They were wrong. Hephaestus thanked them and agreed to become mortal, so that he and Twelve could live out their days together on his beautiful island. He was happy.

The gods were furious and decided to trick him.

Yes, they transformed Twelve from a struggling silver and gold automaton into a beautiful young woman with her whole life ahead of her. But they didn't really make Hephaestus mortal. They took away his godhood, meaning he could never again commune with those powers, but they left his immortality intact. A powerful glamour was cast on him, so that he seemed to grow young again and could age alongside his new wife, but in fact he hadn't changed at all. Underneath the gods' magic, he was still the same old Hephaestus.

As soon as Twelve died—of natural causes, of old age, in her loving husband's arms—the glamour broke and he was once more old and alone and immortal. The gods cast him out of his island and hid it somewhere in the middle of the Mediterranean, behind an invisible shield so that nobody could ever find it again.

Hephaestus limped into the human world alone, grieving, and wondered how he would live the rest of his very long life. He changed his name to Maker and tried to blend in. He made things for people again. He remembered Twelve and the happy years they had spent together, and it was those memories that kept him going during the darkest days. There were many dark days.

It was at that time—at one of his lowest points—that he happened upon a morally ambiguous and yet immortal magus who had need of his ancient skills.

But that is another story.

Acknowledgments

This novel simply wouldn't exist without the major contribution of four people: My agent, Miriam Kriss, who helped me weather some particularly tough times throughout the writing of this book—thank you, thank you! My editor at Flux, Brian Farrey-Latz, who was consistently kind and patient while I was struggling (no matter how much he might have been cursing me behind the scenes!), and who took a severely flawed and unfinished first draft and helped me to make it about a million times better. Thanks so much, Brian. My production editor, Sandy Sullivan, who took the manuscript to the next level and asked all the questions that needed to be asked. And my cover artist, Lisa Novak, who yet again delivered such a beautiful cover in the Iron Witch trilogy. We're three for three, Lisa! Thanks also to everyone else at Flux in the U.S., and at Random House in the U.K. and Australia, for your continued support. I appreciate it more than I can say.

I would also like to thank Jenna Avery and her Writer's Circle, who cheered me on through the many hours of production work on this book. You all rock! And I'm raising a glass to the "real" Demian, whose name I shamelessly borrowed for my demon king—it goes without saying that you aren't evil. Right?

Finally, I couldn't possibly wrap this up without sending big hugs to the Deadline Dames—for Good News Friday and everything else you've given me as a writer (and as a person); Maralyn Mahoney—the best mum (and first reader) anyone could ever have; and Vijay Rana—for putting up with the angst, and not minding (too much) when I only cook once in a blue moon.

© Vijay Rana

About the Author

Karen Mahoney (United Kingdom) is the author of *The Iron Witch* and *The Wood Queen*, the first two books in her trilogy for Flux. She has a highly trafficked blog where she talks about everything from writing books to her lifelong love of Wonder Woman. She is also addicted to Twitter and would love to chat with you there (@kazmahoney).

Visit Karen online at www.kazmahoney.com.

∂₹